SAM MILLAR

DEAD OF WINTER

A KARL KANE NOVEL

BRANDON

First published 2012 by
Brandon
An imprint of The O'Brien Press Ltd
12 Terenure Road East, Rathgar,
Dublin 6, Ireland.

Tel: +353 1 4923333; Fax: +353 1 4922777
E-mail: books@obrien.ie

Website: www.obrien.ie

ISBN: 978-1-84717-343-0

Cover image: Getty Images

British Library Cataloguing-in-Publication Data
A catalogue record for this title is available from the British Library

1 2 3 4 5 6 7 8
12 13 14 15 16

Printed by ScandBook AB, Sweden.
The paper used in this book is produced using pulp from managed forests

DEAD OF WINTER

Winner of many awards, including the Brian Moore Award for Short Stories, and the Aisling Award for Art and Culture, Sam Millar is the author of highly acclaimed crime novels, several of which have sold internationally. He has also written a bestselling memoir, *On the Brinks*. His writing has been praised for its 'fluency and courage of language' by Jennifer Johnston.

Also by Sam Millar

Fiction
The Darkness of Bones
Dark Souls
The Redemption Factory

Karl Kane novels:
Bloodstorm
The Dark Place

Memoir
On the Brinks

Play
Brothers in Arms

www.millarcrime.com

DEDICATION

For Jemma Doyle. You know why.

ACKNOWLEDGEMENTS

I would like to thank all at The O'Brien Press for their hard work and dedication in helping the journey of this book. Mary Webb for her editorial input and keen eye; Emma Byrne for creating such a powerful and atmospheric Karl Kane cover; Ruth Heneghan for all the publicity generated, and Brenda Boyne at sales. Also, to all those behind the scenes, not forgetting Michael O'Brien.

PART ONE

CITIZEN KANE

Che Gelida Manina, (Your Tiny Hand Is Frozen)
La Boheme, Giacomo Puccini

CHAPTER ONE

THE ICE HARVEST

'Down these mean streets a man must go who is not himself mean…a common man and yet an unusual man. He talks as the man of his age talks, that is, with rude wit, a lively sense of the grotesque, a disgust for sham, and a contempt for pettiness.'
Raymond Chandler, *The Simple Art of Murder*

The dark was shifting to early morning when Karl Kane – clad in nothing but a too-small pink bathrobe – discovered the severed hand nestling beside the milk and newspaper delivery on the snowy doorstep of his office/apartment in Belfast's Hill Street.

'Shit…' muttered Karl once the revelation hit home.

From the moist Rorschach-like stains scarring the freshly fallen snow, Karl quickly determined it wasn't all that long ago the hand had been part of the body proper. It looked to be reaching out in a macabre handshake.

A freezing wind skimming off the River Lagan suddenly began whistling up Karl's canyon, making him shudder. Quickly tightening the belt on the bathrobe, he bent on one knee, scrutinising the hand and anything else that could well become relevant, subsequently.

'What the hell...?' The little finger was missing, but unlike the crisp severance of the hand's stump, this seemed to have been gnawed carelessly off.

Suddenly from his peripheral, something between two columns of uncollected bins caught Karl's attention. A mangy, rib-protruding cat, sat sneakily watching, the missing bloody finger housed perfectly between clamped fangs and filthy mouth.

The sight immediately sent a shiver up Karl's willy. Never a lover of cats since his ex-wife, Lynne, threw one in his face, four years ago, scarring him for months, the emaciated creature only helped compound his loathing.

'Bastard!' shouted Karl, standing, faking a wild kick at the thieving feline before slipping unceremoniously onto his arse in the process.

Pain immediately speared him, sending shockwaves radiating from the base of his spine, rocking and shocking the vertebrae.

'Fuck...oh...' Tears formed in his eyes as he tried shifting his weight. To make matters worse, the belt suddenly slipped from the bathrobe, turning him into an instant flasher.

Two passing schoolgirls began giggling, nudging each other until the bloody hand came into sight. Seconds later, they went running down the street, screaming, schoolbags flying haphazardly into the air.

'I just knew in my piss this morning that this was going to be one of those bloody days...' mumbled Karl, quickly regaining his composure before staggering awkwardly towards the warm indoors to call the cops.

CHAPTER TWO

RAGING BULL

'My eyes have seen what my hand did.'
Robert Lowell, *Dolphin*

'**A**ny idea why someone would leave a severed hand at your doorway, Mister Kane?' asked Detective Malcolm Chambers, three hours later, standing in Karl's living room. An open notepad rested in the young detective's hand. Directly behind Chambers, a radio was humming unobtrusively in the background. A song from the seventies playing *Motown* memories.

'I'm more concerned as to what prick alerted the media,' said Karl, sitting uncomfortably on a sofa, his tailbone throbbing with pain. He had yet to offer a seat to Chambers. 'They've been parked outside my door for most of the morning, shouting up at the window and in through the letterbox, scaring away my clients.'

'It certainly wasn't us. The press never make our job any easier.'

'Except when you need them to leak stories for you.'

'The hand,' said Chambers. 'Any idea why it would be left at your doorstep?'

'It's not just *my* doorway. It's shared by twenty other businesses and every drunken bastard taking a piss in the night.'

'We can do without the sarcasm and swearing, Mister Kane.'

'I think we're both of the same mind, that the owner of the hand has been chopped up by the serial killer running about Belfast.'

Chambers stiffened. 'The police don't believe there is a serial killer.'

'Catch yourself on. Two right hands chopped off, and you claim there isn't a serial killer?'

'The first hand – discovered three weeks ago in the dock's area – belonged to Kevin Johnson, a local loan shark. The rest of his body was found shortly after. We've already charged someone for that.'

'Charley Montgomery? That's a fucking joke. Everyone knows Charley never used a knife in his life. His *modus operandi* is a full magazine in the back – and I'm not talking the *Radio Times*.'

'We've got compelling evidence against Mister Montgomery. Two eyewitnesses place him at the scene, and–'

'Bollocks. Keep that shit for the TV cameras outside.'

Chambers' face reddened. 'Please tone your language down, Mister Kane. I'm just doing my job as–'

'Wind your bloody neck in telling me to control my language!' Karl was becoming touchy. His tailbone was killing him, and his haemorrhoids were beginning to flare again. 'How long have you been *just* doing your job as a detective, *Detective* Chambers?'

'I…'

'Well?'

'Six months…'

'Six months? *Six* bloody months!' Karl shook his head. 'I've been wearing underwear for longer than that.'

'I really need you to focus on the questions, Mister Kane, rather than–'

'The last time I saw you was at the funeral of Ivana, about five months ago. Wasn't it?'

'Ivana?' Chambers looked puzzled for a moment. 'Oh, Frank Gilmore, the transvestite murdered by Robert Hannah?'

'Ivan *wasn't* a transvestite. He was transsexual. Can't you even get that right, *detective*?' Karl was becoming irritated. 'Why were you having my photo taken at the scene by a police photographer?'

'I was simply following procedure and orders. Take as many photos as possible of everyone in the cemetery, in case the killer showed up at the funeral. They say a dog always returns–'

'To its own vomit. Yes, I heard that old one when you were still in wet nappies.' Karl was gathering steam. 'Was *I* a suspect?'

'You? No…not that I was aware of.'

'Perhaps Naomi?'

'Naomi?'

'Don't hand me that startled look crap. I've had time to think about that day in the graveyard. Perhaps it wasn't my craggy gob you were interested in, after all, but Naomi's beautiful face?'

'I don't know what you're talking about.' Chambers' face was reddening by the second.

'Have you got Naomi's photo pinned up on your locker, like some pimply-faced adolescent? Eh?'

'I was simply doing my job–'

'Tell your boss, Wilson – my ex brother-in-law, as you're probably aware – to send someone with a bit more experience the next time he–'

The door pushed open.

'Coffee, detective?' asked a young woman, entering the room while carrying a tray crowned with steaming coffee and biscuits. Extremely attractive and lissom, she was dark-skinned with large hazel eyes, and wild black hair cascading in every direction.

'I…yes…thank you…' mumbled Chambers.

'Since when did we start running a bloody café, Naomi?' asked Karl tersely, glaring at his part-time secretary and full-time lover.

'Just ignore him, detective,' said Naomi, placing the tray on top of a table. There was a lovely southern lilt to her voice, and it brought calmness into the room, if only for a second. 'He's always this cranky in the morning. Hasn't had his Weetabix, yet, poor thing.'

'It now transpires that this wee boy was taking *your* picture, Naomi, at Ivana's funeral.' Karl smirked at Chambers.

'I didn't say that, Mister Kane. You're twisting–'

'Chubby bloody Checker twists. I don't.'

'Oh, so that's where I recognised you from, detective?' Naomi smiled. 'Ivan's funeral.'

'I wasn't really taking just your photo. It was every–'

'I hope you got my good side? I'm very vain, you know, when it comes to my face.' Naomi winked, before heading for the door. 'Enjoy the coffee.'

Chambers waited until Naomi left the room before addressing Karl.

'Look, Mister Kane, I don't set the rules. I just obey them, hoping to bring bad people to justice.'

'Wise up, preaching like that to me. You're starting to sound like one of those lying scumbags up in Stormont. Just what we *don't* need. Another fork-tongued and over-paid politician.'

'I guess to you I'm just some naive cadet?' Chambers' face looked pained. 'I'm sorry you think like that, but I intend to carry out my duties to their fullest. If that's old fashioned, then I can live with it.'

Momentarily, Karl looked taken aback by Chambers' frank rawness.

'You sound more like an idealist than a bloody cadet. I hope you know in your profession idealism is dangerous?' Karl shuffled on the sofa. 'Look, we seemed to have started off on the wrong foot – or hand. Sit down and enjoy your coffee.'

'Thank you,' said Chambers, looking visibly relieved before sitting down. He closed the notepad. Sipped the coffee. 'This is excellent.'

'The price I paid for it, I should bloody well think so.' Karl sipped his coffee, eyes peering over the rim at Chambers.

'Can I repeat my question?' said Chambers.

'Which one? I've a terrible memory.'

'Any idea why someone would leave a severed hand at your doorstep?'

'Look, granted I sometimes deal with the dodgiest of characters, but I doubt if any of them would leave a hand at my door. Besides, the hand was obviously dumped in one of the bins.'

'But it was found on the ground, not inside the bins.'

Karl sipped the coffee again. He seemed to be weighing up a response.

'The cat took it out, probably dropping it because of the weight. It just happened to land near my door and–'

'Cat?' Chambers' face knotted. He quickly sat the coffee down on a small table. Re-opened his notepad. 'What cat?'

It was Karl's turn to look uncomfortable. 'The one chewing on the hand's finger. The bastard disappeared with it, down the street. I thought about giving chase, but was practically nude.'

'You should have mentioned that at the beginning,' said Chambers, touchily, scribbling quickly on the notepad. 'That wasn't smart, leaving that particular piece of information out.'

Karl's face reddened. 'If my memory serves me well, when you arrived on the scene, *you* examined the hand. Yet, *you* didn't bother to query about the missing finger? *That* wasn't smart. Six months' inexperience does that.'

It was over an hour later when a frustrated-looking Chambers finally exited.

'You could have been a bit more sociable with that young detective, Karl,' scolded Naomi, entering the room. 'He looked a nervous wreck.'

'If I'd been any more sociable, I'd have needed a condom. Anyway, it'll toughen him up,' said Karl. 'What? What's wrong?'

'Nothing…'

'When you say nothing, with a cliff-hanger voice and *that* look, it's always something. What?'

'I'm worried. You think that hand *was* left by the serial killer, don't you?'

'Well, there's a slight possibility.'

'It's unnerved me.'

'Unnerved *you*? What about me? I almost shit my pants – if I'd been wearing any, instead of your bathrobe.'

'Just for once, can you please be serious, instead of flippant?'

'I am flipping serious. Can't you tell by the way I–'

We're sorry for interrupting this programme, stated a stoic voice from the radio, *but breaking news has just come in. Sources say a shocked member of the public discovered a severed hand in the city centre, in the early hours of this morning…*

'Shocked? I wasn't shocked,' said Karl, feigning shock. 'The bastards better not release my name, otherwise my business will go down the shitter. Who the hell would hire a PI shocked at a bit of blood and meat?'

'You're not going to get involved, are you?' Naomi's face looked troubled. 'I've got a bad feeling about all this.'

'Give me one good reason why I'd want to get involved in one of your bad feelings?'

Other breaking news. An anonymous businessman has said the killings are becoming detrimental for future investments…

'Give that man a cigar,' said Karl, sarcastically. 'All we need now is–'

…and has just announced that he is offering twenty thousand pounds reward for information leading to the arrest of the individual or individuals involved in these heinous crimes…

'Karl? What's wrong?' asked Naomi, her forehead furrowing.

'Wrong? Oh, nothing…'

'When you say nothing, with a cliff-hanger voice and *that* look, it's always something. What?'

'Nothing,' repeated Karl, thinking, *I've just been given twenty thousand reasons to get involved…*

CHAPTER THREE

SWEET VIOLENCE

'Oh the weather outside is frightful...'
Dianne Reeves, 'Let it Snow'

From inside the warmth of his favourite watering hole, Harold Taylor gazed out the window, watching the latest falling of thick snow painting over his beefy Range Rover 4x4, parked a short distance away. The take-no-prisoners snowstorm had long since dulled and diluted visibility on the Antrim Road, but Harold was eager to be heading home. The Rover wouldn't let him down. Of that he was certain.

'You're crazy, Harold, for even thinking of driving in that weather,' said Paul McKenna, manager of the Antrim Arms Motel, watching Harold pulling on a storm-proof jacket.

'I'll *go* crazy if I have to listen to any more of these moaners, Paul,' said Harold, with a shake of the head. 'A wee bit of snow and they're all crapping their knickers about driving in it.'

'I still think you should stay. You heard the storm warning from the weathermen advising drivers to avoid all unnecessary journeys. Besides, the cops love nothing better than to catch drivers under the influence, in this weather.'

'Ha! Don't you worry about me driving in a wee bit of snow.

The Rover's a bit like me. It can handle any situation thrown at it. Anyway, I've only had a few jars. Nothing to worry about if the cops do stop and breathalyse.'

'I still say you should stay. I've got a couple of vacant rooms upstairs. You should grab one before they're gone. Better safe than sorry.'

'Want to bet I won't be home in less than an hour?'

'Knowing you, you'd drive like a mad man just to win the bet. I don't want that on my conscience.'

'What conscience?' Harold smiled, pulling open the large brass entrance door, allowing a whirlwind of biting snow to enter.

Outside, fat snowflakes began caking Harold's face. He moved quickly to the Rover, and once inside, hit the heater full blast.

With little effort he started the vehicle and commenced guiding the brute onto the tree-lined Antrim Road – but not before waving triumphantly at McKenna's wary face at the motel window.

On the road, snow began falling more heavily. Branches were cracking under the weight, sounding like human bones snapping. Wipers squeaked across the windshield, spreading the increasingly dense flakes of snow across it. Visibility lessened. A mist was forming. Harold ploughed onwards. Steady. The twisty road looked eerie. A ghost's entrails.

Within minutes of travelling, the wipers scything the windscreen began leaving chalky smudges in their wake, making visibility even more difficult. He reached to turn the radio on. That was when the obscure figure standing on the edge of the road came suddenly into view.

And he was heading straight for it.

'Fuck!' Pressing down heavily on the brakes, he curved the steering wheel with all his strength. The Rover skidded haphazardly across the road, wheels spinning wildly. Harold held his breath. Seconds later, the vehicle came to a thunderous stop, cushioned by a pyramid of hardened snow leaning against an embankment.

Thankfully, there was no on-coming traffic.

Inside the Rover, Harold tried to regain his composure. Hands were shaking. Skin clammy. He tried steadying his breathing. Had he made contact with the suicidal maniac? He dreaded the thought of leaving the vehicle to investigate; thought about speeding off as quickly as possible, knowing there would be no witnesses in sight.

A movement in the rear-view mirror caught his eye. The figure was moving, seemingly unhurt.

Opening the door, Harold leapt out into the thick snow, quickly going on the offensive.

'What the hell are you playing at?' he growled, walking clumsily towards the figure. 'Trying to get us killed?'

'I…I'm sorry. I didn't see you coming up the road. The snow was blinding me.'

'Well, that's no damn excuse for…' Harold's voice trailed off. The figure was a woman. She wasn't beautiful, but there was something striking about her. She looked terribly frightened. Tiny flakes of snow and ice encrusted her eyelashes. Her lips were slightly parted, dry and chapped from the bitter cold.

'I'm sorry, my car broke down near the Serpentine Road,' said the woman. 'I tried calling emergency services, but no response. Someone down the road told me there's a petrol station nearby. I was on my way to ask for help.'

'Yes…there's one a further mile or so up the road. You'd be mad to walk to it, though.' Harold relaxed the tension in his face muscles, noticing for the first time the oddity of her eyes. One blue. One green. 'You're lucky you made it this far without getting hit by something. Come on. I'll drop you off. I don't live too far from the station.'

Her eyes seemed to look beyond him. A blank stare was the only response, as if she hadn't heard the offer. Another few seconds went by and she still hadn't spoken.

Harold shook his head, turning his attention back to the road. 'Suit yourself, then. Walk. Don't say you weren't warned.' He headed back towards the Rover and got in.

Once seated, he looked in the rear-view. The woman remained standing at the side of the road, defiantly, snow filtering over her.

He started the Rover and began exaggerating the accelerator with his right foot. The metal beast roared like a bull in heat. Harold's eyes never once left the mirror.

'No! Wait!' she shouted, scuttling across the road, slip-sliding awkwardly on icy patches and snow.

Harold smiled. Unlocked the passenger door. Waited.

'Good to see common sense prevailing,' he said. 'Soon have you nice and warm.'

Keeping her eyes on him, she slowly eased onto the leather passenger seat. The extreme shift in temperature seemed to catch her off-guard as she closed the door.

'Thank you,' she said, her voice barely a whisper.

'Don't mention it. That's my good deed for the day. I always say, what goes around comes around. Harold's the name, Miss…?'

'Kerry…' said the woman, hesitantly. 'Kerry Morgan.'

'In this weather we should make it to the petrol station in about twenty minutes. Put your seatbelt on, Kerry. We don't want any more accidents.' Harold's voice sounded all fatherly.

Kerry nervously fiddled with the seatbelt, missing the buckle twice before finally finding its niche.

The belt's strap pronounced her breasts and Harold felt the blood stir in his stomach. He became aware of her womanly smells mingling with the leather aroma from the Rover's seats. A throbbing but pleasurable pain began worming its way into his crotch area, hardwiring pheromone to his brain. He wondered what she would look like naked in the bathtub in his cellar?

'Are you from around here, Kerry?'

'No. I…I live in Bangor. I was heading to Mallusk to visit my parents. It's my mother's birthday, tomorrow.' A faint smile appeared on her face.

To Harold, the smile looked forced. Nerves? Shyness? He couldn't determine, only that the pain in his cock was intensifying. There was only one cure for that particular pain.

It was then that he decided he would hurt her. Badly.

He gunned the Rover forward, showing-off its muscular prowess. The brute roared with satisfaction before munching its way greedily through the snow.

For the next few minutes of driving, silence accompanied them, until Harold finally decided to break it.

'Must have been frightening, travelling from Bangor in all that snow, Kerry?'

Kerry nodded slightly. 'Yes. It was my first time driving in such conditions. I'll never do it again, I can tell you. It was very scary.'

'Well, it's good we don't get this kind of weather too–'

'*Arghhhhhhh*.' Kerry suddenly held her stomach tightly. She buckled forward slightly.

'What is it, Kerry? Are you okay?'

'*Ohhhhhhhh*, my stomach. Stop. I need to get out.'

'What's the– ?'

'Stop! I need to get out, right now!' Kerry began struggling with the seat belt.

'Okay, okay! Take it easy.' Harold quickly eased the Rover over to the side of the road.

'It…it must be something I ate earlier.' Kerry looked queasy. 'I need to go to the toilet, really badly. This is embarrassing. I'm so sorry.'

'Don't be silly,' assured Harold, smiling. 'When nature calls, we all have to answer it.'

Kerry stepped quickly from the Rover, glancing all about, looking lost.

'Down that little pathway,' said Harold, pointing at an old walkway no longer in use. 'Plenty of trees to give you a bit of privacy. Don't take too long, though. It'll freeze the arse off you.'

The woman moved quickly but gingerly down the pathway, gripping onto bushes for balance. She looked back once, and then disappeared behind thickets and uprooted trees long gone to rot.

Harold's eyes never left her.

He tried picturing Kerry on her hunkers, vulnerable and exposed, panties handcuffed around her ankles. The urge to sneak down and watch her was overwhelming. But what if she caught him? That would give the game away. Why risk it? In about forty minutes he would have her all to himself. The thought of her beautiful panties wrapped around her ankles, though, gave him a lovely shiver. The urge became stronger, more intense.

'Fuck it.' He quickly opened the glove compartment. Found the serrated hunting knife. Touched its curved teeth with his index finger. A tingling sensation shot through his body. He licked dry lips before sliding the knife up the sleeve of his coat, careful of the weapon's deadly honed blade.

Stepping quickly out of the Rover, he glanced up and down the Antrim Road. Not a sinner in sight. The urge in his pants began tormenting him again. His cock was quickly becoming rock-hard. The hardwiring in his brain began sizzling with electricity. His skull felt on fire. He wanted her. Needed her. *Now*.

Silently, he tracked the exact same path as Kerry. He could see where her dainty footprints led the way, before being disrupted by a scattering rock formation.

For fuck sake, which way did she go? She can't have got too far in this snow.

Suddenly, he heard a faded rustling sound, just beyond a heavily snowed hedging.

He stopped all movement. His back went taut. He brought the knife out. This would be easy. *There!* He could see the top of her head now, clearly, just beyond the far hedging. She seemed to be standing, looking all about.

His heart began pumping buckets of blood into his brain. His knees felt weak. Wobbly. It had been a long time since he had felt this beautiful sensation.

She disappeared from view.

Fuck! Where'd she go? Probably behind the hedging, squatting on her hunkers. Probably got the shits. He pictured her naked again.

His hands began trembling as he edged closer, desperately trying to control his breathing. He sniffed the air like a wolf hunting down its victim. She was close by. He could smell her.

'*Harold?*' said a whispery male voice behind him.

'What the fuck...?' He turned. His eyes went immediately to the gun pointing directly at his face. A muscle in his cheek jumped. Stomach tightened.

'Who the hell are you? What do you want?'

The man said nothing, just kept pointing the gun. A few seconds later, Kerry reappeared, face flushed.

'Don't you remember me, Harold?' the man asked.

Harold shook his head. 'No, I've never set eyes...' Just as he said the last word, it came to him. The courtroom. The stoic relatives who sat there, day after day. The blood drained from his face, as if his throat had just been cut.

The man smiled. 'Now you remember, Harold. Don't you? This day's been a long time coming, but it's finally arrived...'

CHAPTER FOUR

THE BONE COLLECTOR

'He knows death to the bone.'
W.B. Yeats, *Death*

Karl stood at the office doorway of best friend and forensic pathologist Tom Hicks. The pathologist's face was ghostly green, mirrored by a flickering computer screen. Karl could see ant-size digits running riot on Tom's face and glasses.

'Hello, Tom.'

'Karl...?' said Hicks, glancing up from his computer. 'What the hell are you doing here?'

'Lovely greeting. Haven't seen your grumpy old gob in months, and that's what I get for coming to visit you, down in this dank, cold, bloody dungeon?'

Hicks made a grunting sound. 'This surprise visit wouldn't have anything to do with severed hands and a reward of twenty thousand pounds?'

'You're such a cynic, Tom. Anyone ever tell you that?'

'Yes. You. Each time I catch you out. Anyway, how is Katie doing?'

Karl seemed to hesitate before answering. 'She's taking each day as it comes.' His voice became sombre. 'She's still undergoing intensive therapy after that scumbag, Hannah, abducted her.'

'Young people nowadays are very resilient, Karl,' assured Hicks. 'Katie will soon be back to her old self. Just you wait and see.'

'I...I suppose you're right,' said Karl, believing the opposite.

'What about the locksmith? The one who had his throat cut. Last I heard, his condition was downgraded from critical to serious.'

'Willie?' Hicks' question brought flies buzzing around inside Karl's stomach. He felt slightly queasy with guilt. 'Finally got out of hospital two weeks ago. I visited him yesterday. Recuperating well.'

'According to reports, he was lucky to have come out of that alive – you all were, with the exception of the two killed in the explosion, Burns and Hannah.' Hicks looked accusingly at Karl. 'Blowing up Crumlin Road Prison? Doesn't get much bigger than that, Karl.'

Karl didn't like the direction the conversation was taking. 'I only have condolences for Brendan Burns. Hannah can burn in hell.'

'Burns was the bomber, wasn't he?'

'That's what they say.' The annoying flies were trying desperately to escape through Karl's mouth. He could feel dread creeping across his face.

'According to the report I read, he was also the man who tried killing Wilson years ago, leaving him scarred for life.' Hicks looked accusingly at Karl. 'You knew that, of course.'

'Eventually.'

'Eventually? Sometimes I think you never weigh up the consequences of your actions, Karl.' Hicks shook his head. 'Consequences can be for a lifetime. Burns will end up being one of those consequences, as far as Wilson is concerned. He'll never forgive or forget your association with him.'

'Fuck Wilson. He hates me, anyway. It was a small price to pay for Katie's freedom. To me, Burns was a hero. He sacrificed his life for Katie, while Wilson and his useless crew did ring a ring o' rosies.'

'What…?' Hicks looked taken aback. 'What on earth are you talking about? From all accounts, I thought Wilson pulled out all the stops in trying to find Katie?'

'There are things best not talked about, Tom, for your own benefit. The less you know, the less possibility of you being dragged into any future criminal proceedings?'

'Criminal proceedings? What criminal proceedings? What on earth are you talking about?'

'Let's just drop it. Okay?'

Hicks sighed. 'Okay. Your face is telling me I've reached a dead end. Despite my concerns, at the end of the day I'm always on your side, right or wrong. That will never change. You know, don't you?'

'You don't have to tell me that. I already knew it, the first day we met in school.' Karl grinned at the memory. 'I protected you from all those bullies with wet dreams about beating the crap out of you.'

'You're the only person I know can make violence sound creepily erotic,' said Hicks, approaching a battered coffee machine encrusted with dirt and hardened grease. 'Coffee?'

'I wouldn't say no.'

Karl took a seat while watching Hicks pour the thick liquid into two mugs. Coffee dregs, no larger than full stops, began haplessly rearranging themselves in dodgy oily patterns.

'Enjoy.' Hicks handed a full mug to Karl.

'You could tar and feather some poor bastard with this,' said Karl, taking a suspicious sip before making a face. 'Ghastly shit.'

'How's your father? The last time we spoke, he wasn't in the best of health.' Hicks blew on the coffee. Drank. Unlike Karl, though, he didn't make a face, as if he were immune to the potent oil-like liquid.

Karl thought for a moment before answering. 'His mental health isn't the best. Hardly knows what day it is. These days, I don't even think he recognises me anymore.'

'Oh…I'm really sorry to hear that, Karl. Will you tell him I was asking about him…I mean…'

'It's okay. I know what you mean. Yes, I'll tell him tomorrow. I've a visit arranged up at the nursing home.'

Both men sipped at the coffee. The only sound came from the humming computer.

'You've got about ten more minutes before I kick you out,' said Hicks, finally breaking the silence.

'What's your rush?'

'I've a hand to examine.'

'The one found yesterday?'

'That's right.'

'I feel very close to that hand. Make sure you take care of it.'

'How so?' said Hicks, his left eyebrow suddenly curving into a hairy question mark.

'Because the bloody hand was left on my bloody doorstep, yesterday morning. That's how bloody so.'

Hicks almost spat a mouthful of coffee out. 'You're winding me up.'

'My severed hand to god,' replied Karl, raising his hand to chest level. 'I had Wilson's schoolboy detective questioning me about it. Can you believe that?'

'Detective Chambers?'

'Yes. With him on the trail, the killer – or killers – won't be having any sleepless nights. I thought he was going to faint when he saw the hand and blood.'

'Well, he'll soon be joined by some old warhorse named Harry McCormack, if the rumours are true.'

'Harry McCormack?' Karl's heart popped slightly. '*The* Harry McCormack? One-time heavy with Special Branch? I thought the powers-that-be had retired that dinosaur about two hundred years ago.'

'Do you know him?'

Karl nodded. 'The bastard's nuttier than a squirrel's turd. Face like a car wreck. His wife, Virginia, used to be a cop, too. Hairy Virgina, they were collectively known as.' Karl took a brave gulp of coffee, as if to wash McCormack's name from his mouth. 'What theories is He-Who-Must-Be-Obeyed coming out with concerning the hands?'

'Wilson? The cuts on this new one are so precise he thinks there's a strong possibility that the culprit or culprits could be in the medical profession.'

'Wouldn't have to be a brain surgeon to figure that out. A doctor?'

'Possibly. Could also be a medical student, though.'

'Or nurse. Some of them are as knowledgeable as the doctors – sometimes more so.'

'I never thought of that. Still, hard to believe a woman would be capable of such a grisly act – especially if she were a nurse.'

'Fingerprints?'

'Wilson and his team are working on them upstairs, which means it could take a while.'

'What about the tiny, faded numbers on the hand, saddled between the index finger and thumb? Those were the first things I noted when I scrutinised the hand, before it went all prune-like. The numbers resembled a blue "88". Amateurish. Looked like prison tats.'

'I'll check it out. Didn't notice any numbers in my initial exam-ination, but then, I wasn't looking for them. I'll let you know.'

'What about the body? Has it turned up yet?'

'No. Not yet.'

'What about Kevin Johnson's hand?'

'What about it?'

'Any tats on it?'

'Covered in them. Don't forget, Johnson did long stretches in prison. It would've been against the norm if he didn't have some. The word HATE lined the fingers. An ace of spades and a sham-rock – which looked more like a cabbage leaf – on the back of the hand. Some prisoners collect these things with the passion of a lepidopterist.'

'A lep *what*?'

'Lepidopterist. One who collects and studies butterflies.'

'Why the fuck didn't you say that, then? Oh, that's right. You used to do that shit in school. That's why you were always getting beat up, and I had to rescue you with my fists.'

Hicks glanced at his watch. 'It's time for you to go.'

'Now, can you give my head peace and kindly get going? If I hear anything relevant, you'll be the first I'll contact,' said Hicks, ushering Karl out towards the door. 'Unfortunately, knowing you, you'll probably discover something before I do.'

Tipping an imaginary hat before leaving, Karl replied, 'Make no bones about that, my good friend.'

Once outside, Karl removed the mobile from his pocket and hit a number. After a few seconds, a soft voice answered.

'Dad?'

'How's my favourite daughter doing?'

'Great. Getting stronger each passing day. Oh, did I tell you, I'm thinking of taking driving lessons, then hopefully get a wee run-around?'

CHAPTER FIVE

FOR WHOM THE BELL TOLLS

'A man awaits his end
Dreading and hoping all.'
W.B.Yeats, *Death*

Where am I? wondered Harold Taylor, awakening from a drug-like stupor. A darkened room of sorts. The exact time was a mystery to him. He was stuck in a moment, trying desperately to piece together events. The room was funerary and cold. Walls covered in blood. Pieces of meat barbed with specks of dirty-white bones. Everything bizarre. Unreal.

From his peripheral, he could just about make out a cluster of people lurking nearby. They all seemed to be adorned in gowns, surgical gloves and masks. Each item of clothing looked heavily stained with blood. The sight terrified Harold.

Doctors?

They were whispering. Secretive hushes. They looked as if they were about to perform major surgery on some unfortunate being.

Is that it? Am I in hospital? Did I crash the Rover? What happened to the woman? Kerry...?

Harold tried speaking. Nothing came. Gums dry like cotton. Mouth taped.

Panicking, his tongue began pecking frantically at the tape, trying to get out.

Then the realisation suddenly hit home: he was inverted, naked, dangling from the ankles, hands tied securely behind his back.

As the seconds passed, something dark and sinister began swelling in him. The burden of the closed space created fear. It touched everything and set his mind alight.

Can't breathe...

His heart started pumping madly, as if he'd just sprinted up flights of stairs trying to escape pursuers. Panicking, he began mumbling incoherently, shaking his head and body wildly at the cluster of people, hoping to get attention.

A man's head turned, his eyes looking directly at Harold's. He whispered something to the group before walking slowly forward.

Harold's eyes went straight to the man's hand. The hand housed a large knife, its half-moon-shaped blade glistening in the godless gloom of the filthy room.

Fuck!

More blood began rushing to Harold's head, adding pressure to his stressed brain. He could feel blood spouting from his nose, leaking slowly down his eyes. It stung like acid, blurring his vision.

I can't breatheeeeeeeeeeeeeeeeeeeeeeeee! Oh god, help me!

The man now stood beside Harold, pushing down on a red control button stationed on a steel table to his right. A chain began rattling. Gradually, Harold felt his body moving, snaking upwards like an Indian rope trick. A few seconds later, all movement stopped.

He was now level with the man's masked face, but still inverted.

The man slowly reached and touched Harold's face tenderly with the blade. The touch was gentle. A lover's caress. It made Harold's spine tighten in a very bad way.

'Tick…tock, Harold. See the wall clock?' The masked man was pointing at an old clock on the far wall, his muffled voice barely audible but quite sinister in its sound.

Without warning, the man began slowly swinging Harold's naked body back and forth, like a meaty pendulum hoping to balance time and sanity.

'Do you hear it, Harold? That old clock, ticking away into eternity? Listen to its calling. Tick…tock…tick….tock.'

Harold shivered. Vomit began bubbling in his stomach. With all the strength left in him, he forced it down, fearful of choking on it.

'Surely you remember all that ticking? You sneaking craftily up the hallway, in the silence of your murdering heart? Was that the only sound you heard, Harold? No soft sleeping slumber of children? No voice of conscience? No pity for *their* cries in the darkness?'

Those dreadful, accusing words began conjuring images in Harold's mind – freighted images he would much rather forget. His already stressed bowel abruptly opened. He shit himself, all hot and volcanic, down his bare spine.

A brilliant, white-hot light began filling Harold's head, obliterating vision and all random thoughts. He was sliding towards that hypnological state where the mind and body wrestle to determine reality from dream. Despite this, he understood immediately what it meant. He hadn't until that moment, but the revelation was firmly here and demanded his full attention: Death in all its grisly glory.

To Harold, death had always been real, yet utterly unknowable, just something to be anxiously expecting at all times. But now he knew it had arrived at his door, and there was nothing he could do but wait for it to knock.

The man with the knife began smiling.

'Time to tell us everything, Harold, and depending on how much you want to suffer, I advise the truth...'

CHAPTER SIX

THE ODD COUPLE

'Owl hasn't exactly got Brain, but he Knows Things.'
A.A. Milne, *Winnie-the-Pooh*

Karl entered the dusty hallway in Lower Donegall Street and began pressing the buzzer centred in a 'Do Not Press' niche. Junk mail and soggy magazines carpeted the floor of the building that housed mainly small businesses and a couple of artsy tenants. Stale stench of urine was everywhere, alongside the cloying smell of something indescribably sweet and sickening.

Twenty seconds passed. No response. The buzzer appeared to be banjaxed.

Just as he was about to press it again, Karl heard a metallic voice emitting from the intercom. 'What's the password?'

'Come on, Richard. I don't have time for this crap.' Karl glared into the tiny peephole camera. 'Open up. I need to talk to you.'

'What's the password?'

'I told you before, I can't pronounce that bastard's name. Now, will you open the hell up and stop fucking about?'

'Learn it, or the next time you don't get in.' The door screamed loudly, before squeaking slowly open. 'Hurry into the time capsule. You've five seconds before it shuts.'

Karl mumbled something nasty before entering.

Four flights of narrow stairs later, he knocked at a door plastered with super hero stickers. A large, bloodstained smiley smiled out at him, encapsulating Rorschach, the mask-wearing vigilante from *Watchmen*. **I'm Watching *You***, it proclaimed, in bold black letters.

An eye looked out from the 'o' in *You*.

'Yes?' asked a voice behind the door. 'Who is it?'

'Open up, Richard, and stop being such a dick.'

The door opened. Behind it stood a man with face furniture consisting of cheap sunglasses, anarchist earrings, studded eyebrows and a greasy barcode moustache. His hair was brown and shoulder-length, draping a puffy face with eyes the colour of wet concrete. A saggy, lit joint dangled from his mouth, releasing a sweet pungent aroma. He wore an unwashed T-shirt with the legend: **Don't hit kids – they have guns now**, and a pair of ragged Diesel jeans exposing more underwear than denim.

'I keep telling you the password is *Mister Mxyzptlk*. He's Superman's nemesis,' said Richard. 'I should get you to say his name backwards, just like Superman does to get him to disappear.'

'We can deal with Superman's angst later,' said Karl, pushing into the room. 'Right now, *I'm* the one in need of help.'

Richard Rider was in his forties going on sixteen, a child of the Sixties lost in the years of zeroes. His tiny flat was filled to capacity with superhero memorabilia, including statues, busts and endless rows of American comic books packed neatly into exposed wooden drawers. Posters of numerous mutants and flying beings covered the ceiling like some eerie, claustrophobic skin. A framed picture of Richard smiling alongside legendary *Marvel* creator,

Stan Lee, took pride of place on a desk with multiple computer screens buzzing with artificial life.

'Want some Coke?' offered Richard.

'That's always a dodgy question, coming from you. Any coffee?'

'No. Don't you know caffeine's a killer? I've some weed, if you want to try that?'

'I'm dopey enough, thanks.'

'You being a writer would find it relaxing. Opens up your mind.'

'Opens up your mind, but closes down your brain cells.'

'Suit yourself,' said Richard, sitting down in front of the army of computer screens. 'How's the writing coming along, anyway?'

'It ain't.'

After some more perfunctory chit chat, Karl finally got down to brass tacks.

'What I really need is some info, Richard. I'm hoping you captured it on one of your spy cameras.'

'*Self-containment* cameras,' corrected Richard. 'If you must know, Karl, I'm compiling an electronic account of life in Belfast, for future generations to enjoy. A bit like Samuel Pepys' diary.'

'More like Peeping Tom's, you mean.'

'WWW?'

'What?'

'The information you're looking for. Who, when, where?'

'Oh…me, last Tuesday, outside my place in Hill Street.' Karl sat down on chair beside Richard, but only after removing a nude Homer Simpson doll. 'Roughly seven in the morning.'

'What happened to your cousin, the cop? Didn't he used to supply you with this stuff?'

'He's not my cousin. Ex brother-in-law. It's a long story, so don't bother asking. Besides, no matter what they say about the long arm of the law, your reach is longer. You're a legend.'

'Flatterer.' Richard smiled proudly, broadcasting disjointed teeth enmeshed in silver wire. He began tapping the keyboard.

'Hill Street? *Hmm*. Let's see what we can come up with…'

The screen blackened, and then turned grey. A monochrome picture of falling snow emerged. The picture looked grey and very hazy.

'Is that the best you can get?' asked Karl, not too impressed. 'Snowy static?'

'That's real snow, not static. I'm trying to zoom in without losing perspective or pixel count. What time did you say?'

'Roughly after seven in the morning, or thereabouts. The newspapers and milk had already been delivered a few minutes before seven, according to the shop owner, so it was shortly after that I went out to collect them.'

Richard hit the keyboard. The picture slowly became clearer.

'That's it. That's Hill Street,' said Karl. 'I'd recognise those filthy bins anywhere.'

'Well, let's see what we can come up with…' with his cursor, Richard clicked on a button on the screen.

'There! That's me!' exclaimed Karl, like a kid seeing an early-morning Santa.

'Zooming in,' said Richard, enlarging the picture. 'Nice robe you're wearing.'

Karl began watching himself bending for the newspaper and milk. A few seconds later, he saw himself stand, before going back on one knee.

'What's that you're staring at?' asked Richard, taking a deep suck from the joint.

'A hand.'

Richard laughed. 'No, really?'

'Really? A really real severed hand. Even you must have heard about the nut running about chopping off hands, all over Belfast.'

'No. Can't say I have.' Richard looked dazed, as if trying desperately to remember. 'That's so fucking cool! A severed hand, and you found it?'

'Yes. I'm a lucky sort of bastard when it comes to finding hands other than my own, so stop wetting yourself with admiration.'

'Zombies. Could be something to do with zombies,' said Richard matter-of-factly, blowing smoke down his nostrils like an ageing dragon.

'Stop blowing that shit in my direction, otherwise I'll go out of here higher than the debt those banker bastards have us in.'

Richard turned his attention back to the screen. 'Hey, are you kicking at that wee cat? That's cruel, man. There's no need for such aggression towards a defenceless creature.'

'It was a spur of the moment thing. Couldn't be helped, and I regret doing it. Feel better now?'

'A bit.'

'Besides, it'll live. It's got nine bloody lives and an extra finger.'

'Huh?'

'Nothing. Let's just stay focused.'

Next came the scene of Karl slipping and falling on his arse, and the two passing schoolgirls giggling.

'*Whoa!* That's got to hurt, man!' exclaimed Richard gleefully. 'Right on the old tailbone. And then exposing all your hardware to two little kids. Bit pervy, if you ask me.' Richard played the scene again, freezing the frame exactly when Karl crash-landed. 'Man, that's a pisser.' He replayed it two more times.

'Give it a rest, for fuck sake. Can you backtrack? I need to see if we can catch the culprit, or culprits, leaving the hand.'

'Shit, man, that's cool. I never thought of that.'

'That's why *I'm* the private investigator and you believe in UFOs.'

Richard hit the keyboard again. The snowy scene went retro and slow mo. Nothing. Just falling snow.

'Can't it go any faster? This computer is slower than one of my client's cheques in the mail,' grumbled Karl.

'There's a reason for it going *slowwwwwwwww*. It's called *slow-wwwwwwww motionnnnnnnnnnnnnnnnnnnnn*.'

Then it happened.

'Stop!' shouted Karl, making Richard jump. 'I think I saw a blur of a car.'

Richard quickly hit a key. It was a patrol car, stationed at the top of Hill Street. Then, at the other end of the street, another car began entering before slowing to a halt a few feet away from Karl's office. Ten seconds it lurked there, before a door opened, then quickly shut.

Karl's heart moved up a beat.

'Freeze that, and zoom in,' commanded Karl. 'I thought I saw someone throwing something out of the car.'

Richard zoomed in. The picture was blurred by snow. 'Hard to say, man. Looks like something. Could be that hand. Perhaps not.'

'Can't you get it any clearer?'

'No. That's it to the hilt.'

'What about the car? Plate number or make?'

Richard tried a few more buttons on the screen, but the picture only became more blurred.

'The car looks like a Mercedes, but can't be sure. Forget the plate number. Too blurred. Sorry, man. If this were next week, it would be clearer pictures. I'm getting some great HD shit sent from the States.'

'HD?'

'High Definition. Top of the range shit. From that day onward, I'll be able to see the pores in their skin, instead of this grainy shit. It even comes with crystal clear audio.'

'Would you be able to run this tape through your HD when it arrives, get it clearer?'

'No. Incompatible. Sorry, man.'

'No need to be sorry. You did great, pal. I suspect whoever was driving that car spotted the cops, panicked, and then discarded their unwanted cargo. At least now I can relax. It was random, rather than being deliberately dumped at my doorstep.'

'You...you're not going to tell the cops about this. Are you?' Richard suddenly looked jumpy. 'I could get into all sorts of crap with these cameras.'

'Don't worry. The cops don't even know you exist. The less they know, the better.' Karl slipped Richard a twenty.

'You don't need to pay me. I'm more than willing to do this after you got me a good deal on this place.'

'Stop thanking me. I only did it because you were becoming an eyesore, sleeping in my doorway, scaring away potential clients.'

'You're not the hard man you let on to be.'

'Hard? Me? The only things hard about me are my socks and underwear.'

'Hey, man, now that I have you here. I'm doing a showing of *Star Wars*, back to back, tonight, with a few mates. You're more than welcome to join us. I'll even supply you with a lightsabre.'

'Er, thanks for the offer, Richard, but I've a poker game tonight. Some other time, perhaps?'

Richard looked crestfallen.

'Okay, man. Some other time…'

Karl made his way to the door and opened it.

'One word of warning, though.'

'What?'

'I find out you put my naked arse on the Internet, I'll come back and kill you with one of those ninja swords on the wall.'

Richard's mouth gaped open like a frog's.

Karl smiled wickedly before exiting.

CHAPTER SEVEN

THE NAKED CITY

*'We're all of us sentenced to solitary confinement inside
our own skins, for life!'*
Tennessee Williams, *Orpheus Descending*

Snow was dropping like dead feathers from the heavy night sky as Karl waited for the traffic lights to change. Overhead, telephone wires tensed tightly and deadly, like garrottes waiting for an unsuspecting victim's neck. He glanced from the telephone wires to the luminous face of the impressive Albert Clock, standing in the night's darkness like a sentinel. The hands of the colossal clock were touching the dangerous side of three in the morning.

'Shit. Is *that* the fucking time?' He glanced at his watch. Worst fear confirmed. Ten minutes after three. He'd be in for it from Naomi, having said he'd be home by one. But lady luck had steadfastly refused to leave his side at the poker game, and his endurance was rewarded with a tidy pile of winnings. He'd let Naomi ice-cube him for a day, then, when her anger had defrosted, give her lots of something nice, made of paper with the word fifty written all over them. She liked nice things like that.

'Come on, lights.' The red traffic light seemed to be stuck, its glow washing over his fingers tapping impatiently on the steering wheel.

Glancing out the side window, he could see three scantily dressed women gathering at the corner of Victoria Street, studying him studying the red light. They seemed an apparition in the swampy snow.

It was then he recognised her, and did a quick and illegal U-turn, pulling up alongside the trio, before cranking the window down.

'Lipstick?' he said, to the youngest of the three whose skin was practically a pale blue hue from the cold. Her face was covered in make-up and bright red lipstick. To Karl, the lipstick looked like a bloody mouth wound.

'Hey, handsome. How about you and me doing...? Oh, Karl...' The young girl's forced smiled quickly disappeared.

'Get the hell in!' snapped Karl.

Lipstick's face went serious while reluctantly easing her slight frame into the car.

'Arse is frozen off,' she managed to say, shivering slightly, forcing a smile of sorts.

'Never mind that bollocks. You're out on bail, and only because Naomi was willing to go guarantor and say you wouldn't do any more solicitation. You promised her you'd quit – at least for a few months, until the weather turned and nights got a lot brighter.'

'I'm skint, Karl. I've bills to pay, and no money.'

'Your excuses are getting old very fast. We *all* have bills to pay, Lipstick. Stop feeling so bloody sorry for yourself. Do you want the same thing that happened to you during the summer to happen all over again?'

Lipstick looked away from Karl. 'No...never...'

Karl first met Lipstick – Sharon McKeever – six months ago, finding her cowering in the doorway of his office/apartment, late one night. She had been horrendously beaten by a pimp, but had managed to crawl into the first available doorway, seeking shelter. Thankfully, Naomi took control of the situation, and managed to do essential first aid until an ambulance arrived. The first aid probably saved her life, said the medics. Afterwards, Lipstick was unable, or unwilling, to bring charges against the wannabe tough guy, and so Karl – the genuine article of tough guy personified – decided to teach the scumbag a lesson in tough guy etiquette. The thrashing the pimp received wasn't as horrendous as the one apportioned to Lipstick, but it did leave him needing twenty delicate stitches on his palm tree and coconuts.

The next time, I'll cut your balls off, rather than simply battering them, hissed Karl, into the semi-conscious pimp's ear. *Only next time, there won't be a next time. Here's twenty quid. Get a bus ticket back to whatever rock you crawled out from under. If I even hear your name being whispered in Belfast, I'm going to come looking for you with a few friends of mine who aren't too friendly…*

Ever since that fateful day, Karl had become a protective father-figure to the young girl.

'Still using the protection I gave you?'

Lipstick nodded. Smiling a genuine smile, she put a hand inside her purse and removed an item.

'My knight of the night. Isn't that what you called it, Karl?'

It was a Smith & Wesson Centennial Airweight .38 Special, 2-inch revolver with snag-free configuration, specifically designed for women to pull quickly from handbags.

'You haven't had to use it, I hope?'

'No, just like you said, Karl: poking it in the face of a trouble-maker is enough to make him trouble-free. I only wish you'd have given me more than one bullet. I'd feel a lot safer.'

'One bullet is defence, even in the crooked court of Belfast law. Anything over that, and you're looking at conspiracy or worse. Anyway, once they see that in your hand, they'll run like hell – and that's before they shit their pants.'

Lipstick laughed. To Karl, it sounded rusty, unused, and it almost broke his heart. She was no older than Katie, and he wished he had the magical power to help her leave this seedy world of no-hope and daily danger.

'You called it my knight of the night, but you're really my knight, Karl.'

'You're such a bullshitter, Lipstick. Worse than me,' said Karl, turning the car back into the roadway.

'Where're you taking me?'

'I've a proposition to make to you.'

'A proposition?' Concern immediately registered on Lipstick's face. 'Normally, I'd be happy to, Karl, but you…you're different. I wouldn't do anything to hurt Naomi.'

'Don't worry. It's nothing like that.' From his wallet, Karl removed three twenties, and held them out.

'What's the catch?' asked Lipstick, suspiciously.

'No catch. You come back with me, right now, stay in our spare room for a while – at least until the weather warms up a bit.'

'I go back to your place, and get *paid* for it, without doing anything?'

'I didn't say the money was free, did I? You do some office work, make coffee, and answer the phone. The sort of shit Naomi can't be bothered to do anymore. You get paid weekly – *not a lot* – but you also get free rent at my place. What'd you say?'

'You sure?'

'Sure I'm sure.'

'You're the greatest, Karl.' She kissed him on the cheek and quickly put the money in her faux leather purse.

'Greatest mug, you mean? Just don't get all mushy on me, kid.' Karl turned the steering wheel and made a left into Hill Street.

Halfway up the street, he came to a silent halt at his office. The snow was thickening with each passing minute and he was grateful to be home.

Exiting the car with Lipstick, he prayed that Naomi was sleeping – or at least on talking terms. He doubted both. Bringing Lipstick back, though, was an unintentional inspiration. Hopefully, it would soften Naomi up.

'Strange hours you keep, Kane,' said a voice, somewhere directly behind. Karl turned to see a man emerging from the shadows.

'Who let you out of your cage, McCormack?' said Karl. 'Good to see you're still creeping about in the dark like a sneaky bastard. Old habits die hard, I suppose.'

McCormack was a six-three pillar of brick-hard, shit-house muscle, baptised in the fire of broken-bones, strap-your-balls-on street fights of Belfast. His leathery face was as welcoming as a kicked-in door, and his bald head gleamed with lamplight sheen. In his right hand he held a large tin of Red Bull. The blue tin was not as tall as McCormack's hand was wide. In his left hand he had a half-finished hot dog.

'Oh, I'm not sneaking anywhere, Kane. I'm here for all the whole world and you to see.'

'Well, *I* certainly feel a lot safer in bed, knowing you're outside freezing your nuts off,' said Karl, handing Lipstick the keys. 'I'll see you inside, Lipstick. Make yourself something to eat.'

Lipstick stared at McCormack nervously, before taking the keys and hastily making her way to the building. Seconds later, she was gone.

'You're old enough to be that young girl's father, Kane. Have you no shame?'

'Jealousy will get you nowhere, McCormack.'

'You're one very sick individual, Kane. Know that?'

'What I do know is this weather is fit for neither man nor beast. Then again, looking at you, I guess the beasts must be able to handle it.'

'Fuck you, Kane,' snarled McCormack.

'With my haemorrhoids? No thank you.'

McCormack swallowed the remains of the hot dog, and then drew the can to his large mouth, downing the contents in two greedy gulps. Seconds later, he scrunched the empty can into a wrinkled mess, and threw it into a cushion of snow.

'That's a fifty-pound fine, McCormack. We don't tolerate litter bugs in our swanky neighbourhood.'

In reply, McCormack freed a loud belch of gas into the night air.

'Manners, McCormack. You'll wake the neighbours with that impersonation of a hippo. Is it any wonder your job must be the only one in the world where you start at the bottom and work your way down?'

'You think you're so smart, don't you, Kane? Having a smart mouth isn't the same as having a smart brain.'

'Really? Someone once asked me how I defined ignorance and indifference. My response was I didn't know and didn't care. Sums up my thoughts perfectly regarding you.'

'Well, I think that's all going to change.' McCormack smirked. 'Now that I've been posted to city duties, I've access to numerous cold cases.'

'Cold cases? Is that your idea of a joke, here in the middle of winter?'

'I'm reading the case of two detectives, murdered by some scumbag who thinks he got away with the perfect murder.' McCormack's words hung in the air like a meat hook. He inched closer to Karl. 'In my book, there's no such thing as the perfect murder, Kane. Just an imperfect investigation.'

Karl's chest suddenly tightened as taut as a mousetrap.

'I'd really love to stand here, McCormack, wasting my time conversing with you, but I've a lovely warm bed and even warmer body calling. So, as the "Two Ronnies" would classically say: it's goodnight from me, and it's goodnight from him.'

'For now, Kane. For now…'

Inside, Karl leaned against the door he had just closed, his breathing laboured. His heart was racing madly. He tried calming it. Thought he was on the verge of a heart attack. Thought he could hear McCormack moving about in the snow. He pictured the gorilla, smiling. Waiting…

CHAPTER EIGHT

AN UNFINISHED LIFE

'Is there no way out of the mind?'
Sylvia Plath, *Apprehensions*

Heatherdale Nursing Home looked a perfect winter picture as Karl drove up its long and winding road, by-passing manicured trees, lawns and frozen fish ponds. Yet, no matter how picturesque it looked, Karl could never quite erase the trepidation gnawing his stomach each time he entered the great hall of the Victorian structure, waiting to visit his father, Cornelius.

The cold air had a savage bite to it as he stepped out of the car, before making his way towards the front entrance of the enormous building.

Inside, an eerie quietness patrolled the corridors, tightening the claustrophic atmosphere even further. Karl hated the tranquillity of deafening white noise. It forced his brain to ask questions; questions he would much rather avoid, even though he knew their looming inevitability stalked him like a shadow.

After signing in, he made his way towards his father's room. Just as he was about to tap on the door, an elderly nurse came into view, emerging from a corridor opposite him.

'Karl! Good to see you,' said the woman, loudly, ignoring the

'Silence' signs dotted everywhere. She had the cheerful face of a well-loved aunt, and the body of a well-fed one. 'Cornelius is expecting you.'

Karl smiled at the established lie. The relentless Alzheimer's permitted his father little memory of any visitor, family or friend, coming or going. A scan of the brain, taken three months ago, revealed significant shrinkage and rapid deterioration of cells.

'How's he doing, Sister Margaret?'

'Ignoring staff and instructions, as usual, the old villain.' Margaret smiled cheerfully. 'Got his appetite back, I'm glad to say. Eating like a horse. When were you here last?'

'I…' He thought of lying. Couldn't. 'Two weeks ago. I tried getting up last Tuesday, but—'

'You're here now. That's all that counts. We all have lives to live. Stop feeling so damn guilty, Karl.'

Her comforting words made him feel like a child lost, now found. The guilt eased. Slightly.

'Thanks, Sister…'

'Don't be silly. I see you've brought more coffee.' Margaret smiled. 'He must have twenty jars sitting in there.'

Karl's face reddened slightly. 'I'll try anything.'

'I know. I read the same research article about coffee reversing some of the damages of Alzheimer's. Always worth a try.'

Karl smiled, embarrassed. He couldn't think of any response. He doubted very much she believed the article. In all truth, neither did he.

'Thanks for all the great work you've done for him, Sister Margaret. It's very much appreciated.'

'Just doing my duty.'

'No, you've gone beyond that – you and all the staff.'

She smiled at the words. 'Call in and see me before you go, if you need to talk. We'll have some tea.' She touched his shoulder, before walking towards another corridor and out of sight.

Karl waited a few seconds before tapping meekly at his father's door, almost as if he didn't want to be heard.

No reply.

He opened the door and entered, waiting for the stomach -churning smells to rush him: urine, excrement, boiled unimaginative food, and the most salient of them all, loneliness.

Cornelius was sitting, his head leaning against the window. The breath from his nose kept making cones of haze on the glass. Other than that, there was hardly a movement from his body. A once tall and well-built man, Cornelius had now been reduced to a desiccated husk whose only flesh was prominent on his neck in small accordion folds of skin.

'Hey, Dad,' said Karl, touching his father's arm gently.

'Is it medicine time, sir?' asked Cornelius, glancing from the window, looking directly at Karl.

To Karl, his father's eyes appeared glazed over, as if in a trance. He seemed to have shrunk physically from the last time he had set eyes upon him. Karl looked at the weathered face, now an aged canvas of rough lines and creek-bed wrinkles. Oval creases were forming in dark folds around the eyes, giving them the sunken look of a corpse.

Oh god, Dad… 'It's…it's me, Dad. Karl. Your son,' said Karl, kissing the top of Cornelius' full head of grey hair.

'Son…?'

'Yes, Dad. Karl. Remember?'

'Karl…I remember a Karl…it's hard remembering…'

'I…know, Dad. It isn't easy. Don't…don't be worrying about it.'

'Karl was…he was a good boy…made a promise to me…'

Karl's stomach felt like it had just been kicked. 'I know he did…'

'Karl…'

'Yes, Dad?'

'Karl…' repeated Cornelius. 'He…he was a good boy…a very good boy…'

'And you're a good father, Dad. The best in the world,' said Karl, feeling something uncontrollable welling up inside.

Suddenly, Cornelius gripped Karl's arm, pulling him downwards, closer, whispering, *'Karl made a promise to me. Said he wouldn't let…let me live like this. Not like this. Didn't he understand? He broke that promise. I hate him.'*

Karl tried pulling away, but his father's grip was incredibly strong.

'Said he wouldn't let me live like a vegetable in the dark…'

'I…I know…'

Karl wrapped his arms around his father, gripping him tightly, remembering the time a million years ago, of a young boy crying, fearful of the dark and hiding in the ironing cupboard from the monster with a knife; the same monster that had just brutally raped and murdered the young boy's mother. The same monster that molested and left the young boy for dead.

There is no monster now, son, assured his father, hugging him tenderly. *He's gone forever. I'll never let him touch you again.*

Promise, Dad?

I promise, son. I'll keep the darkness away from you...

'I…I won't let the darkness come to you, Dad…'

Cornelius' eyes suddenly became bright and clear, the glaze dispelling if only for a moment.

'Promise?'

'Promise…'

▲ ▲ ▲

It was late when Karl arrived back at the apartment, haggard and defeated with guilt.

'What's wrong?' asked a concerned Naomi, as soon as Karl entered the living room.

'Besides everything, you mean?'

'Besides that. How was Cornelius?'

'Not good. His mental health is deteriorating rapidly.'

'Oh, Karl…' Naomi walked over to Karl, wrapping arms around him. 'I'm so sorry.'

'He hardly recognised me, and I feel so bloody helpless watching his deterioration. He's…he's like a stranger, lost in a strange world.'

Naomi tightened her grip. 'Oh, Karl…'

'I'm glad I asked you not to come. You wouldn't have recognised him from the giant of a man he once was.'

'He'll always be a giant. You've got to be strong for him, now. That's how Cornelius would want it.'

'I can still feel his big hands, warm on my head, when I left him sitting there in that damn room, all alone.'

'Let me make you some coffee and something to eat,' volunteered Naomi, heading towards the kitchen area.

'A Hennessy would go down a lot smoother.'

'Get some food in you first,' said Naomi. 'Then a bit of rest.'

'Where's Lipstick? Don't tell me she's flown the coop after only one day? Have we really become that boring, Naomi?'

'She said she's away to meet a friend, and that she'd be back by four.'

'Seeing that's it's almost seven, I guess she's disappeared again.'

'We'll, she knows where we live, if she needs a roof over her head,' said Naomi, disappearing into the kitchen.

Karl sat down without removing his coat. Bone tired, he could sleep forever.

He could still hear his father's petrified voice, somewhere in the recess of his head. *Promise?*

CHAPTER NINE

ON THE WATERFRONT

'Slice him where you like, a hellhound is always a hellhound.'
P.G. Wodehouse, *The Code of the Woosters*

Late Thursday night running towards Friday morning. The man eased his tall ageing frame into one of the many abandoned warehouses studded in the docks area of the city. Once inside, he glanced upwards through a broken window. The city skyline had a grim appearance. Floating above, the palest of moons hung like an un-sacked testicle. Rain was coming down, mixed with sleet, and the night air was biting with a vengeance.

He hated this cold weather and the dreary soul-destroying Belfast rain. Quickly pulled the overcoat tightly up to his ears, before lighting a cigarette. Sucked heavily on it, the nipple's glow partially lighting up the side of his face. Smoke began filtering from his nostrils in ghostly grey leakage. He coughed twice, before smothering the third cough with a cupped fist.

Despite the heavy darkness, he knew every square inch of the warehouse, having used the building for numerous backhanders from pimps, drug dealers and corrupt politicians.

Flicking the half-finished cig into the darkness, his free hand touched the damp overcoat tenderly. A necessity. Felt the bulging revolver snuggled warmly up inside. A talisman. His best friend. His *only* friend. He smiled. Assured.

He had arrived half-an-hour early, not wanting to be caught off-guard by any sudden and unexpected turn of events. If things went as planned, tonight's payment would see his dream of a villa in the south of France come closer, and retirement from this dangerous game finally closing for good.

From the outside darkness, eerie sounds came to his ears, slightly unnerving him: rusted chains chirped like wind chimes; battered directional signs squeaked on hinges; doors from abandoned containers knocked loudly up against their outer walls. A lone ship's horn sounded like a dying whale.

For a brief moment, he imagined the sounds of countless shipyard men working like ants, and growling industrial vehicles booming everywhere. But that was a million years ago. Now all that was left was rust. It was everywhere, devouring abandoned boats and every conceivable piece of metal. Even the genuflected weak light from the old lampposts failed to hide it.

His mobile phone buzzed, startling him slightly. He removed it from his pocket and glanced at the screen. He didn't recognise the number, but answered it anyway.

'Hello?'

The sudden coldness of gun metal against his neck numbed him. Momentarily, he became motionless. Then alive.

'A little distraction and deception,' said the gunman, slipping his hand expertly inside the man's overcoat, before removing the weapon. 'I thought it would take your mind off this being in your pocket. I didn't want any accidents.'

'Is this a robbery?' he asked, too late, suddenly recognising the face and realising the stupidity behind the question. 'You've been here all this time, in the dark, watching me?'

'A fox like you has to be outfoxed. It took a while to place you in this position, but I always knew your excessive love of money would be your Achilles' heel.'

He was frightened and incredibly angry; angry for allowing himself to fall this clumsily.

'You…you don't have to do this.' His voice now sounded wooden, desperate.

'You've left me no other choice. If I let you live, you'll become something I'll no longer have any control over. If you want, you can have some time to make peace with God. That's all I can offer you. It's the best deal you'll get.'

'God? I doubt very much if any god would have his ears open for me – or you, come the day.'

'You're wasting valuable time.'

'Well, then? What are you waiting for? Get it over with.'

A flash and a loud crack exploded from the barrel. Silver light filled the warehouse. A few seconds later, the darkness returned, closing down like a fist with something secret in it.

All went quiet on the waterfront.

CHAPTER TEN

A DAMSEL IN DISTRESS

'It was a blonde. A blonde to make a bishop kick a hole in a stained glass window.'
Raymond Chandler, *Farewell, My Lovely*

'**K**arl? There's a Miss Jemma Doyle wishing to see you,' said Naomi, popping her head into the office.

'Bit late for a Friday night, isn't it?' said Karl, reading his horoscope in the tabloid: *Money on its way. And a surprise, for later in the week.* 'Does she have an appointment?'

'No. I told her she needs to make one, but she was insistent. I can send her away, if you wish?'

'No, that's okay. Send her in,' said Karl, quickly discarding the newspaper in the top drawer of his desk. He had tried reading other parts of the newspaper earlier in the day – anything to take his mind off the disturbing visit to his father, two days ago – but couldn't stay focused. Cornelius' pleading voice – like a song or a perfectly crafted line of movie dialogue – continued to play over and over in his head.

No sooner had he closed the drawer than an extremely attractive woman appeared at the door, dressed in a stylish winter coat and skirt, and clutching a large leather handbag. Under the unbuttoned coat a black silk blouse revealed a generous 'v' of perfectly tanned skin. Her eyes were soft and doe-like, with just a hint of melancholy hidden behind them. Blonde hair reached to her shoulders and slightly beyond.

Karl guessed her to be in her late twenties, or early thirties at the most. Everything about her said class.

'Sorry, I know it's late, Mister Kane, but I didn't know I had to make an appointment,' said Jemma Doyle, flashing a perfect smile.

Only now did Karl notice the deep scarring on the left side of her face, not quite camouflaged by the expensive make-up she wore.

'No, don't worry, we were just doing our usual Friday night tidy up. Won't you sit down, Miss Doyle?' said Karl, touching Jemma's hand gently before shaking it rather carefully, as if too much force could dislodge the glove.

'Please forgive the gloves. I suffer terribly from eczema on my hands,' said Jemma, sitting down opposite Karl. 'This cold weather has an adverse effect on them.'

Nodding, Karl asked, 'What can I do for you?'

She leaned in close. Karl could smell her perfume. A musky scent. Expensive. The kind he bought Naomi on very special occasions. There hadn't been too many of those lately. Hopefully his horoscope's predictions would materialise.

'It's my uncle, Thomas Blake. He's been missing for a few years and my family have been trying to track him down. My father – his brother – wants to get in contact with him before…well, my father is extremely ill, Mister Kane…'

'I'm sorry to hear that, Miss Doyle.'

'Jemma. Please call me Jemma.'

'Jemma…' replied Karl, smiling a Colgate smile.

'I know how busy you must be. Your secretary was quite adamant that I come back some other time, but I really need for someone to find Uncle Thomas, before it's too late…' Jemma produced a Kleenex and began dabbing at her eyes. Her voice was quivering, threatening to quit altogether. 'I'm sorry…so silly of me…it's just that all this responsibility in finding him has been put on me, and it's stressed me out.'

'It's okay, Jemma' soothed Karl. 'Nothing like a good cry, I always say. That's what I do when I'm stressed.'

Jemma smiled. It made her even lovelier.

'Would you like some coffee, Jemma? Help warm you up.'

Jemma nodded. 'White, no sugar, please.'

Pressing a button on the intercom, Karl said, 'Naomi? Two coffees. White, no sugar, for Miss Doyle.'

'Get it yourself!' snapped Naomi, her voice as cold as the weather outside.

'Um, sorry, but I forgot that the coffee machine isn't working,' mumbled Karl.

'It's okay, Mister Kane.'

'Karl. Everyone calls me Karl.'

'Karl…I'm so glad I came here,' sniffed Jemma, forcing a smile while blowing her nose on the handkerchief. 'You'll probably think this sounds awfully stupid, but something guided me to this place.'

'Guided you?'

Jemma nodded. 'I was heading home, when my new car just refused to budge. An engine malfunction, apparently. According to the garage attendant, something about the chip in the car's computer.'

'The only chips my car knows are the ones I bring home on Saturday nights, plastered with salt and vinegar.' Karl smiled.

Jemma smiled in return, but the sad eyes belied it.

'The attendant is working on the car right now. Said Friday night's his busiest and it could be a couple of hours. So I just took a walk, while waiting. That was when I saw your business cards attached to a telephone box in Royal Avenue,' explained Jemma, producing one of Karl's cards from her pocket. 'Isn't that strange?'

'Very strange,' said Karl, feeling his face reddening. 'I wonder how on earth that got there?'

'*Kane's Able*,' smiled Jemma, reading the maxim inscribed upon the card. 'I thought that was brilliant.'

'One of my sharper moments, I have to agree.'

'Finding this card and coming here has lifted my spirits.'

'A bit like Lourdes.'

'Pardon?'

'Nothing,' replied Karl. 'When or where was the last time anyone had contact with your uncle?'

'According to my father, about six years ago. They had one of those family arguments over the family business, and neither of them backed down. My uncle left on that particular day and hasn't been seen or heard of since.'

'Nothing like a family to destroy a family business. Any photos of your uncle?'

'Yes,' said Jemma, removing three photos from her handbag.

'These are about the best. My uncle hated his photo being taken. He was a bit superstitious in that regard. I think my father has one or two others. I'll get them to you as soon as I can.'

Karl gave the photos a quick once-over. Uncle Thomas had an over-sized head, crowned with a bird's nest of unruly hair. The face was unsmiling and stern. A keep-well-the-fuck-away-from-me kind of uncle, thought Karl. 'Mind if I hold on to these?'

'No, not at all. You can return them to me once you're finished with them,' nodded Jemma. 'Now, your fee. We haven't talked about it. How much do you charge?'

'I'm not cheap,' said Karl. 'I charge two hundred quid a day – plus expenses.'

'That sounds reasonable,' said Jemma, reaching into the hand-bag again.

'Wish all my clients were as agreeable with my fees.' Karl was warming quickly to this appreciative woman.

'My cheque book. I think I left it at home.' Jemma suddenly looked troubled. 'Do you take cash, Karl, or must it be a cheque?'

'Cash is my preference. I'm actually allergic to cheques. They tend to burn me, on occasions, when the taxman discovers them.' Karl smiled. 'But look, Jemma, I still don't know if I'm going to take the case.'

'I have about one hundred with me,' replied Jemma, thrusting the money into Karl's ever weakening hands. 'I can stop by tomorrow and pay the rest. Would that be satisfactory?'

'We normally don't open on Saturday. Look…okay,' said Karl, resigned, taking the money. 'For now, though, let me do a bit of investigating. We can talk about the rest of the bill later. Agreed?'

Standing, Jemma nodded. She looked on the brink of tears,

once again, as she wrote on a piece of paper. 'You're so kind, Karl. I'll never forget you for this. Here's my phone number, if you need to call me.'

'Listen, Jemma, I have to be up front with you concerning missing persons. Luck plays a major part in finding the person sought – especially if that person doesn't want to be found. Understand? I just don't want you getting your hopes too high on me finding your uncle.'

'All I ask is that you do your best, Karl,' said Jemma, shaking Karl's hand before disappearing out of the office, leaving the fragrance of her expensive perfume floating in the air.

'You can close your mouth now, Karl. Flies are getting in,' said Naomi, quickly entering the room after Jemma's departure. 'A pair of panties and you crumble.'

'How can you be so hurtful?' said Karl. 'Anyway, what's eating you?'

'*We can talk about the rest of the bill later*,' mimicked Naomi, sarcastically.

'You were eavesdropping – *again*. What have I told you about that?'

'Since when did we begin taking deposits?' countered Naomi, ignoring the accusation. 'Miss Jemma Doyle looked as if she could more than afford our *special* client fee, never mind a nominal two hundred.'

'Naomi Kirkpatrick! I think you're jealous.'

'Tell that to the landlord next week when he comes for his money. Guarantee he won't be saying *we can talk about the bill later.*'

'You're starting to sound just like me, and that's scary. Come on. Let's head over to Nick's Warehouse,' said Karl, holding up the five twenties in surrender. 'I'll buy you a lovely evening meal – and I'll even have some expensive candlelight thrown in.'

'Good job I'm *not* the jealous type, Karl Kane.' Naomi smiled, quickly snatching the money from his hands.

'How come every time I get money handed to me, you have the uncanny ability to make me feel skint?'

'We'll order a nice vegetarian meal, washed down with some nice expensive wine.'

'Did I hear you right? Vegetarian?' said Karl, making a face. 'I warned you about trying to impose your sick beliefs on me. I want a good piece of meat, not some bloody dead plant or withered flowers.'

'No meat tonight. Come on. No more arguing,' said Naomi, putting on her jacket. 'A strange coincidence, don't you think, Jemma Doyle finding your card like that?'

'That's your suspicious mind working overtime, Naomi.' Karl grabbed his jacket, and began easing into it. 'I've no problem with coincidences – provided they only happen once and are entirely accidental. '

But as he turned the lights off in the office, his own suspicious mind went into overdrive. Actually, he hated coincidences, especially those introduced by beautiful women.

CHAPTER ELEVEN

ANALYZE THIS

'Nothing is perfect. There are lumps in it.'
James Stephens, *The Crock of Gold*

It was early next morning when Karl awoke to a million wasps rattling about inside his eardrums. Elsewhere, another type of noise was sounding, somewhere in the bedroom.

'Huh...?'

It was his mobile phone, resting on the bedside table.

He tried ignoring the incessant screeching, but the more he tried, the more the migraine headache drilled its way into the side of his skull.

Surrendering, he reached and lifted the annoying piece of plastic to his ear.

'Hello?' he asked in a groggy, injured tone.

'Karl? What the hell took you so long?' asked an annoyed voice. 'I was about to hang up.'

'Tom...? Sorry...I...oh, my fucking head...' moaned Karl, hand squeezing tight against his forehead. 'It's Saturday morning. Don't you ever go home?'

'Sounds like you over-indulged in something, and I'm not talking about vitamins.'

'Went out for a meal last night with Naomi. Got blocked out of my head. I think she spiked my drink. She'll do anything to get me into bed.'

An elbow shot into Karl's ribs.

'*Oh!* That hurt, Naomi,' protested Karl. 'Thought you were sleeping?'

'*Keep me out of your conversation,*' hissed Naomi, rolling over, taking most of the blankets with her.

'Karl? Are you there?' asked Hicks.

'Sorry, Tom. Go ahead.'

'I've got some news on the severed hand found outside your place.'

'Oh?'

'I had one of the lads take a picture of it and enlarge it by ten.'

'And?'

'You *were* right. It is the number eighty-eight.'

'Hate to say it, but I told you so.'

'I also did another re-run on the Kevin Johnson hand, but, although he had plenty of other tats, there was no sign of the number eighty-eight.'

'Bang goes another of my grand theories of Johnson and the serial killer.' Karl thought for a second. 'Could be a cult of some sort. Witchcraft, perhaps?'

'Don't be ridiculous. I doubt very much we have a coven of witches running about Belfast.'

'You wouldn't be saying that if you'd witnessed some of the women I went out with years ago.'

'Can you stop the nonsense, just for a second?' said Hicks, obviously tiring of Karl's puerile prattle.

'Could be bingo aficionados.'

'What's that supposed to mean?'

'Eighty-eight. Two fat ladies. Those bingo fanatics would kill for a thrill.'

'I've got to go.' Hicks sighed. 'Talk to you later.'

'Before you kiss me goodbye, could you do me a really big favour?'

Silence at the other end.

'Tom? I know you're there. I can hear your heavy, sexy breathing.'

'What is it?' sighed Hicks.

'I need you to check the records for a Thomas Blake. He's a missing person, but could be dead.'

Karl could hear Hicks scribbling something.

'Okay, but that's you favoured-out for the rest of the month,' replied Hicks. 'If I discover anything, I'll let you know. Give my regards to Naomi.'

Turning the phone off, Karl squeezed in closer to Naomi's deliciously warm body. She stirred and growled in protest at the coldness of his touch.

'That dirty old bastard, Hicks, said he wanted to ravage you,' said Karl, nuzzling her neck while stroking her warm arse. 'I told him I would kill any man who even dared look at you.'

'Get your roaming hands off my bum,' protested Naomi.

He could tell she was smiling, and began pressing harder against her arse. His erection added an exclamation mark between her warm, firm buttocks.

She groaned softly. 'Anyone ever tell you, you're a *bad*, man, Mister Kane?'

'Bad relationships, bad debts and a lot of bad business in between, will do that to a man once good.' Karl began whispering into her ear. *'What do you say we stay in bed all day and do nothing but dirty things to each other?'*

'What kind of dirty things, good sir?' responded Naomi, merrily. *'Do you want to cane me, Mister Kane?'*

'That can be arranged for later, you naughty girl, but right now I was thinking of that jar of honey in the kitchen. I would just love to put it—'

The mobile phone suddenly screamed again on the bedside table.

Karl ignored it.

The phone stopped ringing.

They both smiled.

It rang again.

'Shouldn't you answer that, Sugar Kane?' whispered Naomi, hoarsely, face slightly flushed. Her hands were cupping his balls, as if weighing them.

'Answer what? I don't hear a thing except the sound of someone playing Tubular Bells *on my globular balls.'*

'Could be important.'

'What's more important than having sex with the woman I love?' murmured Karl, ice-skating his nails over her left breast and nipple.

'Business!' said Naomi, swatting his hand away while reaching for the phone. 'Hello? Oh…yes, one second, please.' Making a face, Naomi mouthed, *Jemma Doyle…'*

Taking the phone, Karl said, 'Hello? Yes, Jemma. No, you didn't catch me at a bad time.'

Naomi rolled her eyes.

Less than a minute later, Karl clicked the phone off.

'She has a few more photos of her uncle for me.'

'Why didn't you ask for the fees?'

'I will.'

'I have to pee,' stated Naomi huffily, getting out of bed.

'Be quick, my dearest. I have a rocket for your pocket.'

'Get stuffed,' she pronounced, walking towards the bathroom, breasts bouncing seductively, small buttocks seesawing mischievously.

'Hurry, my dearest…'

She mumbled something nasty before scurrying into the bathroom, slamming the door loudly behind her. A few seconds later, Karl could hear the toilet seat falling, followed by familiar tinkling sounds.

'I have something for *youuuuuuuuuuuu*,' he sang out loudly. 'It's hot and getting bigger by the second.'

'Really?' shouted Naomi from the bathroom. 'Well, until you get more money from Miss Jemma Doyle, you can put your tiny dick back in its matchbox. It's not lighting my fire any time soon…'

CHAPTER TWELVE

BLOOD WORK

'Oh! God! That bread should be so dear,
And flesh and blood so cheap.'
Thomas Hood, *The Song of the Shirt*

'Hello, Tom? Karl,' said Karl, holding the phone while guiding his car into a wasteland of grey buildings and mangled steel frames, three days later. 'Listen, I think all those cop mutts are barking up the wrong tree.'

'Really? And what tree should they be barking up?'

'The tree where I'm heading, right at this moment. The only abattoir in Belfast.'

'The abattoir? Are you serious?'

'Why not? I don't necessarily believe it has to be a doctor or medical student. A good butcher is as skilled at slicing meat as any surgeon. I was at the Continental Market yesterday, at the City Hall, and watched German butchers working on a pig. Horrible to look at, but they were brilliant, the way they did it. That's when I got the idea.'

Karl could hear Hicks making a grunt of scepticism. 'I think you're way off, Karl, and wasting your time.'

'Admittedly, I'm thinking outside the box, but this was once owned by the Shank family.'

'The Shank family? The name doesn't immediately ring a bell.'

'I'll explain it all to you when I get back.'

'Just be careful. Those sort of places have a terrible safety record,' said Hicks. 'In the meantime, I've got some news on the fingerprints on the hand found at your doorstep. His name is – or *was*, assuming he's dead, of course – Billy Brown. A very bad boy, indeed, according to police and prison records.'

'Oh? What did Bad Boy Billy Brown do time for?'

'You name it, he's done it. Rape, arson, attempted murder, to list a few.'

'An impeccable CV. Anything else?'

'He was originally from London, and a member of the neo-Nazi BNF.'

'The British National Front?'

'Yes, plus he was wanted in England for the attempted murder of a young black man in the London Underground, four years ago. Been on the run ever since, and was apparently hiding over here, sheltered by loyalist paramilitaries in Limavady, Coleraine and Ballymena, to name just a few small towns.'

'As if we haven't enough of our own locally grown scumbags, we're now importing them,' said Karl, bringing the car to a halt. 'Perhaps someone within the paramilitaries killed Bad Boy Brown because he was bringing too much heat?'

'We'll never know unless we find the body – *if* there is a body to be found.'

'Time will tell. Anyway, I've got to go. I'm at the abattoir now. If all goes well, I'll brass neck it, and ask for a few free steaks for you.'

'Just watch yourself.'

'I didn't know you cared, Tom Hicks,' replied Karl, blowing a kiss down the phone before snapping it shut.

The abattoir was located near Duncrue Street, a desolate, so-called industrial area where men were men – and even some of the women, too. Shells of shuttered factories landscaped the grey-brick background, like shantytowns of desolation. Walls of putrid garbage did eerie slow-motion movements, caused by burrowing rats gnawing everything in sight. An abandoned train with dilapidated carriages sat glued with rust. Mountains of disused car tyres snaked in dark coils, resembling giant anacondas awaiting victims.

Exiting the car, Karl could see, too late, that the women and men of the night had obviously been busy plying their trade. A minefield of used condoms were splattered everywhere, mimicking a post-paintball fight. To make matters worse, bloody spillage from the slaughterhouse mingled with the condoms and other unmentionables.

'*Shit!*' he uttered, accidentally walking into the collateral damage of dead sex and animal leakage. Gingerly, he began shaking away the sticky sheaths from the sole of his shoe. 'What a fucking mess.'

Outside the abattoir gate, he gazed over the building, taking in its Gothic-like appearance. It was a mammoth, grey cement structure begging to be demolished. Grim was an understatement. Dull lights peered dimly from behind numerous frosted-glass windows. The smell of rainy ozone on tarmac floated heavily in the air, at once familiar and strange, and for a very brief moment Karl felt the specific sensation of everything being unreal.

'Creepy fucking place…'

Dove-grey smoke drifted upward from a massive industrial chimney, like a ghost, formless yet controlled. There was something eerily unsettling and intimidating about the place, a chill that caused the hairs on the back of his neck to stand on end. A sensation Karl always dreaded.

Above, the evening sky had become menacing.

'What the hell are you doing here…?' he mumbled, seconds before entering a decrepit office furnished with a laminated table, two battered yellow chairs, one occupied by a middle-aged man, and a couple of metal cabinets diseased with rust spots. On the table sat a bust of a severed pig's head, its languid tongue resting between yellow and bloody teeth. The place reeked of confinement, with the added unattractiveness of a post-war kitchen. Dying fluorescent tubes flickered overhead, spitting annoyingly.

'Hello, there. Are you the owner?' asked Karl, tapping at the door, looking directly at the man.

The man had skinny streaks of grey hair, yellow moustache and the bluest eyes Karl had ever seen. He seemed engrossed in a newspaper. An ancient pipe rested in his mouth, despite the large 'No Smoking' sign spiked against the far wall. The stench of burning tobacco was everywhere.

For a few seconds more, the man continued reading the newspaper, before placing the smouldering pipe in a filthy ashtray nailed to the table's top.

'No, I'm the manager. John Talbot's the name. The owner, Geordie Goodman, is over at the pens, taking stock, and very busy right now, Mister…?'

'Kane. Karl Kane,' replied Karl extending his hand. Despite

Talbot's face being mottled with age, Karl quickly discerned that the old dog still retained a greatly part of a once-formidable build, and that his bite would be a hell of a lot worse than his bark. 'Everyone calls me Karl.'

'How can I help you, Karl?' asked Talbot, standing, shaking Karl's hand. Talbot's grip felt like cold iron. He was Karl's height, about 6-3 or so, but stooped. Across the shoulders, he was two of Karl.

'I'm a film scout, looking for a good location for Channel Four. They're making a horror movie, about zombies. I hope you're not easily insulted, John, but this place looks perfect to use for the film.'

'Zombies?' Talbot suddenly released a howl of laughter. 'You've come to the right place. Most of the so-called workers in here *are* zombies!'

Karl joined in the laughter, some forced, some appreciative.

'I'll have to remember that one, John, when I go back to the studio and file my report.'

'You'd have to see the boss for the final say, of course, but I can give you a quick tour of the place, until then. That's if you're up to it?'

'Would you? That's terrific.'

'Think nothing of it. Here. Put this on,' said Talbot, handing Karl a battered hardhat, red in colour. 'Ready?'

'Yes.' Karl squeezed the hat on. It was a right fit.

'Come on. This way,' nodded Talbot, walking towards the door. 'I should warn you, though: you better have a strong stomach. It can be a bloody horrible sight.'

'A bit like my ex-wife.'

A quick bark of a laugh burst through Talbot's nose. 'Yes, I have one of those myself. *Axe*-wife, I call her.'

'I love your wit, John. There could be a part in this movie for you, if you're interested. Wouldn't be much, of course.'

'You're kidding? Me in a movie? Bloody hell!'

'How did you know the title of the movie?'

'What? Oh! Now you're winding me up. Come on. Over beside those two doors.'

The two enormous steel doors opened automatically, and a shiver touched Karl despite the freezing temperature already mounting throughout the building.

The noise of skull-rattling machinery was suddenly everywhere. Karl could feel its strength tremble beneath him. It made him uncertain.

'No point in standing there if you want to see inside,' said Talbot, a rubbery smile on his face. 'They won't bite – at least not yet.'

Tentatively, Karl entered, immediately feeling as if an invisible hand had slammed against his stomach. The place was massive and seemed to have no boundaries. It was breathtakingly horrible, like the Sistine Chapel bloodied by barbarians. Its dank coldness reeked with tension and void of all things human. The enormous floor was littered with sawdust chips speckled red with bloody imperfections. There was a sense of danger about the place; a sense that someone was going to be killed before the day was complete.

To Karl's left, gangs of sad-looking cows were being herded up a metal gangplank affair, led by a bizarre-looking creature.

'Is that a goat?' quizzed Karl, pointing at the scruffy animal with a head crowned by blonde curly locks.

Talbot nodded gleefully. 'That's old Martin, the Judas Goat. He keeps the cows calm, as if on a picnic. Unbeknown to them, they're following him obediently up the ramp to their doom. They haven't a clue what's waiting for them.'

To Karl's amazement and horror, old Martin suddenly slipped into a tiny hideout, leaving the cows alone and looking bewildered. Karl could have sworn the old goat was grinning from ear to ear just as it made its exit.

'The cows can usually smell a trap, but like all good traps, they can't escape it. After the trap comes that…' said Talbot, pointing at the far wall.

Suddenly, from behind hidden panelling, a group of young women appeared, stun guns in hands. Seconds later, they placed the stun guns behind each cow's head and pulled the trigger, releasing a plunging bolt directly into the unfortunate creatures' brains. The pneumatic hissing of the stun guns was everywhere, sounding like a million disturbed snakes.

'Ten thousand volts of pure kick applied to the head renders each animal unconscious,' continued Talbot. 'The stun gun prevents adrenaline from entering the animal's bloodstream, ruining the tenderness and beauty of the meat.'

'*Dear Lord…*' muttered Karl, feeling the violence of the act recoiling in his stomach.

'Don't worry too much, Karl. It's all humanely done. They hardly feel a thing.' Talbot winked. 'At least that's what we tell the public and the media.'

Without warning, each cow went keeling over in a thunderous thud, as if on ice, shit, piss and blood rocketing from all natural cavities. Legs broke. Necks snapped. Eyes popped from their enclosures.

*Fuck the night…*thought Karl, turning quickly away from the horrendous scene.

'Come on, Karl. Down this way, into the butchering arena, where the real kings reign.'

Seconds later, Karl entered the arena and almost immediately his nostrils began flooding with a stomach-churning smell of salty iron. The same stinking stench from outside the building was coming at him with force, but more powerful, more tangible in its taste of freshly slaughtered meat.

Air. Need some fucking air, thought Karl, trying desperately to hold control of breath and stomach.

Blood-splattered butchers were performing an opera of death, knives flowing fluently as conductors' batons, cutting sinew and meaty parts expertly. With the animals' hearts still capable of pumping blood, the legs were being removed from just below the shoulder by hydraulic shears.

Karl steeled himself to watch, wondering which of these butchers wouldn't think twice about slicing and dicing a human being?

'The arteries are severed and the heart pumps most of the animal's blood from the body in less than two minutes,' said Talbot's blasé voice, in what sounded like a well-rehearsed explanation. 'The draining blood flows through that floor grate and into a collection system for final processing into fertilizer and other uneatable items.'

The butchers continued hacking at the warm meat, ignoring Karl and Talbot. To Karl, the butchers' faces seemed to be filled with hypnotic madness. Women saturated in blood began packing the hacked parts into plastic containers.

'Those are the labourers,' grinned Talbot, almost dismissively, pointing at the women. 'Are you feeling okay, Karl? You look pale. You're not going to be sick, are you?'

'I'm fine…I think I've seen enough…' His stomach suddenly felt like a springboard. A vile acid bile rose to his mouth. He forced it back down, and felt its kick in his stomach.

'Actually, Karl, you lasted longer than most people do when they first come here and have a wee tour of–'

'What on earth is that contraption?' asked Karl, pointing at an enormous metal container stationed at the far side of the room. The huge device had all the appearances of a medieval torture chamber, with leather straps and numerous levers and buttons protruding outwards. It was caked in blood and rust, and to Karl, resembled something out of an Edgar Allan Poe nightmare on acid.

'Oh, that's the Slaughter Restraint,' said Talbot.

'The what?'

'The Slaughter Restraint. That's where the Jewish butchers do their kosher cleansing. *Shechita* they call it.'

'*Shechita*?'

'The ritual slaughter of animals according to Jewish dietary laws. They cut the cow's throat with a great big bloody knife called a *hallaf*. God the night, you want to see the blood! Buckets of it. You've got to see it to believe it.'

To Karl, Talbot seemed to be relishing the details a little too much. 'Sounds absolutely horrific.'

'Not at all. It's quick and painless, but a lot of those interfering do-gooders and animal welfare organisations have disputed this.

What the hell would they know? They're not getting it done to them, are they? That's logical.'

Not wanting to argue with Talbot's take on logic, Karl said, 'Sounds awfully complicated just to eat a piece of meat.'

'Well, these Jews are a complicated people. That's how their God tells them to eat. If the hindquarters of the animal are to be eaten, they must be stripped of veins, fat, suet and sinews. Do you read the Bible?'

'No…I mean not on a regular basis.'

'Well, it's all in there, if you ever feel that way inclined.'

'Are any of your butchers specifically assigned to do this?' said Karl, the gears in his brain moving nicely with suspicion.

'Ha! They're not even allowed touch the cow, never mind butchering it for them. Jews have strange customs. They think us Gentiles are unclean – though they'll never say that to your face, of course. They're afraid we'll contaminate their grub. No, what they do is get one of their rabbis to do the killing. That keeps them right in the eyes of God. If you read the Bible, you'd know all that, just like me.'

'What part does the Slaughter Restraint play in all this?'

'The Slaughter Restraint is connected to that room above.' Talbot pointed to a room directly above the Slaughter Restraint. 'Once the animal – usually a cow – is forced into the Slaughter Restraint, it's immediately clamped in tightly by two buffers, before being inverted by the turning mechanism inside the chamber. Then the cow's upside down head pops over that half-moon ledge, exposing the lengthy neck.' Talbot stretched out his own neck, and made a slicing motion across it. 'That's when the deed is done, slicing through to the jugular vein.'

'I think I get the picture…'

'You have to see it to believe it.'

'I'd rather not,' replied Karl, quickly. 'This chamber is used exclusively by the Jewish community?'

'Not necessarily. Muslims use it, too, and a couple of trendy restaurant owners. When it come to money, we don't have any religious discrimination,' chuckled Talbot. 'How about a tea, before you go?'

'Coffee, if you have it,' said Karl, doubting that his stomach would hold it down.

▲ ▲ ▲

Five minutes later, Karl sat at the table watching Talbot rummaging through a battered and paint-peeling cupboard. He removed a near-empty bottle of Bushmills.

'Medicinal purposes. Works wonders,' said Talbot, winking.

'Just like WD-40.' Karl grinned.

'I know I had some coffee here, somewhere.' Talbot began pushing items out of the way. 'One of the thieving bastards has sneaked in when they saw me on the floor. Probably nicked it. You need eyes in the back of your head for this job.'

'Don't trouble yourself, John.' Karl glanced at his watch. Almost two and a half hours had passed since he first arrived. He needed to get moving. 'I really have to be—'

'No trouble at all. I know someone who has loads of the stuff. Back in a tick,' said Talbot, quickly exiting the door, ignoring Karl's protestation.

Never one to allow a golden opportunity to slip by, the moment Talbot was out the door, Karl stood before hastily walking to one of the cabinets marked 'Employees' Payroll'.

Sliding open the top drawer, he immediately began scanning

the folders for something, anything, to jump out at him.

Unfortunately, it was Karl doing the jumping.

'What do you think you're doing?' asked a calm but firm voice at the door.

'Shit!' exclaimed Karl, almost slamming the metal drawer on his fingers.

A young woman, walking stick in hand, stood at the door, glaring at him. Her eyes were mirrored bullets, lethal in their intensity. He could almost feel the heat coming from them. She was small, 5-5, but Karl knew that dynamite can come in small packages, and if ever he was looking at living explosives, this was it. He couldn't help but notice the braces looping the outside of her legs like a miniature steel construction. They seemed to be the only thing stopping her from toppling over.

'You better have a good reason for searching private property,' she said, threateningly. 'Just who the hell are you?'

'Never mind who I am, just who the hell are *you*?' said Karl, shaken, but brave-facing it with a bluff.

'If that's the way you want to play it, we'll let the police do all the questioning.' Producing a mobile from her pocket, she hit a few numbers. Placing it to her ear, she said, 'Hello? Yes, I'd like to report a break-in at—'

'Whoa, there. Let's just think about this for a few seconds and not be too hasty, Miss…?'

'One moment, please, officer…' she said into the mobile, before looking straight into Karl's eyes, glaring even more intensely.

'Okay. You win. I'm a private investigator,' said Karl, removing one of his business cards and holding it out.

'Place it on the table. Sit down. Don't make any sudden moves.'

'The way you're talking, you'd think that was a gun in your hand instead of a cane, Miss…?' said Karl, complying.

'Don't let the walking stick fool you. I'm more than capable of defending myself from the likes of you.' Lifting Karl's card from the table, the young woman appeared to be scrutinising it. A few seconds later, she spoke into the mobile. 'Sorry, officer. False alarm. No…everything is okay. Thank you.'

'I guess that means you believe me?' said Karl, watching her pocket the phone.

'I rarely believe anyone, least of all strangers. Luckily for you, I remember the name *and* face. I saw you on the TV, not so long ago. Something to do with finding a kidnapped girl. A university student, wasn't it?'

Karl nodded. 'My daughter, Katie.'

'Oh…she's okay?' The woman's face softened slightly.

'As much as can be expected, considering what she went through, Miss…?'

'Goodman. Georgina Goodman. Everyone calls me Geordie,' she replied, approaching the table before sitting down, resting the walking stick on top.

'*You're* the boss…?'

'That's correct. *I'm* the boss. You look shocked. Don't think women can handle being bosses?'

'No…nothing like that. It's just…this abattoir. Not the most glamorous of places, or what I'd expect a young woman to be in charge of.'

'It once belonged to my father. But that, as they say, is another story. Now, what exactly are you doing here, searching? And no bullshitting.'

'No, I'm sure you get enough of that in the pens,' said Karl, forcing a smile but receiving only a stony stare from Geordie. 'Look, to be honest with you, I know a bit of history about this place, the killings a few years back.'

Geordie suddenly stiffened. Her eyes narrowed. 'If you're here to do some sort of blackmailing, then you're wasting your time. It's all public knowledge, what went on here back then, with my father and sister.'

'No, I'm not here to dig up the past, I can assure you. You're aware of the body parts discovered in and around the city, I assume?'

'The mysterious severed hands? Of course. Who isn't? They're the talk of Belfast.'

'Yes, well the cops think it could be a doctor, but I think—'

'You think it could be someone working here, because of its grisly history.' It was a statement. 'The police have already been here, last week, asking questions.'

'What…? Oh…I thought…'

'That no one else had checked us out?'

'Something like that. My ego has been slightly dented now.'

'The cops seemed to be more interested in free steaks, rather than any answers.'

'Greedy corrupt bastards. They're all the same. Can't watch them.'

'I doubt very much that we've a serial killer running about the place, Mister Kane. I told the police the same. The people working here may look frightening with all that blood on their faces and hands, but it actually washes off at the end of a hard working day. Sorry to disappoint you.'

'I didn't mean to insult the workers, but this is the only abattoir we have in Belfast.'

'Not forgetting its bloody history, of course?'

'Well, yes…' Karl was beginning to look uncomfortable. 'Admittedly, I could be a mile off track, but then again, I could be a couple of inches near.'

Geordie sighed. 'I can see you're not going to drop this, Mister Kane, so what exactly do you want from me?'

'Have you noticed any unusual behaviour from anyone working here? Someone keeping odd hours, out-of-the-normal absenteeism? Anything of that nature?'

'I'd have to go through all the files, again, just like I did for the police. That's going to be time-consuming. We've only recently started to computerise the business. My father wasn't a great believer in computerised technology or–'

'Got some!' said Talbot, entering the room. 'If I get my hands on that thieving bastard…oh, Geordie. Didn't see you sitting there. You've met Mister Kane, then? He's a scout for Channel Four. They're thinking of shooting a movie here. Can you believe it?'

Karl's face reddened.

Geordie smiled wryly. 'Yes, John. Mister Kane has been explaining in great detail his line of work to me.'

'Look, I don't think I can stop for that coffee, after all, John,' said Karl, standing. 'Just remembered another appointment.'

'Oh, you're going?' said Talbot, looking slightly disappointed. 'Sorry I took so long.'

'Don't worry about it, John. Hopefully, the next time I'll get a chance to savour it,' said Karl, before looking directly at Geordie. 'You will let me know your decision, Miss Goodman?'

'It's *Mrs* Goodman,' said Geordie, forcing herself up from the table before reaching for the walking stick. 'Goodbye, Mister Kane. Be careful on the way out. The lighting isn't that great.'

Karl thought he could detect a slight warning in Geordie's voice.

Outside in the cold air, Karl cleared his lungs of the lingering stench bottled inside. He spat a few times, his mouth cotton dry. He knew it would take a longer time to rid himself of the taste lingering in his mouth.

Just as he was about to get into the car, his phone rang. It was Hicks. He sounded annoyed.

'Why'd you have your phone turned off? I've been calling you for over an hour.'

'Just got caught rummaging through a woman's drawers.'

'Huh?'

'Nothing. What's wrong, dear Tom?'

'Just calling to let you know that I'll have the information you wanted on Blake, tomorrow.'

'Excellent. How about I drop by in the afternoon?'

'Make it morning – *early*. I've a court attendance before noon.'

'Very much appreciated, Tom. See you in the morning, first thing.'

Karl clicked the phone dead and began easing the car out in the direction of the road. As he looked in the rear-view mirror, he could have sworn someone was watching from the abattoir window. It looked like Geordie Goodman.

Tiny mice suddenly ran up his spine. He shuddered in a very bad way. He hated when his spine moved like that.

CHAPTER THIRTEEN

A TOWN CALLED BASTARD

'She had eyes like strange sins.'
Raymond Chandler, *The High Window*

It was early next morning when Karl showed up at Hicks' office.

'Don't offer me any coffee, Tom. My stomach's not feeling the best,' said Karl.

'You really should consider cutting down on the booze. It's not doing you any good, from the looks of it.'

'Booze has nothing to do with it. It was all that bloody blood in that hellhole called an abattoir. What have you on Blake?'

'Done time. Nothing major, it would seem. Released from prison three years ago. Burglary, a few years back. Last known address to be the town of Ballymena.'

Hicks gave a possible street address, explaining that the information was sketchy at best.

'It's better than nothing,' said Karl extracting a beaten docket, and scribbling on it.

'What're you writing?'

'Good plans always start with a piece of paper. No matter how you figure it, adding and subtracting comes to zero. It's what's in between that gives the final sum. No need to be concerned.'

'I'm *always* concerned when I give you information. I hope you're not going to do anything illegal with it?'

'Nothing *too* illegal.' Karl smiled. 'I'm getting paid, so I'll take a wee trip out to the backwoods of the Bible belt, later today. See if I can coax uncle Thomas and Lassie to come home, all is forgiven.'

'You shouldn't be so hard on Ballymena. It gets a bad rap from outsiders.'

'Bad rap? Don't make me laugh. Their very own paper, the *Ballymena News*, stated that there are at least two hundred and thirty heroin addicts living in the Ballymena area – that's a staggering seventy per cent of the province's heroin users. And I can still remember the excellent exposé the *Guardian* did, a few years back.'

'Those figures are probably embellished.'

'Embellished, my arse. Did you know that heroin is easier to purchase in Ballymena than hard liquor, condoms, clean air and good neighbours? Suicide is very high – though not high on the fundamentalist Christian agenda of saving the dead rather than the living.'

'Christians are an easy target, Karl. You're starting to sound like a bully.'

'Good Christian people is the term Ballymenians normally use to refer to themselves, ignoring the ingrained sectarianism devouring their town. Ballymenians may indeed be legendarily humourless, but it can't be denied that they don't have a strong case for irony.'

'There's a lot of culture in that wee town.'

'Culture?' Karl shook his head and walked to the door. 'Bacteria's got more culture than bloody Ballymena. I'll talk to you later, when I get back.'

It was four hours later when Karl parked his car in an underground car park on the edge of Ballymena town centre. The night was quickly coming on outside and he wanted to get to a bar inside; hopefully one contained within the cut-price motel he was planning to book into. He didn't feel like doing too much walking tonight.

Exiting the car with a scuffed leather grip bag in hand, he spotted two men playing cards outside a makeshift office. One was elderly and in a wheelchair; the other much younger, dressed in grease-monkey garbs.

'Do I pay now, or later?' asked Karl, directing his question at both men.

'Where d'you think you're at, big lad? Pay now, of course,' said Grease Monkey, grinning a row of black and missing teeth. He smelt strongly of car oil and stale body odour. He had mean, tiny tight eyes, and looked as if he hadn't shaved since King Camp Gillette was in nappies.

Karl had difficulty deciphering the man's broad Ballymena drawl, and immediately though of *Duelling Banjos,* Grease Monkey making his way through the swamps of Ballymena, shotgun in hand, looking for virgin male passageways. A yellowing poster above the office door alerted him to the mindset of Grease Monkey and Co: '*Immigrants are like sperm. Millions get in, but only one works*'.

'How much?' said Karl, going for his wallet.

'How long?' said Grease Monkey.

'One night,' replied Karl, carefully erasing *I hope* from the sentence.

'Ten quid. Be back before this time tomorrow, otherwise you pay double.' Grease Monkey grinned annoyingly, again, before throwing down a three of clubs on the table.

The older man quickly lifted the card. Smiled all gums. Threw out a different card in return.

'I got a straight run, Jimmy boy.' The old man proudly displayed the cards in his hand.

'That's not a straight, Chester. All the cards need to follow each other. Told you that before.'

Karl could see that neither man was actually playing with a full deck, but, deciding to direct his questions to the man in the wheelchair, he asked, 'The Motel Royal. How far am I from it?'

'Depends how far you want to be.'

Grease Monkey grinned at Chester's reply.

'Could you walk there?' asked Karl, getting annoyed, before realising his Freudian slip.

'What the hell's that suppose to mean?' asked Chester, clearly upset. 'You trying to be a smart arse? If I could walk *at all*, the first thing I'd do is sink my useless boot into your big city arse.'

Grease Monkey giggled like a big girl on her first kiss.

'I'm...I'm sorry,' mumbled Karl. 'I meant...could *I* walk there, or would I need to call a taxi?'

'When you get outside, turn left,' said Grease Monkey. 'Two streets down make another left. Cross over to Burger King. Directly behind it, three streets to your left and you'll see The

Royal. Don't go down the street directly beside Burger King, though. Take the one beside the burnt-down school and abandoned police station, but avoid Dog Turd Avenue, if you know what's good for your health.'

'Thanks.' Karl handed Grease Monkey a ten spot.

'Though, if I were you, I'd take a taxi,' stated Grease Monkey, an oily hand quickly taking the money. 'Not the safest part of town, where you're heading. Just last week we had two men stabbed to death in a drug fight, not a kick in the dick away from where you're staying. Lots of skegheads roaming about.'

'Skegheads?' The tag sounded like a bad sci-fi movie.

'Heroin junkies. You'll recognise them by their yellow skin and lack of beef. Those lads or lassies would cut you for a penny. There's a load of them roaming about out there at this time of night.'

Karl's stomach did a little bend. 'Know something? I think I'll take your advice and call a taxi. You wouldn't happen to have the number of a reliable taxi place?'

'Sure. That's my taxi, over there beside the exit. Hop in. I'll take you,' said Grease Monkey, throwing down his cards. 'Look after the place, Chester. Won't be long.'

Inside, the taxi was packed with Christian pamphlets and hymnbooks with Ian Paisley's name plastered all over them.

Ballymena isn't known as the Bible belt of Ulster for nothing, or being forward in its backward way of thinking, thought Karl, easing the hymnbooks out of the way.

'You can have one of those, if you're Christian-inclined,' said Grease Monkey, starting the car-cum-taxi wreck. 'No charge. We never charge for the Reverend Paisley's word being spread.'

'Thanks,' said Karl, reluctantly lifting one of the pamphlets, trying not to offend. 'I'll read this later on. There's nothing I like better than to snuggle up to a good read and cup of cocoa in bed.'

Grease Monkey smiled approvingly.

Less than a minute later, Karl was travelling down an unmarked dirt road, where a featureless and flat housing estate dissolved into squalor, infested with the rotten stench of grey hopelessness.

'Motel Royal,' said Grease Monkey, halting the car on skidding wheels. 'If there's anything you need while staying in our lovely town, just give me a howler. Everyone knows me. The name's Grassy Noel.'

'Grassy Noel?'

'It's my street tag. I sell a little bit of weed on the side. Can have some for you in about ten minutes, if you want? Bring it right up to your room.'

'No thanks. I gave up gardening a long time ago.'

'If you're worried about getting caught with it, don't worry. I have a saying: on the street, always be discreet.'

'You should send those charming words to Seamus Heaney. I'm sure he'd appreciate them.'

'Who?'

'How much for the ride?'

'Four quid.'

Karl handed over a fiver.

'I don't have any loose coins on me.' Grease Monkey smiled, and once again Karl thought of *Duelling Banjos*.

'Keep the change. You've earned it.'

Grease Monkey smiled even broader, before doing a Steve McQueen back down the road into total darkness.

The Motel Royal looked neither royal nor a motel; more of a fleapit where even the fleas had the intelligence to flee. The concierge barely acknowledged Karl – though he did scrutinise the twenty-pound note handed to him for payment.

The elevator wasn't working so Karl was grateful for room thirty-six being on the second floor. The thin carpet in the hallway was balding and depressing, and covered in every stain imaginable and unimaginable.

Karl quickly entered the room and flicked on the light switch. The room was lit by a naked bulb dangling from a ceiling covered in damp patches that stretched like leprosy.

Glancing at the World War Two furniture, he began to appreciate the bad lighting. The bed looked saggy and overused. He doubted if it could accommodate his large frame. The sheets looked like they had been washed last week – in body stains.

Throwing Big Ian's words into an overflowing wastepaper basket, Karl glanced out at the street below filled with drab buildings and walls scarred unmercilessly with graffiti. Among the many uplifting messages, one was in army-green paint: *Dublin the heroin capital of Ireland? Big deal. Ballymena's the heroin capital of Europe!*

Defeated by the drab landscape, Karl decided on a quick shower and a bite to eat, washed down with something other than water.

Quickly stripping, he pulled the scum-coated shower curtains open, and gingerly reached to turn the water on. A streak of dark orange rust immediately trailed down from the showerhead, covering the tiny area in dark stains.

Karl tried erasing from his thoughts what the stains reminded him of as he stepped timidly into the lukewarm spray. The shower water stank of ozone, sputtering and stopping at ten second intervals. The bathroom faucet dripped rusty brown, and the pipes beneath the sink were held together by a filthy pair of lady's torn nylons.

'Fuck it.' He stepped quickly out, and twenty minutes later, made his way downstairs to the bar.

'*Please Do Not Ask For Credit As A Punch In The Mouth Often Offends*', was the first sign he saw, nailed over the bar's cracked mirror. He hoped it wasn't a portent of things to come.

The bar was humming with sea shanty music. A bizarre mixture of maritime and Dolly Parton portraits hung precariously on the plaster-decaying walls, alongside the odd photo of politicians. Very odd politicians. Ian Paisley smiled from one. He appeared to be staring down into Dolly's ample cleavage.

'No wonder you're smiling, big lad,' said Karl, moseying up to the bar's counter and parking his formidable bulk on a stool.

Removing a ten spot from his wallet, he glanced about the bar. Two customers, bearded and smoking pipes, sat docked at the other end, each nursing their own brand of poison. They looked like defeated sailors, forced to become dreaded landlubbers because of the recession or their age. The pipes dangling from their toothless mouths were releasing as much smoke as a small freight train. The smoke covered the bar in an eerie mist.

Karl wondered if the no-smoking laws introduced years ago had reached the backwoods of Ballymena yet? One other customer lingered in the shadowy background, an empty glass her only companion.

'A Hennessy, when you get the chance, me old shipmate,' said

Karl, to the large barman cleaning glasses from an old jawbox sink. The barman's massive Popeye-the-sailor-man forearms were plastered in nautical-themed tattoos, and nude ladies with questionable anatomies.

Seemingly in no hurry, the barman eventually placed a Hennessy on the counter, removing the ten spot at the same time.

'Haven't seen one of those old jawboxes in ages,' said Karl, by way of conversation. 'I used to get washed in one of them.'

Placing the change on the counter, the barman looked Karl straight in the eye. 'Bit big for that, aren't you?'

'They're now very trendy, apparently,' replied Karl, ignoring the sarcasm oozing from the man's mouth. 'All those home shows on TV call them Belfast Sinks. I suppose that's appropriate, when you consider the Titanic was built in Belfast.'

The unreceptive barman went back to cleaning the glasses.

'What's there to do in this lovely wee town on a Friday night, friend?' asked Karl, straight at the barman's back.

The barman didn't even bother to turn around, opting instead to glance at Karl through the cracked mirror. 'You're already doing it, *friend*, so don't be getting too excited.'

'Ignore Colin,' said one of the old seafarers, edging up towards Karl. The man had an alcohol-ruptured nose and a mottled pink complexion. 'The name's Johnny. Johnny Walker. And you can forget about cracking any old whiskey jokes. I've heard them all a million times before.'

'Please to meet you, Johnny,' said Karl, shaking Johnny's hand. Johnny's gnarled fingers felt like serrated steak knives wrapped in wiring. 'Don't worry. I'll make it my business not to crack any whiskey jokes.'

'Colin doesn't have much to say. You'd think he was getting charged for each word coming out of his gob.'

'Wish my ex-wife had been like that.' Karl smiled. 'Can I get you a drink, Johnny?'

'Thanks. I've a thirst something shocking. I'll have a jar of Guinness,' said Johnny, cheerfully, grabbing a handful of salty nuts resting in a bowl.

'Colin? A pint of your blackest black stuff for Johnny, and another Hennessy for me. Have something for yourself,' said Karl, producing a twenty spot this time.

Johnny kindly offered the bowl of nuts to Karl.

'Er...no thanks,' said Karl, knowing that most drunks never wash their hands after going to the toilet. The thought of all those unwashed urine-stained hands groping the bowl of nuts was off-putting, to say the least.

Colin placed the drinks on the counter, before mumbling thanks to Karl for the free drink.

'I didn't catch your name,' said Johnny.

'Jim. Jim McFadden,' said Karl, his lie as perfect as a politician's face on polling day.

'Staying upstairs, Jim?'

'Yes, just for a night, probably. I'm trying to trace an old school friend from years back. I heard he's living somewhere in this lovely wee town.'

'Perhaps I know of him? What's his name?'

Before Karl could reply, the other customer from the end of the bar squeezed tightly in beside him.

'You were asking what's there to do in this place on a Friday night, big fella? Plenty, if you ask me.'

Karl's jaw nearly fell off his face. It was a woman, the pipe and beard camouflaging any feminine features donated to her face. She had bigger forearms than Colin the barman – with an equal amount of tattoos. Her breath stank like dead flowers, and her teeth had obviously been unzipped from her mouth.

'I…' Karl was lost for words.

'No one asked for your company, Marion Dunlop,' said Johnny, rather huffily.

'Nor yours, Johnny Walker. Just keep your beak out of it,' retorted Marion, adjusting her arse on the stool. 'Jim here is looking for some nice female company. Isn't that right, Jim?'

Karl felt ice fingers tighten on his balls. He shuddered inwardly. 'To be honest, Marion, I'm dead tired. I was just having a wee drink before going to bed.'

'Exactly my sentiments, Jim!' winked Marion, nudging Karl playfully in the ribs.

'Stop being a pest, Marion,' said Colin, bringing his face close to Marion's. He spoke with the confidence of someone not used to having to repeat himself. 'Head back over to your end of the bar, or leave.'

Karl felt like reaching over and hugging Colin.

Marion's eyes rolled. She mumbled something vile before heading back to her patch of the bar.

'And I'm keeping a good eye on you as well, Johnny Walker,' said Colin, before heading back to the sink.

'She's a head-melter, that one,' said Johnny, giving Marion a scornful look. 'Lost her mind in sixty-nine and never got it back. Now, before we were so rudely interrupted, you were about to tell me the name of the friend you're searching for.'

'Thomas Blake. Know of him?'

Johnny shook his head. 'Can't say I do.'

'I do,' said a voice directly behind Karl.

It was the woman with the empty glass. Exceptionally lovely, she was wearing strawberry-coloured hotpants, tight buttocks protruding provocatively, legs all the way to her shoulders. To Karl, she looked like something out of a Robert McGinnis painting, the kind of woman who could whistle 'The Derry Air' magnificently on her magnificent derrière.

She eased close enough for Karl to smell perfume from her skin and the booze on her tongue.

'Want to buy me a drink, stranger?' she asked in a husky, kittenish voice.

'No one invited you into our company, you Jezebel you,' exclaimed Johnny. 'Just keep your–'

Like lightning, the woman reached and grabbed Johnny by the balls and began squeezing.

Terror and pain registered on Johnny's face.

Colin smiled a crooked smile from the mirror, seemingly enjoying the ball-crunching entertainment.

'Please,' said Karl, staring directly into the woman's composed but determined face. 'I'm sure Johnny didn't mean what he said. Just the booze talking.'

'Just the booze talking, Johnny?' asked the woman. 'Shooting off stupid words with that shotgun mouth of yours?'

Johnny made a whimpering sound. Nodded continually, like a cat with a small creature lodged in its mouth.

'Okay, Johnny,' she said, calmly. 'When I release my grip on your tiny balls, you'll do an about-turn and head straight for the door. No back-lip. Deviate whatsoever from my instructions, and I'll crush what little you have left. Am I clear?'

Johnny nodded quickly. Tears began forming in his eyes.

The woman released Johnny from her death grip, and watched him staggering out, doubled-over with pain.

'You can call me Sandy and buy me a drink,' said the woman, putting out her hand to Karl.

'Jim…Jim McFadden.' Karl shook the hand that had just squeezed the life out of Johnny's balls. The hand felt terribly warm. 'That's some grip you have, Sandy, if you don't mind me saying.'

'In my business, you need to have a good grip on *all* things, otherwise, you're dead – just like Johnny's balls.'

'What would you like to drink?' asked Karl, reluctant to ask Sandy just what *exactly* her business was, even though he could hazard a decent guess.

'A g and t.' She smiled, and suddenly looked very gentle.

'A gin and tonic for the lady, Colin, and have another for your good self.'

'Which room are you in?' asked Sandy, becoming all business-like.

'I…' He didn't want to go there – at least for what he suspected Sandy wanted to go there for. 'To be honest, Sandy, I'm not really looking for company. I'm dog tired.'

'You're gay? I can accommodate that.' From her impressive handbag she produced an extremely large dildo, pink in colour.

'Shit…' Karl's haemorrhoids suddenly began flaring. His skin went clammy. 'No…no thanks. You can put that weapon away.'

'Is it the colour? I've others.'

'The shape. I'm not gay I'm not even in a gay mood, to be honest with you.'

'*Hmm.* You're not gay? And you don't want to fuck an attractive woman? What do you not like about me?'

'What's *not* to like? Don't be insulted, Sandy, it's just that I already have a beautiful woman whom I'm madly in love with.'

'Old fashioned morals? That's a rarity in the men I usually meet. I like that in a man.'

'That's me. Old fashioned and boring.'

'You want info on your *long lost friend?*'

The hairs on Karl's neck suddenly nipped his skin. The way she pronounced the last three words told Karl there was at least one person in Ballymena not buying his long-tall-glass of a story.

'Yes,' said Karl. 'I'd appreciate any info you have, Sandy.'

'Now that we both know where we stand, which room are you in?'

'Thirty-six.'

'That's one of my all-time favourites. Not a lot of noise comes from the springs. Mattress isn't too comfortable, though.' Sandy smiled again, but this time Karl could see the damage in her eyes.

Colin interrupted the conversation by placing the booze on the counter. Handed Karl his change. Mumbled a thank you. Returned to the sink.

'Come on,' said Sandy, taking her drink. 'Let's go. More privacy up there.'

Reluctantly, Karl eased away from the bar and followed her.

'Like what you see, *Jim*?' said Sandy, tilting her head over her shoulder, before smiling at Karl.

'I…' Karl, for the second time that evening, was lost for words.

Sandy pulled the strawberry-coloured hotpants up tighter. 'I'm not a good Christian girl, but I'm more than willing to turn the other cheek.' She gave Karl a cheeky wink.

A very *cheeky wink,* thought Karl, trying not to grin like an oaf. Even soulless Colin managed a grin.

Marion glared with disgust as Karl and Sandy progressed up the stairs to the room.

'I always liked this room,' said Sandy, before sitting down in a rickety chair. 'Simple decor and bare necessities.'

'Yes, I'm sure it's seen a lot of bare things.' Karl smiled.

Sandy returned the smile. 'I like your attempt at wit, *Jim.* A man who can make me smile is very special – even if he is a cop from Belfast. Going to arrest me for solicitation?'

Karl's face froze for a second. 'Cop? You've got me all wrong, Sandy. If I gave you the impression of being a–'

'You're a cop or cop *something*. I can smell it a mile away. Let's not argue over semantics, *Jim*. Now, who are you and what exactly is it you want to know about Blake? If you start with more lies, I'll leave immediately.'

'I…' Karl thought quickly. Reached inside his wallet, before handing Sandy one of his business cards.

Sandy studied the card. 'Karl Kane. Private investigator. Wasn't too far off the mark, was I?'

'I'm trying to trace Blake because his brother is dying. The family need some sort of reconciliation or closure before death. Nothing sinister.'

'Want my advice, Karl? Go back to Belfast. Tell his family you couldn't find him.'

'Why would I do that?'

'Because Blake is a scum bucket. Drugs. Loan sharking. Runs a brothel in the town centre. Anything the devil's invented, Thomas Blake had his hand firmly in it.'

'Oh…'

'I know that look on your face, and what you're thinking. Here's a woman, a hooker, and she has the audacity to complain about a brothel.'

'I might be thinking you're trying to get me to lean on the opposition.'

'If you saw how he treats the women in that place, then you'd understand.'

'I've seen enough of it in Belfast to understand fully what women go through in those places, Sandy. Why don't you just make a confidential call to the cops, make them disrupt his business, if you're so concerned?'

'He opens the cops' palms with drug money and they close their eyes. Free membership to the brothel thrown in.'

'Just like Belfast.' Karl shook his head. 'I wish I could be of help, Sandy. I really do.'

'Then you're not going to take my advice?'

'Tell his family I couldn't find him? No. Once I take a job on, I see it through. It's a bad trait, I know, but I'm kind of stubborn that way. I usually end up in a mess of trouble because of it.'

Sandy stood. Walked to the door. Opened it. 'You're a good man, Karl Kane. You've got decency written all over you. I wish I'd met someone like you about ten years ago.'

'If you'd seen the state of me ten years ago, you'd have run a mile, Sandy,' said Karl, walking to the door.

'If you ever tire of that lucky woman in your life, come and look me up – anytime.' She smiled, and then kissed him full on the mouth. It burnt his lips. 'You'll find Blake's brothel over at Princes Street.'

'Thanks for the info, Sandy, and the kiss. Very much appreciated.'

'One word of warning, Karl. When you come to a ghost town like Ballymena, just be careful that you don't leave as a ghost. Goodnight, and probably goodbye.'

Less than five minutes later, a fully clothed Karl lay on top of the soiled linen and saggy mattress. He tried not thinking about the warning Sandy had given him, but something about it rattled him.

Removing his mobile, he hit some numbers. Placing it to his ear, he listened to the tone. She'd probably be sleeping, but he needed to hear her lovely reassuring voice.

'Karl?' said the groggy voice of Naomi, a few seconds later. 'What's wrong?'

'Nothing.'

'Oh…'

He pictured her in bed, warm and snuggled under the sheets, and suddenly felt terribly lonely.

'What're you doing?' he asked.

He could hear her moving slightly, getting herself comfortable.

'I was sleeping until some big hunk woke me. What're *you* doing?'

'Me? Just finished having great sex with a lovely lady of the night.'

'Good. You deserve it. How's that hotel?'

'Don't ask. The only thing this dump has in common with any hotel is four of its letters spell hole.'

He could hear her yawning.

'What're you wearing?' he asked, knowing she was probably wearing her Winnie the Pooh and Tigger Too, pyjamas. Her "comfy zone", as she liked to call them.

'I'm nude. You?'

'Same, except for a pair of cowboy boots and a sheriff's badge pinned to my hairy chest.'

She giggled.

'I've been thinking of that lovely arse of yours, Naomi. Making me feel very sporty.'

'How so?'

'I'd love to be playing handball on it.'

'I think you need to get a good sleep, Mister Kane.' Naomi yawned loudly.

'Okay,' said Karl. 'I get the hint. Goodnight, darling.'

'Come home soon. Keep safe. Love you.'

He gave a loud kiss into the phone, and then clicked it shut, wishing now he had brought his Royal Quiet DeLuxe portable typewriter. He could have finished another chapter of his latest manuscript, hoping to have it completed before year's end. Ironically, the dodgy motel and some of its even dodgier characters had given him some new ideas; ideas he hoped to convey onto paper when he got home.

'Colin, barman by day, serial killer by night…'

Before long, though, fatigue and Hennessy sent him hurtling into disturbed nightmares of a dead mother, dead cops, and a monster with a bloody knife and grin. His father was there, also, crying in the dark. *Help*, he kept pleading, over and over again. *Please help me get out of the darkness.*

CHAPTER FOURTEEN

ANGELS AND DEMONS

'Such a lot of guns around town and so few brains.'
Raymond Chandler, *The Big Sleep*

Karl arrived in Princes Street early the next morning, parking the car a little down the way from the address given to him by Sandy. The brothel was squeezed between an antique shop seemingly selling everything but antiques, and a bookie's selling more than it promised. A peeling poster outside the bookie's stated: *'Things to do in Ballymena.'* The remainder of the poster was blank, with the exception of a red pen scrawl from a local wit: *Fuck all to do in Ballymena.*

In the car, Karl's breath kept making a blush of cold vapour on the windshield, so he rubbed a clear streak at eye level with bare knuckles, while negotiating the car's dodgy heater.

Heater on, he began checking the digital camera loaned to him by Naomi, trying desperately to remember the arcane instructions she had given.

'Whatever happened to the simple push-the-button days?'

Frustrated but finally finished, he brought the camera to his face and zoomed it at the brothel. The clarity both startled and amazed him.

'I can see the bloody splinters on the door…' He shook his head with delight, instantly becoming a convert to modern-day ingenuity and technology.

Making himself comfortable, he opened a McDonald's bag, extracting a greasy hash brown and large coffee. Removing the lid, he sipped contentedly, while watching any activity in and around the brothel.

By all accounts, it appeared to be quite popular with the male population of Ballymena – mostly balding, big-bellied bruisers – coming and going. Occasionally, young women would emerge from the doorway, kissing the dodgy clients before waving them on their merry way.

'Home from bloody home. All they need is "Ernie the Milkman" to deliver some of his famous–'

Someone tapped on the side window, startling him. Karl turned to see a pretty young woman with stringy fair hair staring in at him. She wasn't dressed for the freezing weather, wearing skimpy summer clothing instead. Her face – like the rest of the amorphous body – was emaciated, like one of L.S. Lowry's anorexic stick people.

She was shaking terribly. Mostly from heroin withdrawal, Karl suspected. Hatchings of small scars covered her arms. She looked like she hadn't slept in days, yawning continuously while indicating for Karl to crank the window down.

'Yes, love?' he asked in his gentlest voice, complying with the window.

'What can I do for you?'

She forced a smile. 'I'm Rosie, and it's what *I* can do for you, love. A blowjob or handjob for a fiver. Full fuck for ten. Cheapest and best in Ballymena – or Antrim, if you care to know.'

Karl shook his head. 'Not today, love.'

'Please, mister. I need the money. Badly.' Rosie began scratching madly at her arms and head, as if covered in invisible insects. 'I'll do anything. Look, see her, over at the wee shop?'

Karl glanced over his shoulder. Another young girl stood in the shuttered doorway of a rundown shop, yawning and sneezing. Despite wearing a navy-blue Linkin Park hoodie, she was shaking, and held her stomach tightly, as if being attacked by cramps.

'That's my wee sister, Tina. Only fourteen,' continued Rosie. 'Smooth as Vaseline. No condoms, if you want bare back. She's a dream. You can have both of us for fifteen quid. How's that sweet taboo sound to you?'

'Look, Rosie, I'm just visiting a friend over at–'

'Friend, my fucking arse! You're taking photos of Blake's girls, aren't you? I've been watching you for the last ten minutes. Think we're not good enough, me and my wee sister?' Rosie suddenly became extremely agitated. 'What are you? A peeping Tom perv? Can't handle the real thing?'

Karl thought about driving away. Come back in an hour's time, hoping the young girls had moved on – or had *been* moved on. He doubted both.

'Okay…call your sister over, and get in.'

Rosie smiled and started waving frantically to her young sister. 'Tina! Come on! Move your arse!'

Tina began staggering across the street, holding her stomach tightly. A few seconds later, she accompanied Rosie into the back of the warm car.

Prettier than her older sister, Karl doubted very much that Tina had reached teen years. A crop of pale ginger hair sprouted from beneath the Linkin Park.

'You look like you need medical treatment,' said Karl, concerned at the pain etched on Tina's young face.

'It's nothing,' cut in Rosie. 'Just stomach cramps. She needs to be smacked.'

'What?' said Karl, immediately shocked and angry. 'No-one's smacking anyone. Do you hear me?'

'Don't be a fucking scally, mister. Not smacking. *Smacked*. A *hit*. Some smack. Heroin. She'll be okay after that. Won't you, Tina, wee love?'

Tina nodded robotically, all the while sniffing snot back up her nose.

'What if we go to McDonald's, get something to eat? A Happy Meal, or something?' suggested Karl, regretting it the minute he opened his mouth.

'You really a fucking perv?' asked Rosie.

'Let's forget the last suggestion,' said Karl. 'Just trying to be helpful.'

'With an unhappy meal at *Mickey Dick's*? I don't think so. Time is money, mister. Let's get down to business. Who do you want? Me first, or Tina? Or can you handle both of us?'

'*I'm cold and hungry, Rosie,*' whispered Tina. '*Can't we get something to eat first?*'

'Stop being such a fucking ginger whinger, Tina. We'll eat when I say so. Just shut up.'

Karl sighed. 'Look, what if I told you I'm willing to give you twenty quid to do nothing, other than go and get yourselves something to eat? What would you say?'

Rosie's eyes tightened. They looked hardened and a little frightened.

'What's the catch?'

From his wallet, Karl removed the twenty.

'No catch. I see you back in this area any time soon, I'll have an old friend of mine take you to jail, let you stew there for a few days. Understand? He'll make you go cold turkey.'

'You're a cop? I knew it.' Rosie looked slightly worried. 'Why give us money instead of nicking us?'

'I've bigger fish to fry, *at the moment*. You're a distraction I can do without. But don't push it. I've been known to eat sardines, when hungry. I'm going to be driving over towards Hope Street shortly. I don't see you both there, in that little cafe at the corner, stuffing your faces with grub, I'll hunt you down. Trust me. You'll not enjoy where you end up. Now scram.'

'Come on, Tina! Didn't you hear the man? Move it!' said Rosie, grabbing the money, while moving for the door. She was quickly followed by Tina.

'Don't forget what I just…' Karl stopped in mid-sentence. They were away, scampering down the street, Rosie leading, with Tina a very close second. He doubted they would be heading to the cafe. Probably the nearest drug den. 'Don't give money, they lose. Give money, they lose…'

Karl stared at the almost-finished coffee in his hand. The sisters' plight made him think of his darling Katie, and the evil that men do to those most vulnerable and weak in society. Never a firm believer in any god, each passing day seemed to vindicate his atheistic principles.

'A terribly depressing little town…' He sipped at the coffee, but was no longer in the mood to finish it. He suddenly needed to pee, and regretted buying the greedy-pig sized cup. Cranking the window down halfway, he began dumping the lukewarm liquid out the window. That was when he saw the two men emerging from a flashy Audi that had just pulled up at the brothel entrance.

Karl quickly glanced at the photos given to him by Jemma. Much older now, but there was no mistaking Blake's towering structure or thick nest of unruly grey hair crowning his over-sized head. Two large Doberman Pinschers stood rigidly at Blake's side, looking menacing. The other man accompanying Blake was of slim build, and had an uncanny resemblance to Lee Marvin. Both men seemed deep in conversation.

Karl quickly brought the camera up. *Click!* Nice close-up of Blake. *Click! Click!*

'Beautiful ugly mug…' *Click!*

Blake turned. Glanced up the street towards Karl's car.

'*Fuck!*' Karl instinctively ducked down behind the steering wheel. Had Blake or Lee bloody Marvin spotted him? '*You careless bastard…*'

Easing his head slowly up, he glanced out the window. Both men gone.

'*Shit! They've scampered back inside.*'

Deciding not to push Lady Luck too far, Karl began reversing the car slowly out of Princes Street. Just as he reached the middle of the street, a loud explosion shattered the wing mirror.

'*Fuckkkkkkkkkk!*' He quickly glanced in the rear mirror. A figure aiming a brute of a pump-action shotgun was preparing to fire again. It was the Lee Marvin look-alike, his face knotted with anger.

Karl ducked, but not before being confronted by one of the Doberman Pinschers forcing its mallet-shaped head through the half-opened driver's window. Karl could smell the dog's stinking breath as fangs snapped at his face.

'Fuck off!' he shouted, landing a wildly thrown punch on the creature's nose. The dog yelped loudly, retracting its head quickly from the window.

Just as Karl gathered his breath, the second dog went on the offensive, squeezing most of its body in through the window. Lunging for his arm, the dog secured it, biting down viciously with its vice-like jaws.

'Fuckkkkkkkkkkkkkk!' His arm felt like it was being put through a mangle. He punched at the brute's face, but it was a feeble and awkward attempt. To add to his worries, Lee Marvin was aiming again.

Instinctively, Karl pressed his weight on the accelerator. The car roared towards the end of the street, but not before a flash and simultaneous explosion rocked inside.

The back window shattered, and a millisecond later – hardly time to cue his next thought – the windshield rained down on his head, covering him and the attacking dog in fragmented glass.

His stressed bladder unloosed.

'Bastard!' The crushing explosion of glass triggered a primal reptilian response. He spun the steering wheel with one hand, taking a left in a 'No Left Turn' zone, narrowly missing two on-coming vehicles. The Doberman continued biting through his coat, then stopped abruptly as a speeding car took off the crea-

ture's rear parts, scattering them across the motorway.

Headlights flashed and angry horns blasted. Someone shouted an obscenity, but he was too shocked to hear it or care. Seconds later, the car hit a grassy embankment, slamming Karl against the dashboard, forcing a halt. By the time he managed to look back through the now gaping hole, his attacker was gone.

For one full minute, Karl sat in the driver's seat, stunned, shaking terribly, trying to get his brain's gears back on track. The dead Doberman's head and upper body clung ghoulishly to his arm.

'Bastard...' he said, prying its jaws open before shoving the bloody mess out the window.

Cautiously, he looked in the rear-view mirror. An ashen face looked back, slightly bloodied. Thankfully, nothing in his body seemed broken – unlike the car. By the time he pulled to the side and looked back through the now-open space, his pursuer was gone.

'Stinking bastard...' he eventually said, no longer thinking of his narrow escape, but the bill to have the car restored and cleaned, plus the humiliation of having pissed his pants in broad daylight.

Gingerly removing his coat, he began checking for any damage done to his arm by the dog's fangs. Thankfully, the skin wasn't punctured, but an ugly swelling was already forming.

Cars continued speeding by, their drivers seemingly in too much of a hurry to investigate the accident.

'Thanks for your concern,' said Karl, warily guiding the car back onto the motorway in the direction of Belfast, praying not to be stopped by the cops.

No sooner was he on the motorway than his phone started

ringing. He answered it.

'Tom? What's happening?'

'What's wrong?' asked Hicks. 'Your voice seems shaky.'

'Ballymena's bacteria has made my stomach queasy. Someone let the dogs out, and gave me a grand *au revoir*. Why're you calling?'

'This is a shocker. A body's just been discovered in a disused warehouse in the dock. Been there for a few days before being discovered by some homeless man looking for shelter.'

Karl didn't like the edginess attached to Hicks' voice. Ten seconds of silence slithered in between the two friends. Hicks seemed to have hung up.

'Are you going to tell me *whose* body, Tom, or do I phone a friend or ask the audience?' said Karl, almost dreading the answer.

'Edward Phillips. Not official yet, so don't be saying anything until it's confirmed.'

It took a couple of seconds for the information to sink in. When it did, it made Karl feel even queasier. Tiny bats began fluttering in his stomach. The skin on his face dampened.

'Detective Phillips? One of Wilson's old crew before he retired?'

'*Forced* to retire. Remember? Something to do with getting money from drug dealers.'

'Shit. What's the speculation?'

'Quite a bit, to be honest. Whispers from rank and file are saying it's drug-related, that Phillips must have become too greedy, dipping his hands into some drug dealer's dirty money.'

'Hands? Not the most highly sought-after word at the moment, Tom.'

'That's all of Wilson's original squad of detectives dead, and all by violent means. Someone must have placed a curse on that whole team, if you ask me.'

Karl's head began throbbing. Hicks' voice was sounding like an annoying metallic echo. He wished Hicks would just shut the hell up, talking about Wilson's squad.

'Karl? You still there?'

'What? Oh…yes…yes. Just pulling into a petrol station. Listen, I've got to go, Tom. You'll keep me informed of any developments, of course?'

'Of course. You know you don't even need to ask that.'

As Karl clicked the phone dead, the bats in his stomach went into a feeding frenzy. He had a bad feeling about Phillips' murder. A very bad feeling, indeed. One that could very well find its way to his doorstep.

CHAPTER FIFTEEN

SOMETHING'S GOTTA GIVE

'He looked like a nice guy if you didn't crowd him. At that distance and in that light I couldn't tell much more, except that if you did crowd him, you had better be big, fast, tough and in top condition.'
Raymond Chandler, *Playback*

Tuesday morning in Belfast. Karl phoned Jemma Doyle to say he had some info on Uncle Thomas.

'That's fantastic, Karl,' said Jemma, her voice filled with elation. 'When can we meet?'

'I've to see another client, over at Victoria Square, in about twenty minutes. How about if we meet, say between eleven and eleven-thirty?

'That's perfect.'

'Do you know Costa Coffee?'

'Yes.'

'We'll meet there. Okay?'

'Costa Coffee it is. Thank you.'

Just as he clicked off the phone, Naomi entered the room, her face full of concern.

'I still think this is a case that you should drop, Karl. Now, rather than later.'

'We went through that all over the weekend, love. I'd never have become a private investigator in the first place if I let myself be intimidated by thugs. Besides, you know I just can't drop every case that suddenly turns sour.'

'This didn't just turn sour, Karl; it turned violent.'

'I know, but believe me when I say–'

The phone rang.

It was Hicks.

'Tom?'

'Keep this under your hat for now, but another hand was found, in the early hours of this morning, over beside The Odyssey. Had the numbers eighty-eight etched into it, just like the last hand.'

Karl gave a soft whistle. 'There can be no question now of a serial killer. It'll be interesting to hear how the cops put a spin on this for the public.'

'There's to be a press conference later today.'

'I give you odds of ten to one that our great leader, Wilson, won't be doing it. Not good for the image, looking like a dick in front of all those cameras.'

'The owner's name is a Harold Taylor, last seen coming from a motel on the Antrim Road. A bit of a thug with a criminal record. He was reported missing four days ago.'

'Looks like we have a Charles Bronson running about, dishing out instant justice.'

'The courts of law are justice, Karl. What we don't need is more vigilantes or so-called street justice in Belfast. Those bad days are supposed to be behind us.'

'They'll never be behind us. Anything new on Phillips?'

'It's official. It *was* Phillips' body in the warehouse.'

'Shit. Poor bastard. I was sort of hoping it wasn't him.'

'His funeral's on Wednesday, just in case you want to attend.'

'Bit quick, isn't it?'

'Not really. Autopsy completed. His ex-wife won't be attending. Says she's not going to be a hypocrite.'

'Ex-wives. Diplomats in the making.'

'I'll be at the graveside. If you're there, I'll see you.'

'I'll do my best to attend, provided something doesn't come up. Take care,' said Karl, clicking off.

'What was that all about?' asked Naomi. 'I heard you mentioning Charles Bronson.'

'Charles…? Oh, Hicks was just discussing his all-time favourite actor. He's into all those rock-jawed macho guys.'

'Karl, don't laugh if I tell you something. Promise?'

'So long as it isn't funny.'

'I want you to drop this case. Please. For me. I had a terrible nightmare last night. I kept seeing a strange girl, standing over you with a knife covered in blood.'

'That was Lynne.'

'Please, Karl, I'm serious.'

Naomi looked as if she were about to burst out crying. He reached and touched her.

'Look, tell you what, my dearest. I get no more information in the next twenty-four hours, I'll drop it. Okay.'

For the first time that morning, Naomi smiled.

'Is that a promise, Karl?'

'Scout's honour,' he said, kissing her on the lips, before grabbing his coat. 'Now, I've really got to get a move on. See you in the afternoon.'

▲ ▲ ▲

To Karl, the dazzling glass dome atop the impressive Victoria Square shopping complex looked like a giant magnifying glass, while he stood waiting patiently for Jemma Doyle at Costa Coffee. The winter sun was beaming through the dome, covering the inhabitants in a ghostly Tuesday afternoon shroud.

Almost to the second, at two o'clock Jemma appeared. She seemed breathless, as if she had been running.

Karl ordered two coffees, before finding a table at the busy coffee oasis.

'What's the information on my uncle?' asked Jemma, gripping the steaming coffee with gloved hands.

'I don't know if it's what you want to hear.'

Jemma's face seemed to pale right before Karl's eyes. 'He's… he's not dead?'

'No, nothing like that. Sorry for giving that impression. How well do you know him?'

'Not very well, I suppose. I haven't seen him in years. To be honest, Karl, if not for my father, I probably wouldn't be searching for him. Why? What did you find out?'

Karl removed an envelope from his inside pocket, before handing it to Jemma.

'Open it up. That's what he looks like now.'

Jemma opened the envelope, removing the photos one at a time. Studying them, she seemed engrossed.

'He's aged a lot – at least from the photos I gave you.'

'You weren't being fully honest with me when you asked me to take this assignment, Jemma, were you?'

'What…what do you mean?' Jemma looked taken aback.

'Uncle Thomas's been in jail, and that's the good news.'

'Jail?'

'Are you going to tell me the truth about him, or do I get up and walk away?'

'I…I don't know what you mean.'

Karl stood abruptly. 'Have a nice day, and all that, Miss Doyle.'

'No! Wait!' Jemma grabbed Karl's hand. 'Okay…'

Karl sat down.

'It's…not easy for me to talk about this, Karl. My uncle stole most of our money – my father's money, I mean. He swindled people. He was violent towards my grandmother.'

'Nice uncle. So why track him down?'

'My father…my father's a proud man, Karl. He's on the verge of bankruptcy. The money Uncle Thomas stole can help get my father out of the mess he's in.'

Karl sighed. 'And you thought Uncle Thomas would just hand it all over?'

'I…' Tears were forming in Jemma's eyes. 'We're desperate. The shame of all this. My father's health is deteriorating each day. I need to find a way to get that money back.'

'The way you described your uncle beating up your grand-mother is almost nostalgic, compared to the present-day Thomas.'

'What…what do you mean?'

'He runs a brothel in Ballymena, among other things. Prob-ably involved in drugs, also.'

'A brothel…' Jemma looked as if Karl had just slapped her face. 'Drugs? Are you certain?'

'I wish I was as certain with the horse I'm betting on at three o'clock.'

'This…this is shocking.'

'Sorry for being so blunt, but he's turned out to be an even bigger scumbag than what he was. One of his…associates thought he was on a duck-hunting trip last Saturday morning, and that I was a sitting duck.'

'I don't know what you mean.'

'Took a few pop shots at me with a gun that fired everything *except* pop.'

'*What?* Oh my God. How dreadful. Are you okay? You weren't hurt?' Jemma seemed genuinely concerned.

'Pride, plus a new pair of underwear.' Karl forced a smile. 'Let's just say that I won't be going back to the town of Ballymena any time soon.'

'Did the police arrest your attacker? Is he in jail?'

Karl shook his head. 'Private investigators are a bit like priests. We never divulge other people's sins. That's why we're called private. Isn't good for business spouting to the cops. Besides, the less the cops know, the more I get to manoeuvre.'

'Isn't that dangerous? Couldn't the gunman come looking for you?'

'I doubt very much an inbred from Ballymena will venture up to Belfast, just to come looking for me. Past experience has shown me that most thugs don't like venturing out of the safety of their mucky ponds.'

'I feel responsible for bringing all this to your door, Karl. I'm so sorry. Truly I am.'

'Don't worry. I'm a big boy and can look after myself.'

'Can I ask how you were able to locate Uncle Thomas? My family tried every known organisation, from The Salvation Army to the police, but with little success. The police in particular were of little help, and didn't seem in the least bit interested.'

'My contacts in the police are a bit more…helpful. Had your uncle not been in jail, years ago, I doubt very much if we would have ever found him.'

'My family will be devastated when I tell them about the brothel and drugs.' Jemma Doyle suddenly looked very tired. 'My father will be ashamed. He comes from the old school of moral righteousness.'

'Here's your uncle's address,' said Karl, handing a note to Jemma. 'At least you know where he is, if you or your family want to make contact with him. Someone gave me advice to forget him. I'm giving you the same advice I ignored, Jemma. You really should take it.'

'Thank you for all you've done, Karl. I'll think about what you've just said.' Jemma scanned the note. 'Can I have the photos I gave you of Uncle Thomas? They're my father's.'

'Of course.' Karl fished in his pockets and handed the photos to Jemma. 'Sorry I had to be the bearer of such terrible news.'

'Nothing to be sorry about.' Standing, Jemma pocketed the photos, before handing Karl an envelope. 'The remainder of your fee. Thank you once again, Karl.'

'Any more problems, you know where to find me, Jemma,' replied Karl shaking her gloved hand. 'Take care.'

'You too, Karl. Good day.'

He watched her leave, taking the escalator to the ground floor. She seemed to have the weight of the world resting on her shoulders.

'Poor girl…'

Karl was just about to head back to the office when his phone began buzzing in his pocket. He didn't recognise the number on the screen.

'Hello?' he asked.

'Mister Kane?'

'Yes. Who's this?'

'Georgina Goodman.'

'Sorry?'

'Geordie. The abattoir?'

'Of course! What can I do for you, Mrs Goodman?'

'I've a bit of information. Don't know if it's relevant to what we discussed last week, but if you want to drop by, you can decide for yourself.'

'I could be there within the hour, if you're not too busy?'

'No, not today. I'm leaving on a business trip. I'll be back on Thursday. Does that suit?'

'Yes, that's perfect. I'll see you on Thursday,' said Karl, turning off the phone, feeling the hairs on the back of his neck suddenly rise.

CHAPTER SIXTEEN

THE DEAD

'The hour of departure has arrived and we go our ways – I to die and you to live. Which is the better, only God knows.'
Socrates, quoted in *Plato's Apology*

If Edward Phillips' life had been measured by the number of people attending his funeral, the measuring tape would not have stretched too far, thought Karl, watching the small pocket of mourners gathering in the mucky field of death.

Tired blades of mottled grass were shimmering in the early morning ice drop. On the horizon, thin black strands began unlacing, allowing small measures of deluded sunlight to knife through filthy grey clouds. Birds were noisy in the trees, gossiping, declassifying the lonely silence of death below.

'Not a great turnout,' said Hick, as if reading Karl's thoughts.

'I don't think he'll be overly concerned,' said Karl. 'Anything new on his murder?'

'He was shot in the back of the head, at close range. The impact took off most of his face. Rats and feral cats devoured what remained. It wasn't pretty.'

'No, Phillips wasn't the most handsome of people, admittedly, though I still find it hard to believe he's gone – not like this. He wasn't the worse of that scumbag crew.'

'I always had time for Phillips, but he seemed more and more troubled, each time we spoke.'

'Troubled? How?'

'As if he were hiding something he was ashamed of. Now I know it was the drug dealing and dirty money, just like everyone is saying.'

'You still think drug dealers had something to do with it?'

'Particles of cocaine were discovered between his fingernails and in his nostrils.'

'Cocaine,' said Karl, shaking his head. 'I never took Phillips for a coke head. What about the bloodstream? Any traces there?'

'Nothing as such. Minuscule traces, but they could just as easily have come from the painkillers he was apparently addicted to.'

'What's Wilson's take on it?'

'Haven't really spoken to him, but heard through the grapevine that he's totally devastated. Vowed to find the person or persons responsible.'

'I'm sure they'll be shaking in their underwear, hearing that news.' Karl began pulling the collar of his overcoat tighter to his throat, fending off the icy wind.

'You'd think the Force would have at least sent a few lads just to make up the numbers.'

'There were more attendees at the Last Supper, but I suppose you could argue that the free grub was an incentive to attend that particular august gathering.'

'I know the Force doesn't want to be associated with drug dealing, and all that jazz, but whatever happened to innocent until proven guilty?'

'At least that bastard Wilson has had the decency to show up,' said Karl, spotting his ex brother-in-law speaking to a mourner. 'I have to give him a wee bit of credit for that, I suppose.'

Detective Inspector Mark Wilson's poker-straight frame stood like a deep-rooted tree at the edge of the newly dug grave. His cropped, marine-short haircut was shaped like a smoothing iron, and just like the man himself, totally unmoving in the brisk, icy wind. The extreme haircut accentuated a face badly pitted with pockmarks. Not caused by acne, but by a shotgun blast to his face, many years ago by a person now dead: Brendan Burns, a man who had recently sacrificed his own life for that of Karl's daughter, Katie.

'Wilson doesn't look at all well,' said Hicks. 'All this is obviously playing hard on him.'

'Anything on the gun used to shoot Phillips?' asked Karl, not liking any sort of sympathy being delegated to Wilson.

Hicks nodded. 'He was shot with a forty-five calibre. Ballistics have yet to match the fragments found in the brain with anything used before. Strangely, the forensic report stated that the warehouse where the body was discovered yielded nothing.'

'Why strange?'

'Locard's theory, of course.'

'Of course, the old Locard's theory.' Karl smirked. 'I hate when you're so smug. What the fuck is Locard's theory, smart-arse?'

'I really wish you would start reading some of the books I gave you. Edmond Locard was a prominent French forensic scientist who built the first crime laboratory in the twentieth century. Locard's exchange principle states that *with contact between two items, there will be an exchange.*'

'An exchange of what, to be precise?

'Every contact leaves a trace. There has to be an exchange of *something*, be it sweat, hair, dust. Almost anything.'

'DNA?'

'Yes, and also other trace evidence like soil, cloth fibres etc …'

'Why the hell didn't you just say that instead of that long-winded spiel?'

'All I'm saying is the killer was extremely careful. Either he – *or she* – stayed long enough to check that nothing was left behind.'

'Not only has the killer got balls to kill an ex-cop, but takes his time departing. Obviously not your average dope-on-a-rope drug dealer or off-the-wall killer. It should be fun watching Wilson and McCormack becoming Holmes and Watson trying to solve this one.'

As if he could hear every word, Wilson turned and looked directly over at Karl and Hicks. The look was anything but cordial.

'Wilson's ears must be burning,' said Karl, staring straight back. 'He's sighted us with his rifle-scope eyes.'

'You're not going to cause another commotion at a funeral, are you?' said Hicks, looking slightly worried. 'I had enough of that disgraceful nonsense the last time you and Wilson decided to roll in the muck at a funeral.'

'I'm above that sort of behaviour now. As Doctor Jekyll said to Mister Hyde: I've changed.'

'Why do I always find that so hard to believe?'

'Anything more on the hand found at The Odyssey?' said Karl, ignoring the accusation.

'Mostly what I already told you. His name was Harold Taylor, a local businessman from the Glengormley area.'

'You said he had a criminal record.'

'Intimidation and racketeering. He also had done time for raping a young woman, about ten years ago. Left her covered in blood and with broken bones.'

'Nice chap.'

'He was last seen leaving a motel on the Antrim Road. It was the day of that terrible blizzard. He seems to have simply disappeared off the face of the earth.'

'And only a bloody hand to tell a tale. I have the feeling these hands are being deliberately left to be found.'

'Like a calling card?'

'More likely a warning to someone. A bit like sending a Jack Russell to sniff out rats. Make them all nervous.'

Karl's phone buzzed.

'Hello?'

'Mister Kane? Geordie.'

'Oh, Mrs Goodman. I thought it was tomorrow, our meeting?'

'I just called to let you know I won't be able to meet you – at least not this week. I've been delayed on my business trip. Sorry about that, but how about next Monday, in my office, early?'

'Sound as a bell. Monday morning would suit me fine, if that's okay with you?'

'Monday morning it is. See you then, Mister Kane.'

Karl switched the phone off. His face looked uncertain.

'A client?' asked Hicks.

'No, not exactly. I really haven't figured this little lady out, just yet. She has ice in her veins and no heartbeat. To be honest, she gives me the creeps. It appears she's trying to avoid me, or perhaps it's just my suspicious nature kicking in.'

'You? Suspicious? No.' Hicks smiled.

'Very funny. Comedians. They're everywhere. Even in grave-yards.'

CHAPTER SEVENTEEN

DETECTIVE STORY

'Stinking cops. Nobody socks me around like that.
Nobody. I get even. I always do.'
Gene Barry in *Naked Alibi*

Early Saturday morning found Karl parked in the seat of his local barber's, Ben's Hair, listening to owner Ben Causeway's encyclopaedic ramblings on local politics and scandals.

'Looks like it's all coming back to bite her in the bum, all that holier-than-thou shit she's been mouthing against the gay community,' said Ben, clipping at the thickness of Karl's greying hair.

Belfast was abuzz with a politician's wife's scandalous affair with a much younger man.

'Why're you so shocked, Ben? I keep telling you that politicians are *all* the same. A bunch of lousy thieving hypocrites,' said Karl, nodding in the mirror. 'I blame the mugs who vote for them, hail, rain, or snow.'

'I don't vote,' said Ben, defensively, gliding the scissors expertly across Karl's mane. 'Anyway, she's old enough to be the guy's granny.'

'Too much information. Let's change the subject. And mind

my bloody ear, Ben. You almost clipped it.'

Leaving the barber's thirty minutes later, a neater-looking Karl began making his way in the direction of Chapel Lane to place a hotly tipped bet in Ladbrokes the bookies. There were closer bookmakers for him to lose his money to, but the fact that this particular establishment was sandwiched between a chapel and church always seemed to bring him closer to a god he didn't believe in. In addition, Kelly's Cellars and the Hercules pubs would help comfort the blow of defeat later in the day, if things didn't go according to plan.

Just as he turned the corner to enter the bookmakers, Karl became aware of the dark and sinister-looking car cruising directly behind.

'Kane!' shouted a booming voice from the car.

Karl turned to see Detective Harry McCormack easing his bulky frame from the passenger-side door.

'Well, if it isn't Mister Congenial,' said Karl.

'Why don't you get in, keep us company for a while?' said McCormack. It wasn't a request.

'I've urgent business to attend to, McCormack. You'll just have to wait until I'm finished.'

'I won't ask again. The car or the station. Your choice, Kane.'

'Can't it at least wait until I place this bet? The race is about to kick off in a few minutes. It's a sure shot. I'll even let you bet on it.'

'Get in the car. Now.'

'Thought you said you wouldn't ask me again, McCormack?'

Reluctantly, Karl walked to the car and was quickly shoe-horned inside where another burly giant of a detective sat, silently observing. To Karl, the man resembled the Incredible Hulk – only white, and less handsome. The driver of the car was equally silent, looking bored and smelling of last night's booze. The heat and body odour in the car was overwhelming.

'What's this about, McCormack? It better be good. I was on my way to winning a small fortune.'

McCormack smiled painfully. It looked like a knife wound. 'Always with the mouth, Kane. You never know when to shut it, do you?'

'That's a trick question. How am I to answer without speaking?'

White Hulk made a grunting sound of impatience and looked out the side window of the car, before elbowing Karl violently in the stomach.

'*Fuck!*' Karl buckled immediately, winded.

'You know the old story of good cop, bad cop, Kane?' said McCormack, pulling Karl back into the seating position. 'Well, we dispensed with good cop, just for you. We only have bad cop and bastard cop.'

For a brief moment of madness, Karl thought of saying something smart again. Thankfully, sanity came to his rescue, forcing him to say nothing.

'Do you know a Laura Fleming?' asked McCormack.

Karl thought for a few seconds. The name didn't ring a bell.

'No…'

From his pocket, McCormack produced a small, clear bag, the word 'EVIDENCE' stapled boldly across its lip. A tiny item clung to the inside of the bag.

'Recognise this?' asked McCormack, holding the bag inches from Karl's face.

Upon close inspection, Karl could see that it was one of his business cards, a smudge of red staining its pale lettering.

'Looks like one of my business cards.'

'It *is* one of your business cards. See the red smudge? Care to hazard a guess as to what it is?'

'Lipstick, perhaps?'

'Blood. Laura Fleming's blood. Care to tell me how it got there, and what she was doing with your business card?'

'My business cards are everywhere. I don't have any control over where they end up. I haven't a clue how the woman's blood got on it. Besides, I've already told you, I don't know her.'

'Know? *Knew.* I forgot to tell you. She was found murdered in a hotel, three days ago. She had been raped and tortured, before having her throat cut, almost separating her head from her shoulders. Your *everywhere* business card was forcefully clamped between her teeth.'

'What…?' Karl felt like he had been slapped. His stomach began tightening.

'Ever been to a fleapit called The Motel Royal, in Ballymena?'

Karl's stomach tightened further. It was slowly beginning to dawn on him where the questioning was going.

'I…yes, a couple of weeks ago…'

'Good job you admitted that, smart mouth. After showing your picture to a few customers, they confirmed you were there, but using a different name. Jim McFadden, apparently. Some of the customers in the bar section of the motel informed us that you had a drink before going upstairs and having sex with the woman you never heard of.'

'Didn't know it was lawful for cops to carry pictures of people without criminal records, McCormack?' Sweat began trickling down Karl's spine, pooling between his buttocks.

'You learn something new every day, don't you? I had your photo with me to clarify things at the motel.' McCormack smiled his knife-grin again. 'Now, what about this murdered woman you claim not to know, but had sex with, just the same?'

'I…I didn't know her real name was Laura Fleming. Told me it was Sandy.'

'You're a disgusting and immoral bastard, Kane,' said McCormack. 'You travel far to use your cock, but that's fine with me, because eventually it'll become a rope to hang you with.'

'There was no sex involved.'

'I see. You just needed a shoulder to cry on?' McCormack smirked.

'A client hired me to search for someone. A missing relative. The trail led me to Ballymena.'

'Name of client and missing relative?'

'Confidentiality. You know I can't divulge such information.'

'Bollocks to that, Kane. A woman's been brutally tortured and murdered, and you've the cheek to talk confidentiality?'

'It's not cheek. It's the law.'

'Okay, then, if sex *wasn't* involved, you won't mind giving a swab, just to eliminate any DNA from other suspects?'

'Am *I* a suspect?' Karl bristled.

'How about that swab?'

'You get a warrant, you get the swab.'

White Hulk made another sound of impatience.

Karl braced his body for the blow. None came.

'There was a shooting in Ballymena the day you were there.

Know anything about *that*?'

'Shooting in Ballymena? That's news?'

'Apparently some old paedophile was having sex in his car with two children, before a good citizen chased him off, rescuing the children.'

Karl felt his face redden slightly. Tried controlling it. 'Good for that good citizen.'

'The story doesn't stop there, Kane. Apparently, this was a rather persistent and sneaky paedo, and he came back later, only to be blasted by a few shots up the arse from a old rusty blunderbuss, before he fled the scene for good, shit running down his legs and out his car door.'

White Hulk made a sound like laughter.

'Where's all this going, McCormack?' asked Karl.

'I was able to track down the children involved. Two young sisters. Saintly wee things. I asked them for some description of the perv. Even managed to show them some photos I had in my pocket, one of which was of you. Know what they said?'

'No, but I'm sure you're going to tell me.' Karl began steeling himself for whatever damaging revelation was coming next.

'Quote: "That ugly bastard? We'd never forget *that* face, had it been him!"'

McCormack and the driver both laughed out loud. Even White Hulk managed a weak grin.

Karl laughed, also, nerves kicking in. 'I guess sometimes it pays to be ugly.'

There was almost half a minute of silence before McCormack finally spoke.

'You can get out now, Kane, but I'll have a few more questions for you in the very near future. You can place a bet on *that* sure thing.'

'Just make sure you contact my solicitor,' said Karl, easing himself back out of the car. 'I'm sure your boss, Wilson, will have his phone number.'

'Be seeing you, Kane…' said McCormack, pulling the door shut.

Welcoming the whisper of cold wind on his damp face, Karl watched the car slink out of view before turning and throwing up all over the pavement.

'*Ah fuck…*' he muttered, wiping the spillage from his mouth.

'Disgusting,' said an old lady, tut-tutting, before making her way into the church. 'Drunk at this time of the morning. Disgraceful animal.'

CHAPTER EIGHTEEN

THE CONVERSATION

'He had a battered face that looked as if it had been hit by every-thing but the bucket of a dragline. It was scarred, flattened, thick-ened, checkered, and welted. It was a face that had nothing to fear. Everything had been done to it that anybody could think of.'
Raymond Chandler, *Farewell My Lovely*

'And this man's name is Thomas Blake?' said Detective Chambers, taking notes in Karl's office while sitting down facing Karl. 'You suspect Blake had something to do with Miss Fleming's rape and murder in Ballymena?'

'Suspect? Something a bit stronger than that.'

'Any proof?'

'Unfortunately, no. He has a partner, looks a bit like Lee Marvin and—'

'Lee Marvin?'

'Do you have to be so bloody young? Lee Marvin was an actor – one of the best. Anyway, this bastard is the spitting image of him. He likes wielding and firing shotguns in public – preferably at people looking like me.'

'Firing guns in public? Have you any proof of that?'

'No proof, *per se*. I didn't stay around long enough to have my face blasted into oblivion when he was pointing that mother of all guns at me. But even the dogs in the street know – and I mean that both literally and figuratively.' Karl folded his legs, trying to get comfortable in an uncomfortable situation. 'No, better make that *dog*, singular, not plural. One of them had a slight accident with its rear end when it was rear-ended.'

Chambers scribbled something into his notebook, and then looked Karl straight in the face.

'Why'd you ask for me specifically, Mister Kane? Why not Detective McCormack? He's the one in charge of the case.'

'I like the freshness of your face. Very homely and honest.'

'Can you never answer a question without sarcasm?'

'No.'

'Detective McCormack reported that you refused to give any information when he questioned you two days ago. Why the change of heart now?'

'Questioned? Is that the word he used?' Karl forced a smile.

'What word should he have used?'

'Intimidation and bodily force, for starters.'

'Are you saying he hit you, Mister Kane?' Chambers looked slightly uncomfortable.

'Him? No. Never touched a hair on my pretty head. Even a thick-neck like McCormack is a bit too smart for that. But the gorilla with him did.'

'The gorilla?'

'Face and built like King fucking Kong. Only hairier. Has a piece missing from his left ear, and bigger pieces from his brain. Would talk the leg off a stool.'

Chambers smiled. 'Oh…that's Detective Carson, probably. A

strange one.'

'Strange? If he had two dicks, he couldn't have been any stranger. Anyway, to answer your question as to why the change of heart. The last two days have been hell. I can't get Laura Fleming out of my head. The thought that this scumbag Blake or Lee Marvin will get away with murdering her was something I couldn't live with.'

'We still have no proof of anything you've just told me, but I promise you that I will look into this, even if it means angering Detective McCormack.'

'I kind of thought you would, seeing how you're such a believer in law and order.'

Chambers shook his head. 'You're a very hard person to like, Mister Kane, if I'm to be totally honest with you.'

'Honesty is always the best policy, I find. Works wonders for the soul, if not the bank account. Now, are you finished here? Some of us have work to do.'

'Okay. Have it your way.' Chambers stood to leave. 'I'll look into the allegations you've just made against Thomas Blake and his associate. I'll be in contact, if I need to ask you anything else.'

'You do that. One word of advice. I'd be careful of letting McCormack know what you're doing behind his back. He might not like that. He's very…sensitive, when it comes to police work.'

'Thank you for that. I'll try and remember it. Though to be honest, I think it's Detective McCormack who should be careful.' Chambers smiled, and immediately Karl saw a different young detective standing before him in the smile. 'Good day, Mister Kane.'

CHAPTER NINETEEN

THERE WILL
BE BLOOD

'Anyone checked you for a heartbeat lately, lady?'
J.T. Walsh in *The Last Seduction*

'**T**here's been nothing out of the ordinary from any of the workers in their time schedules, other than a few sick notes,' explained Geordie Goodman, in the makeshift office, handing Karl a collection of beige-coloured folders. 'But on further examination, I discovered a few irregularities in the logging-in of a businessman, a Mister Tev Steinway, one of the Jewish butchers.'

'How so?'

'He comes here about two in the morning, twice a month, to do his slaughtering.'

'Why so late at night?'

'The place is basically empty at that time, with only a few maintenance men checking wear-and-tear throughout the abattoir. This gives Mister Steinway privacy. No curiosity seekers witnessing the slaughtering ritual.'

'Have you ever met Mister Steinway?'

'A couple of times. He's been here since my father ran the place. One of the few customers who didn't desert us in bad times. Never any trouble. A real gentleman. Keeps himself to himself…'

'But…?' coaxed Karl.

Geordie seemed reluctant to proceed. 'Mister Steinway has been here *six* times in each of the last two months. I just found out from one of the night security that Mister Steinway's been bringing in whiskey and food for the main security guard, asking for a blind eye to be turned by not logging-in every visit.'

'How'd you find out?'

'Petty jealousy. An anonymous whistle-blower phoned John Talbot, a couple of days ago, told him what was going on. Obviously someone with a grudge against the security guard. Wanted him in hot water.'

'Why would Steinway not want the log-ins recorded?'

'He's charged each time he uses the facilities. It can all add up, I suppose…'

'I suppose you're supposing something else, though, aren't you?'

She seemed to be assessing before answering. 'We've never had a problem with his bills. Never squabbles like some of the others using the facilities. Payments always on time; correct amount. I just…I don't know…'

'You think his nocturnal activity has something to do with the severed hands?'

'No, of course not! I…I just want to make sure that there's nothing illegal being done in my business. I had to fight tooth and nail with Belfast City Council to keep this place open, after what went on here years ago.' Geordie's face tightened. 'I'm not going to allow it to be closed – for *anything*. Especially something I know nothing about. Even if it is by a loyal client, like Mister Steinway.'

'You want me to do you a favour by making sure that every-thing really is *kosher* with Steinway. Is that it?' Karl smiled.

'I thought I was the one doing you a favour, passing on this information?'

'Okay. We'll call it evens on that. What about the guard? Has he been spoken to yet about turning a blind eye?'

'Not yet. He's been off on his two-day break. He's back tonight. I was going to question him about it, tomorrow, first thing.'

'Do me a favour. Let things be, for now. Don't tell the guard he's been caught out. That way, if Steinway *is* involved, he won't be alerted. Do you a have photo of Steinway on file?'

'Yes. We've security photos of everyone working here, as well as those using the facilities. I can have a copy for you in a few minutes. What're you going to do?'

'Oh, a little bit of nocturnal surveillance, I suppose. Noth-ing else for it, unfortunately.' He was dreading the thought of it, what it entailed. 'Fancy taking turns?'

'No,' said Geordie, rather coldly. 'You run your business; I run mine.'

'I'll have to remember that.' Karl stood to go. 'I'll call you later, with some instructions.'

'Fine. Good day, Mister Kane.'

Exiting the building, Karl couldn't help feeling just a little apprehensive about doing business with the strange, stoic young woman and her *bloody* business.

CHAPTER TWENTY

STAKEOUT

'When you commit a crime, there are a hundred ways to fuck up. If you think of fifty of 'em, you're a genius. And you ain't no genius.'
Mickey Rourke in *Body Heat*

Overcoat wrapped to his ears, Karl sat huddled in the car and watched punishing slabs of grey rain battering the outside. The heater wasn't working – hadn't been since he left the car in to be repaired. He should have had it seen to when having the new rear window replaced after the shooting. Now he was paying for his neglect through chattering teeth and dripping nose.

The inside of the car was quickly becoming as cold as the abattoir when he had visited Geordie three days ago, discussing the information she'd uncovered about Tev Steinway.

From the glove compartment, Karl removed the security photo of Steinway, giving it another once-over for the umpteenth time.

'Forgive the pun, Tev, but you're built like a bloody bull. Would hate to piss you off.'

Steinway's handsome face was leathery and weather-beaten, looking more like that of a seafaring man than butcher. His thick grey hair matched the grey eyes staring at Karl. The eyes gave away nothing about what was going on behind them.

'Despite your impressive size, you certainly don't look like a killer,' said Karl, a wry smile on his face, before placing the photo back in the compartment. 'Of course, neither do most killers…'

This was the third consecutive night of sitting in the darkness and cold, watching for Steinway, and each night seemed to be stretching longer than the previous. Worse, there was no guarantee that Steinway would show; no guarantee of the Jewish butcher's involvement, either. And what of Georgina Goodman? Was she to be trusted? As a betting man, he wouldn't place too much money on the odds, preferring the bookie's favourite: the M1911 Colt .45 automatic pistol, snuggling warmly in the inside pocket of his coat, just in case.

A stakeout at an abbatoir? Probably should rename it a *steak-out*.

Unscrewing a thermal flask, Karl poured his fourth coffee of the night. He sipped it for the warmth. The liquid had gone to rot, tasting like foul ink.

Suddenly, a loud tapping at the window startled him, making him spill a goodly amount of the coffee onto his crotch area.

'For fuck sake!'

A grinning face stared in at him.

'What the hell are you doing!' shouted Karl, staring back at the face, while cranking down the window. Almost immediately, the cold rain came rushing into the car, splattering his face.

'Haven't seen you about here before, *big* fella,' replied the hooker, smiling. The rain was running off a battered umbrella in her hand and snaking down the sleeves of her jacket. She seemed immune to it. 'I'm Joanie. You looking for a bit of warmth on this ball-freezing night?'

'Thanks, Joanie, but my balls are warm enough right now thanks to all that coffee you made me spill on them.'

'Don't be like that. Want someone to rub your magic lamp?' continued Joanie, undeterred. 'See what we can conjure *up*?'

'My genie's nice and snug,' replied Karl, now noticing that Joanie was more of a Johnny, with muscularly chiselled facial features. The masculine voice only added to the peculiarity.

'*Cum* on. Don't be like that,' coaxed Joanie. 'How can I get you to change your mind, honey?'

Shaking his head, Karl said, 'Honey, you aren't wealthy enough, and I'm not desperate enough. Now, disappear before I forget my manners.'

'Fuck you!' shouted Joanie, spitting into Karl's face.

'Right. That does it!' snarled Karl, quickly exiting the car. 'I never hit a lady, but with you not being one, I'll make an exception.'

No sooner had the words left his mouth than the unexpected hit him: a punch to the chin so hard that his head snapped violently back.

'This lady don't take shit from no faggot-arse thug,' Joanie said, batting the umbrella perfectly perfectly across the bridge of Karl's nose.

'Fuck!' Karl instinctively brought his hand up to his nose. It was bleeding.

'I'm going to teach you how to respect a lady!' Joanie aimed the umbrella like a spear, before thrusting it towards Karl's left eye.

Barely managing to move out of the way, Karl balled his fist and connected awkwardly with Joanie's forehead. She went staggering backwards into a pile of discarded cardboard boxes stuffed with rotten fruit.

Down but not out, Joanie administered a spine-shattering kick to Karl's balls, buckling him over like a flipped coin.

'*Ohhhh…*' moaned Karl, genuflecting to the ground like a monk saying matins.

Almost immediately, eager fingers began rummaging through his pockets. He felt his gun being removed from the inside of his coat.

'Don't you fucking move!' shouted Joanie, pointing the gun at Karl's petrified face. Her hands were shaking.

'Take…take it easy. You don't want to–'

'This'll teach you to disrespect me!' Joanie pulled the trigger. *Click!* Nothing. She pulled the trigger again. *Click!* Same result.

'Please…' Karl pleaded.

'Faggot!' Joanie shouted, escaping into the darkness with the gun.

Minutes passed before Karl was able to stand, unsteadily, catching his breath, grateful for Joanie's lack of understanding of guns; her inability to take the safety off.

Warding off vertigo with deep gulps of air, his head suddenly felt lighter. He quickly checked his pockets. Wallet gone too.

'*Bastard…*' he hissed, easing back into the car, gingerly checking that his nose wasn't broken.

Less than ten minutes later, chalky headlights lit up the interior of the car, casting wilting shadows across Karl's face. Then, just as suddenly, the darkness returned.

Karl watched the blue Merc halt at the security gate for a few seconds, before the barriers eased upwards, permitting entry.

Quickly leaving the car, Karl ran to the abattoir's side entrance, and began working the key, given to him by Geordie, into the lock. It was proving stubborn.

A leprous rat watched Karl's edgy manoeuvres, its yellow eyes making him even more edgy.

'*Scat!*' The rat quickly disappeared under a deep scar in the ground.

'*Come on!*' mumbled Karl to the reluctant key, cold and adrenaline making it almost impossible to negotiate the tiny cavity.

At last the key turned and the door opened.

Inside the massive grounds, he could hear guard dogs barking in the distance. The sound made his stomach do involuntary flip-flops, despite being assured by Geordie that the dogs were primarily trained not to attack, only to frighten off would-be thieves. He had a problem with the word *primarily*. Too ambiguously grey. He also had a problem no longer having a gun, and debated whether to cancel out tonight, in favour of some other night, hopefully a lot more favourable.

'Fuck it. Get it over with…'

Making his way cautiously across the unruly expanse of tarmac and cement, he soon discovered there was little light, except what glowed from the tired moon silhouetting the different buildings into apocalyptic scenes of desolation and solitude. The night seemed to be closing in all around the abattoir, painting it darker and darker.

Just like Karl's mood.

'*It can't get any worse, surely?*' he mumbled, resisting the urge to use the pocket torchlight in his pocket, thankful that thieving Joanie hadn't liberated that, as well. '*Where the hell is the abandoned tunnel?'*

The tension in his spine was horrendous. Every nerve in his body was tingling with adrenaline. He kept hearing Naomi's voice questioning his actions. *And what about this Georgina Goodman? You don't even know her. What if she's setting a trap? You read the newspaper archives about her and her insane sister and father. I told you I had a bad feeling about this…*

Naomi's dire forecast – balanced against the uncertainty of whatever waited ahead – wasn't helping the situation. The need to maintain a calm demeanour was paramount if he was to see this through.

To his relief, the entrance to the abandoned tunnel came slowly into view. Covered in thick bushes and triffid-like weeds, he almost missed it.

'What a fucking dump…' he muttered, entering.

Only now did Karl yield to the necessity to use the torchlight. His anxious face was a pale spot framed by the fragment of moonlight sneaking in through the broken stones marshalled all along the makeshift tunnel – the one-time pathway leading to the back of the abattoir. It had remained idle for years, after the crumbling stonework had fallen, killing one of the workers making his way home on a Saturday afternoon. Always a favourite shortcut with the workers, it now remained unused and condemned. Too dangerous.

Old, corroded water pipes that ribbed the grey, peeling walls, hissed and spat in his face, blinding him periodically. He began sweating. Since the time of his mother's murder, dark and claustrophobic spaces had always bothered him, and he was finding it extremely difficult to stay orientated or to regulate his breathing.

A crafty wind came suddenly rushing down the tunnel, carrying a medley of nauseating animal stenches. Manure, muck and dead blood all banded together along the slimy floor of the tunnel. Karl could taste it in his mouth. Extremely unpleasant, it gave off some kind of vibration, like a tuning fork punctuated by too much feel. He felt his stomach heave, but managed to control it with sheer willpower.

At last the side door leading to the main building came mercifully into view. A few seconds later, he was easing it open, slipping inside while extinguishing the light from the hand torch.

The building appeared empty of people, even though lights were flickering, shapeless and indistinct, through frosted glass. In the distance, soft sounds of machinery hummed quietly, in sharp contrast to its normal daily grind.

Quiet as a bloody tomb…

A succession of steps guided the way to the main floor, and Karl took them two at a time, silently, halting only to listen. His heart kept banging in his chest and eardrums.

Less than five minutes later, he stepped onto the deserted main floor, and quickly tried orientating his bearings, hoping to chart some sort of direction from his mind's map.

Which way?

Moving carefully, he headed along a corridor leading to the large doors of the main floor, thankful now of Talbot's ghastly tour. The doors opened automatically, waiting for him to enter.

It always baffled Karl – when watching the occasional horror movie with Naomi – how anyone could be so daft as to enter the haunted house. Any fool could see that nothing good would come of it. Yet, here he was, doing the exact same brainless action

– albeit on a bloodier scale.

He entered cautiously, expecting Vincent Price's laughter to sound out, mocking him. Instead, he caught an unwelcome glimpse of the malevolent Slaughter Restraint lurking in the shadows. The huge device looked even more intimidating and appalling in diluted light. It seemed alive, like an enormous Venus flytrap waiting for a succulent victim to embrace.

Proceeding up the last flight of stairs in the direction of the room above the Slaughter Restraint, Karl suddenly stopped dead in his tracks, alerted by a noise directly overhead.

'*Ohhhhhhhhhhhhhh…*' moaned a voice.

What the fuck? Karl let his breath out carefully, so it couldn't be heard.

The voice continued moaning. '*Ohhhhhhhhhhhhhh…*'

The moaning became louder, more urgent. Had someone hurt themselves on one of the machines? One of the night staff, perhaps?

Debating whether to remain hidden or call out to the injured, Karl quickly realised he had no alternative other than to do the right thing.

'Hello! Where are you? Give me some directions!'

Nothing. The moaning had stopped. All he could hear was his own breathing.

Moving cautiously up the staircase, he began using the shadows as cover, wishing he had his gun.

'*Ohhhhhhhhhhhhhh…*' The moaning suddenly commenced again. The sound seemed to be quivering. It was coming from inside the room above the Slaughter Restraint.

'Hello? Where are you?'

DEAD OF WINTER

Deathly silence.

Just as he halted outside the door, Karl spotted a red runnel of thick liquid beneath, partially gathering in a pool. The crimson diffusion slithered to where he stood, touching the lip of his shoes like a swarm of squashed tadpoles.

The hairs on the back of his neck suddenly began spiking. Something wasn't right, and he was standing right in the middle of that something.

'Blood? Fuck...' he muttered, seconds before something hit him hard across the back of the head, turning all lights off in his dark and bloody world.

CHAPTER TWENTY-ONE

DEAD MAN'S SHOES

'The unmentionable odour of death…'
W.H. Auden, *September 1, 1939*

Karl slowly awoke from a foggy stupor in a dimly lit room, feeling as weak as dead man's piss. His throbbing head seemed to have been cleft open. He reached to touch the wound, only to discover that his hands were tied firmly behind his back.

A fractured mirror on the wall shockingly revealed that he was inverted, naked, hovering directly over the evil-looking Slaughter Restraint. His feet were secured at the ankles. A bloody rag filled his mouth, which was taped shut. The pupils of his eyes had gone bloodshot, resembling deep wounds. The scars of boyhood horror that covered his body looked like a giant map of the world in the dull light.

He shivered. A mixture of foreboding and cold. He had never felt so cold in all his life. A large wall clock ticked loudly in his upside-down world. With difficulty, he figured he had been unconscious for at least twenty minutes. Thirty at the most.

His eyes began scanning the room. Bulky blocks of foul-looking meat were pyramided in corners, wet with blood. A large metal counter in the centre of the room resembled an operating table, pieces of newly hacked meat on top. Bloody utensils rested beside the chunks of meat. With sudden horror, Karl realised that the meat was human.

Three figures covered in bloody overalls and wearing facial masks stood a small distance away, mingling in the shadows, whispering. One glanced at Karl before touching the others, as if in a warning.

Seconds later, the same figure approached, stopping directly beside Karl before pressing a button ensconced in the wall.

Karl suddenly felt his body moving upwards, jostled by some unseen device. It sounded like rusted chain.

'I'm going to take the rag from your mouth and ask you some questions,' said the man, voice muffled, a serrated knife in his hand. 'If you try and scream, I'll gladly remove a finger. Lie, and I'll remove something a lot more personal. Nod if you understand.'

The stench of the bloody rag was burrowing all the way to Karl's stomach. He wanted to throw up. It was difficult nodding upside-down. He did his best.

'Good,' said Knifeman, ripping the tape off, before removing the bloody rag.

'*Arghhhhhhhhhhhh!*' Karl felt as if his lips had been torn from his face. He quickly began sucking in great gulps of air, choking on its taste.

'Why have you no ID?' asked Knifeman, pressing the knife against Karl's nose.

Knifeman had young eyes. Untested by the world. The kind of eyes that made Karl nervous.

'I...it was stolen from me, less than an hour ago. I was

attacked by a woman.' Karl suddenly became aware of the mutilated corpse, several feet away, brains squeezed from the skull like puréed strawberries. The corpse's bloody face seemed to be looking straight at him, a resigned smirk on its face.

'Attacked, by a *woman*?' snarled Knifeman, mockingly.

'I meant a man. A man stole it from me. A cross-dressing prostitute.'

'Very original.' Knifeman began pressing a smaller button on the wall.

Karl immediately felt his body being slowly lowered into the Slaughter Restraint. A sound of steel clanging, and he was jerked roughly to the side. His battered head banged against metal. He began moving in slow motion, rotating at an awkward angle like a hog on a spit, bringing him closer and closer to the face of the corpse anchored below.

'What…what're you doing?' Karl tried controlling the panic in his voice.

Knifeman said nothing, all the while continuing to rotate Karl's body.

Karl was certain the tiny stepping-stones of his spine were popping out from their enclosure.

'*Fuck!*' He began gritting his teeth. The pain was becoming unbearable.

For twenty long seconds Karl's battered body rotated, then stopped. His nose was touching the corpse's head. The dead man's skin felt rubbery and damp, making Karl shudder. Ears were missing from the face, along with parts of the right cheek. A horrible jigsaw face.

In his mind, Karl started replacing the missing parts of the fleshy puzzle. When he was done, there was little doubt in his mind that the bloody head had once rested on the shoulders of Thomas Blake.

Almost immediately, a warm reek of bile sat in Karl's throat like a piece of badly swallowed apple. He wanted to throw up again.

Knifeman's hands suddenly grasped Karl's head, positioning it in a half-moon clasp.

Karl immediately thought of a guillotine. Tried struggling. No use. His head eased backwards, exposing his neck. Talbot's grisly words rushed at him: They cut the cow's throat with a great big bloody knife called a *hallaf.*

Panicking, Karl began squirming like a worm on the end of a line. Without warning, a set of wooden vice-like clamps squeezed tightly against his head and body, stopping all movement.

'Bastards! Filthy murdering bastards! You'll not get away with this!'

'If you scream again, I'll punish you in such a way you'll never want to scream again,' said Knifeman, calmly, running a hand smoothly over Karl's exposed neck. Knifeman could easily have been a barber, carefully checking the facial terrain of one of his regulars. 'I'll ask you one more time. Why have you no ID?'

'I've already told you the fucking truth, you sick bastard! It was stolen from me!'

Knifeman reached for Karl's hand. 'First, I'm going to remove your index finger…'

'No! It's the truth!' exclaimed Karl, trying desperately to ball his hand into a protective shell. 'Outside the abattoir I was accosted and–'

'How many others have you brought with you?'

'Others…? There are no others. I'm…I'm on my own. I swear.'

'Liar. You'd swear your mother's life away,' hissed Knifeman, finally securing one of Karl's fingers.

'I'm a private investigator, for fuck sake!' shouted Karl, feeling the coldness of the knife on his index finger.

'I warned you not to lie!'

Just as Karl waited for his finger to be chopped, another man emerged from the shadow. Even though most of the man's face was masked, Karl suspected it was Tev Steinway.

'Wait!' commanded Steinway's muffled voice, directing his stare at Karl. 'What's your name?'

'Kane…Karl Kane…'

'Kane?' A flicker of recognition seemed to appear in Steinway's penetrating eyes. 'How do I know you're telling the truth?'

'Why would I lie? My car's parked in the wasteland, at the side of the abattoir. You can't mistake it. It's a silver Ford Cortina GT, originally used in "The Sweeney" TV show. You can't miss it. Take my keys. They're inside my coat pocket.' Karl gritted his teeth. His back felt ready to snap. 'Go check the glove compartment. You'll find a load of my business cards and some other scraps of ID.'

Steinway seemed to be weighing up Karl's words. He waited a few seconds before speaking to Knifeman. 'Take his keys. See what you can find.'

'He's lying. Can't you see he's just stalling for time? He's after the blood money.'

'What blood money?' asked Karl, hoping his face didn't betray him.

'The twenty thousand pounds,' said Knifeman. 'Stop pretending not to know. We're not fools.'

Karl's mind instantly separated into two camps of thought – deceitfulness and truth – before finally opting for the latter.

'Look…I'll admit at the start of this investigation, money *was* the motive–'

'I told you!' exclaimed Knifeman, looking directly at the other two men. 'What more do we need to know?'

'Go and find his car,' instructed Steinway to Knifeman. 'Bring back anything of importance. Make sure you are not seen – *by anyone.*'

Mumbling under his breath, Knifeman glared at Karl for a few seconds, before quickly leaving the room.

A fucking psychopath, thought Karl, glad to see the back of the mad bastard.

'If you *are* lying to us, stalling for time, it will be all the worse for you,' said Steinway. His voice had a commanding calm.

The calm before the storm, thought Karl, trying to angle his neck, hoping for a better view of Steinway.

'Why *were* you spying on us?' said the third man, speaking for the first time. Directly above his left eyebrow, the man had a small but deeply rooted scar.

To Karl, the scar resembled a pitted star.

'I've already told you. I'm a private investigator. When your friend comes back, he'll confirm everything I said.'

'You'd better hope he does,' said Starman. 'Luckily for you, we found no trace of certain tattoos on your skin. If we had, we wouldn't be having this conversation.'

'You mean eighty-eight?' replied Karl, seeing from the reaction in Starman's eyes that he had probably hit pay dirt – though admittedly more dirt than pay.

'What do you know about the numbers?'

'Nothing, other than the fact they've been on the hands of victims discovered in and around the city.'

'I wouldn't use the word *victims* when describing filth.' Starman's voice sounded agitated. 'Now, we need you to remain quiet, until we find out a little bit more about you.'

It was forty long minutes later when Knifeman finally returned, a bunch of papers held tightly in his right hand. He looked less than pleased.

'I found these. *Cheap* business cards,' said Knifeman, handing them to Steinway. 'Unpaid parking tickets and crumpled-up betting dockets. But other than that, no photo ID confirming his name. He also had *this*, hidden in the glove compartment.'

It was the photo of Steinway given to Karl by Geordie.

Almost immediately, Steinway began whispering into Knifeman's ear. Seconds later, Knifeman produced a mobile phone and took a photo of Karl's face.

The stench of the place was finally getting to Karl. He needed to throw up. Just when he thought things couldn't get any worse, the pain in his back began intensifying.

'My fucking back's breaking!'

'*Shut up!*' hissed Knifeman.

Less than a minute later, the mobile phone sounded loudly in the hushed room, making Karl jerk as if tapped with an electric cattle prod.

Knifeman glanced at the mobile's screen before showing it to the other two men.

'Who gave you this?' asked Steinway, holding the photo close to Karl's face.

'I…I stole it when I was searching about in the office, a few weeks ago. No-one even knows it's missing. I can put it back just as easily.'

'You're not a very good liar, Mister Kane. Did Mrs Goodman give it to you? Or was it Talbot, the foreman?'

'I already told you–'

'What you already told was a lie. Don't compound it with another, please, even if it is commendable that you think you're protecting your source. Now, what's Mrs Goodman's involvement?'

Karl let out a sigh before answering. 'She's not involved in *anything*, other than trying to save her business. She just wanted me to check that everything was above board with *all* her clientele, that none of them were breaking the law. I'm sure you're aware of the history of this place, and her father and sister, what they did?'

Steinway nodded. 'Yes, it's public knowledge: all the killings Mrs Goodman's father was involved in before he himself was killed.'

'Then you'd agree that the last thing she would want is a prying private investigator like me bringing any undue attention to this bloody place? She asked me to check, and then get out of her life and abattoir for good.'

'That sounds feasible, if somewhat convenient.' Steinway glanced over at Starman.

'What guided you here in the first place, Mister Kane?' asked Starman.

'I'd like to boast it was brilliant brain-storming, but it was nothing more than a hunch. I decided to give it a try to see what I could discover, clearly wishing now I hadn't.'

'What exactly *did* you discover?'

'The more I found out about the…' Karl almost said victim, but quickly substituted the word. '…*owner* of each hand, the less inclined I became to find those behind the dismembering.'

'Even though you discovered what scum they were, you don't approve. I can tell by your voice,' said Starman. 'Perhaps you think everything is black and white? People like you, Mister Kane, can never truly understand that life is sometimes made of grey, and ruled by the past.'

'I understand the darkness of grey, perhaps more than you do. But I've also learnt from the past that a blood-trail is a stain easily created but damn hard to erase.'

'He's saying what he thinks we should hear, just to stall for time!' exclaimed Knifeman, becoming more agitated. 'Don't you see? He'll do anything to get the blood money.'

'I've already admitted that the money was the motivation at the start of this investigation. *Was*. Past tense.'

'And now?' asked Steinway.

'You see these scars covering my body?' said Karl directly to Steinway and Starman. 'Want to know the story behind them?'

'*No!*' hissed Knifeman. '*We have no interest in–*'

'Let him speak,' said Steinway, his calming voice once again taking control. 'Go on, Mister Kane. I was more than slightly curious about them, I have to admit.'

'My mother was raped and murdered when I was eight,' said Karl, his voice almost a whisper. 'I was stabbed over twenty times, and left for dead by the same monster. These scars are a daily reminder of what he did. Each time I look at them, I see him, grinning, warning he'd be back to finish the job.'

Steinway looked totally shocked at the revelation.

'Years later, as an adult,' continued Karl, 'I had the chance to avenge my mother's murder by killing the man responsible. I didn't take it. Had I done so, two young girls wouldn't have been brutally raped and murdered by the monster a few days later.'

'Why didn't you kill him?' asked Starman.

'You think killing someone you don't know can be done cleanly and neatly because it's done with detachment?'

'That's your reason?'

'Cowardice or conscience, perhaps. Even after all these years, I still debate with myself each night before I try to sleep.' Karl's voice was on the verge of breaking. 'Still think I don't understand the grey between the black and white? Think again.'

Everything in the room came to an eerie hush. Karl's laboured breathing was the only audible sound. It was left to Steinway to break the silence.

'Release him, and put him in the chair,' Steinway instructed Knifeman.

'You can't be serious?' said Knifeman. 'What if he tries to get out?'

'He'll not get out. Place him in the chair.'

Mumbling under his breath, Knifeman began manoeuvring Karl out of the Slaughter Restraint. To Karl, Knifeman was a lot slower taking him out than he had been placing him in the damn contraption.

Finally upright, Karl was eased into a wooden chair, hands and feet still bound. Muscles were limp and unresponsive. His head felt light, yet despite the hellish situation, it was heavenly to be sitting again.

'Go back and finish your work,' Steinway ordered Knifeman. 'We haven't much time.'

The last sentence caused a shiver to run up Karl's battered spine. His stomach suddenly became a bucket of rats.

'What…what are you planning to do with me?' he asked, not really wanting an answer.

In the stillness, broken only by the ticking of the clock, Steinway seemed to be reflecting. 'I haven't decided yet.'

Suddenly, Knifeman came rushing forward. In his hand he held a cleaver newly wet with blood. 'He knows too much! Don't you see? He's playing mind games. We have no other choice than to dispose of him.'

Steinway shook his head wearily. 'You would spill innocent blood, mingle it with the guilty?'

'*He's* not innocent. He wants the blood money, and that makes him as guilty as the filth we've disposed of. Don't you understand? We'll go to prison for life, and they'll have won.'

'*Won?*' said Steinway, shaking his head. 'Is that what this is about? Winning? Have you lost sight of justice?'

'No…no, of course not…' Knifeman's voice became subdued.

'I give you my word that I won't go to the cops – or anyone else,' said Karl, marvelling at how calm his voice sounded, contradicting his frayed nerves.

'*Your* word?' Knifeman's eyes narrowed. 'A bounty hunter's words?'

Steinway slowly removed his mask, before looking directly at Starman. 'I'll not have this man's death on my conscience.

What do *you* say?'

To Karl, Starman seemed to be taking forever to say something. He looked at Karl, then over towards the visibly agitated Knifeman, before looking back at Steinway. Finally, he spoke. 'There's a great possibility that Kane will go straight to the police and tell them everything, the moment he's released. Of course, two of us do have the advantage of anonymity. He only knows you.'

'I can live with that,' said Steinway. 'The police will get nothing from me if I'm arrested. You have my word on that.'

'I don't need your word. I've always trusted your decisions. This time will be no different. But this I say, and I want it understood by Kane.' Starman turned his attention to Karl, looking directly into his eyes. 'If *anyone* is ever arrested and charged, I'll hold you personally responsible. I don't care where you try to hide. I'll find you – at any cost. Do you understand?'

Karl did his best to nod. 'I believe you. Hopefully, you believe me.'

'Untie him,' Steinway told Knifeman. 'Help him get cleaned up. Give him back his clothes. We've a lot of clearing up to do.'

'You can't be serious?' said Knifeman. 'We're finished the moment he walks out of here. He'll go straight to the police. And what about Goodman?'

'We're finished here – forever. Enough blood has been spilt. As for Mrs Goodman, Mister Kane's final report to her will say there was nothing to be concerned about. She'll go along with that, once I tell her I've decided to retire. Besides, Mister Kane won't jeopardise the safety of those he loves,' said Steinway, turning his gaze on Karl. 'Isn't that right, Mister Kane?'

CHAPTER TWENTY-TWO

THE SCARLET LETTER

'People think that Hell is fire and brimstone and the Devil poking you in the butt with a pitchfork, but it's not. Hell is when you should have walked away, but you didn't.'

Gary Oldman in *Romeo is Bleeding*

'**Y**ou come back at six in the morning, cuts and bruises all over your face and body, and smelling of God knows what, and say you just slipped on the snow?' Naomi dabbed yellowish medicinal liquid on Karl's face, while he sat on a chair in the living room. 'You expect me to believe you just *slipped*? Really?'

'Really.' Karl wore only underwear, exposing a body badly bruised by its ordeal on the Slaughter Restraint. His swollen lips had turned as rusty as the liquid Naomi was administering, while the back of his head still throbbed terribly.

'Well, for your information, Karl Kane, I'm not buying what you're trying to sell.'

'It's easy slipping, once you know how, Naomi. Simply place one left foot in front of the other left foot, and just add ice plus a sprinkling of hardened snow. Works every time for me. Even better when I've had a few brandies for winter fuel.'

Naomi released a sigh of disgust. 'Your lips look like someone tried to rip them off. That wasn't a fall.'

'It was a kissogram gone wrong.'

'Stop trying to be smart when you know you're anything but.' Naomi dabbed the liquid on roughly.

'*Fuck sake!* Careful with that bloody stuff. You're rubbing it on just a little too enthusiastically. That's my face, not dough, you're kneading.'

'Stop fussing like a big girl's blouse.' She dabbed some more. 'So, are you going to tell me about your little nocturnal shenanigans, or do I rub a little harder?'

Karl thought of the last four nightmarish hours. Rolled them into a split second. Shuddered involuntarily. Another nightmare to add to the mounting toll.

'It was all a waste of time and money. I was totally wrong,' he finally said. 'Nothing suspicious about that bloody place, or any of the even bloodier people working in it. If I've learned anything this day, it's the fact that I'm a failure when it comes to hunches.'

'I won't have you being so self-critical. So stop it.' She gently kissed the top of his throbbing head.

He felt the kiss burning through his hair, all the way to the scalp, like a magical balm. Loved it. Loved being back with the woman he loved; her perfume, her voice. Her very presence was solace to his soul. Just wished he didn't have to lie to her. How things could have ended so differently. Never seeing her again. He shuddered.

'Karl? Are you listening to me?'

'Oh…sorry, love.'

'I said, what about Geordie Goodman, the owner? Nothing

suspicious about her?'

He had wondered the same, but Steinway's concerned words had cleared her. No, Geordie Goodman wasn't involved in this particular grisly case, but something else, perhaps? He really didn't want to contemplate the thought, but had a sneaking suspicion that their paths would cross again, sometime in the future. It wasn't Goodman he was thinking of, anyway, but the woman claiming to be Jemma Doyle, how she had fooled him into setting up Thomas Blake to be tortured, then murdered. He had phoned the number she had given him, but as he suspected, it was no longer in service. What a sad, pathetic sucker he had been.

'No. Not a thing about Georgina Goodman. From the little I uncovered, she's as clean as a nun's bum. But I'll tell you something, after visiting that terrible place, I'm gonna do my best to eat less meat."

Naomi slowly sat down beside him, her lovely face suddenly terribly serious.

'Are you trying to wind me up, Karl?'

'Not unless you have a key sticking out of your back.'

'You'll really try?'

'I'll *try*. Cross my heart and hope to die.'

'She threw her arms around his sore neck, hugging him tightly.

'Easy, for fuck sake, Naomi. For such a wee thing, you've got the grip of a wrestler. Let go, will you?'

She slowly released him, kissed his torn lips, and stood.

'Could you manage a cup of nice coffee, if I make it special, just the way you like it?'

He put on a limp voice. 'I'll try…but only for you.'

She giggled, before quickly heading for the kitchen.

Music started filtering from the kitchen, just as the doorbell down below began ringing insistently.

He quickly grabbed Naomi's pink bathrobe and made his way awkwardly downstairs.

The bell rang and rang.

'All bloody right! I'm coming!' he shouted, halfway down the stairs.

It was Sean, the postman, wrapped up as if for a polar expedition.

'Couldn't you've just dropped any mail through the letter box, Sean? All that irritating ringing like Quasi bloody modo.'

'And a good morning to you, too, Karl. That colour really suits you.' Sean grinned. He held out a large brown envelope. 'This envelope is too big, and anyway it has to be signed for. It's from a solicitor. I thought it might have been from a publisher accepting one of your rejected manuscripts.'

'Cut the sarcasm. It's too early in the morning.'

'Just sign inside the window.' Sean handed Karl the envelope and a black plastic signing device.

'Who the hell invented this piece of crap?' complained Karl, trying to negotiate the pen-like tool onto the screen.

'Be as quick as you can. It's Baltic out here, Karl.' A frosty mist escaped Sean's mouth each time he spoke.

'Stop complaining. You get paid for getting your nuts frozen off.'

'You must have been pollaxed last night. You look like you got a good hammering.'

'It was Thor. So if you happen to see the long-haired prick on your rounds, give him a good kick up the *Ass*gard for me.'

'You know what they say? A bad morning is usually the result of a good night.'

'Thank you, Socrates,' mumbled Karl, awkwardly scribbling an illegible scrawl, before handing the device back.

'Have a nice one,' said Sean, throwing the mailbag over his shoulder before leaving the doorway.

Back inside, Karl glanced quickly at the printed solicitor's name. *T. P. McGuigan*. His heart moved up a notch. He didn't like letters from solicitors – especially ones he had never heard of. He wondered if it was from Lynne, looking for more money? It was just the sneaky sort of shit she'd get up to: changing solicitors to confuse him.

Upstairs, he threw the large envelope on the sofa, debating whether to open it or leave it for Naomi to hit him gently with any bad news it might contain. A cup of hot coffee sat on the table beside his chair. He could hear Naomi moving about in the bathroom.

'To hell with it…' He slit the envelope open with a pen and began removing the contents. A paperclip attached a page to another envelope. His name was scrawled across the envelope's face like an unhealed scar. He sat the envelope down, concentrating on the page first.

Dear Mister Kane,

Please find enclosed letter from one of our clients, now deceased. Should you need any more information, please do not hesitate to contact me.

Yours sincerely,

Thomas P. McGuigan

Karl's intuition began kicking in. *Deceased?* He didn't like the sound of that particular deadly word.

As if handling a booby-trap bomb, he began gingerly removing the contents from the other envelope. One typed page. Small key taped securely to it.

Well, Kane? Bet this comes as a bit of a shock to you?

Karl quickly ran his eyes to the bottom of the page, hoping to determine the sender. The name screamed at him: Edward Phillips.

'Shit…'

If you're reading this, Kane, then I guess I didn't manage to die of old age in my bed, and have probably ended up a victim of a mysterious or violent death. If so, I've given instructions to Tom (McGuigan, my solicitor) to ensure this letter arrives safely in your capable, if somewhat dodgy, hands.

Remember that day we bumped into each other outside headquarters, all those eons ago? My pension had been withdrawn by that fuck of a brother-in-law of yours, and I was on my way to confront him? I was slightly intoxicated. Remember?

Karl remembered. Too well…

▲ ▲ ▲

Karl had just emerged from Police Headquarters when he bumped into Phillips. Phillips had recently been drummed out of the force, with loss of pension and benefits. Rumour said it was something to do with shaking down drug dealers.

Upon seeing Karl, the ex-detective had engaged him in conversation, the effect of booze obvious in the way he slurred some of the words. The short version of his story was that he was heading in to see his old boss, Wilson, and was going to make him reinstate what was owed to him.

'Good luck with that,' Karl had said.

'Luck's got nothing to do with it when you've got good, solid insurance and just the right amount of secrets.' Phillips had seemed very confident.

'Secrets? What kind of secrets?'

'As juicy as a box of oranges, or should I say, figs from King David's garden.' Phillips had winked knowingly.

'King David?'

Karl remembered Phillips leaning in confidentially before he said, 'Listen, Kane, I've always liked you, despite the fact that you probably shot two of my old workmates, who, likely as not, had it coming to them.'

'That booze is making you talk shit, Phillips,' Karl recalled saying. 'I had nothing to do with Cairns or Bulldog being killed.'

Phillips had shrugged. 'I'm only saying I always liked you, and just to prove it, if some unfortunate accident should befall me, I'll make sure my solicitor sends you a little something in the mail.'

With that, Phillips had headed towards the door of HQ. 'Be seeing you, Kane.'

What the hell was all that about?, Karl had wondered at the time.

Maybe now he was going to find out.

▲▲▲

'You were wrong on that account, Phillips. You never did see me again.' With difficulty, Karl sipped the coffee before continuing with the letter.

A numbered key should be enclosed with this letter. It opens a private postal box in the train station at Great Victoria Street. Open it. Once you do, you'll find a nice wee surprise from me. A sort of going away gift, we'll call it. There will also be another letter. Read it and weep, Kane. Discover the truth about your so-called moralistic brother-in-law. Remember what I said about the King David Syndrome?

See you about, Kane. Some place…

Edward Phillips

A scraggly signature was scrawled over the typed 'Edward Phillips'.

And there was a PS: *Oh, I suppose there's a possibility that this communication has fallen into the wrong hands. If so, I guess it's not you reading it. Probably, just like me, you're dead also.*

The coffee no longer tasted honest in Karl's mouth. He sat the cup back down on the table.

'Karl?'

'Naomi! What the hell are you doing, sneaking up on me like that?'

'I'm not sneaking anywhere.' Naomi was leaning against the bathroom door, her arms folded, a frown on her face. 'What's wrong? You look like you just saw a ghost.'

Or felt one pissing on my grave. 'It's this awful coffee. Where the hell did you get it? *Miser Mick's*? It's bouncing.' Karl desperately began balling Phillips' letter.

'What's that in your hand?' asked Naomi, ignoring the sarcasm in Karl's voice.

'What?'

'*That*.' Naomi pointed at the offending hand. Bits of the letter spiked out between Karl's fingers.

'Oh! *That*? Would you believe, another rejection letter? Those heartless publishers show no mercy, always kicking a man when he's down. That's the third this week. They're relentless and ruthless.'

'Oh, Karl. I didn't know.' Naomi walked over and began comfort-hugging him. 'Try not to let them bother you too much. I'm sure even Shakespeare got rejection letters.'

'Please don't compare me to that old plagiarising bastard. He stole more notes than the Northern Bank robbers. At least they had the decency to wear masks.'

'Don't let those silly publishers get you down,' said Naomi, planting a kiss on his cheek. 'You'll prove them wrong, one day. Promise me you won't let them get to you.'

'I'll try, my wee love, but it's not easy being me.' He stood and returned the kiss, while stuffing the letter hastily inside the pocket of the bathrobe.

'Go for your shower, Karl. I'll have something else for you to slip into, once you get back, and it'll be a hell of a lot warmer than my bathrobe.' Naomi grinned, giving him a playful slap on the arse.

'Such a tease.' Karl moved quickly for the shower, grasping the key so tightly it began cutting his skin.

CHAPTER TWENTY-THREE

THE STRANGER

'And there shall be no night there;
And they need no candle,
Neither light of the sun;
For the Lord God giveth them light:
And they shall reign forever and ever.'
Revelation 22:5

Sarah Cohen stood silently at the grave of her three children, staring at the simple inscription on the tombstone:
Benjamin, Nora and Judith.
Always with you.
And the spirit shall return unto God, who gave it.

▲ ▲ ▲

Fat snowflakes were falling heavily on Sarah's uncovered hair and long black coat. She appeared immune to them, as if stuck in a moment, or in an unexplained mystery. Snow and ice encrusted her eyelashes, preventing any more tears. Her lips were quickly becoming chapped from the bitter cold.

Although early in the afternoon, the relentless snow was already creating a dull darkness over the area. The graveyard was quickly emptying, with the exception of an elderly woman two rows down, and a tall, well-made man directly across from her.

Both seemed deep in meditation.

Sarah lifted her head slightly, before glancing over at the man and woman, wondering if they also were weighted down with inconsolable sorrow?

The elderly woman – now finished – began trudging through mounds of swampy snow, making her way towards a parked car a small distance away.

Less than a minute later, she started the car and began guiding it slowly out towards the main entrance gate. Just as she was about to ease through the gates, the engine began spluttering, forcing the car to stall.

Sarah could clearly hear the ignition being sparked up, the ageing engine spluttering and wheezing. She hoped the woman wasn't going to be stranded in the snow.

The snowfall was becoming noticeably heavier, with the winter wind increasing its fierceness. Sarah moved to go.

'There's always some comfort here,' said a voice directly behind Sarah, startling her. 'Perhaps not a lot, but some, once you find it.'

Sarah stared at the man. He looked like a preacher, garbed in sombre clothing. Features were difficult to decipher in the dull light, but his skin was pale like the snow, eyes the colour of dead coffee. They had a cold distance in them.

'It took me a while to find you, Sarah.'

Surprised, Sarah said, 'How…how do you know my name?'

'Patience and time. Everything eventually finds its way home.' He held out his hand. A tiny item rested in it. 'Take it.'

'Take it? Why?'

'I created it especially for you.'

'I…I don't understand.'

'There is no longer any need for understanding. Take it… please.'

She backed away, her eyes on the tiny offering, her hands pulled defensively aagainst her chest.

'What am I supposed to do with it?' she asked nervously.

'Do? Keep it.' He smiled. The smile looked borrowed. Like something he'd just bought in a pawnshop. 'It will be yours to cherish forever.'

Sarah shivered before quickly glancing beyond his shoulders, towards the woman in the car. The vehicle was still wheezing with effort. Sarah thought about running towards it, but her feet seemed unable to move, as if glued to the snowy ground.

'She can't help you,' he said, producing a bulbous gun with a long-nosed silencer attached. 'Besides, if she tried, who would help her after you're gone? This is just between us, Sarah.'

Sarah's heart began beating furiously. Words were sticking in her throat.

'I…I don't understand. Why…why are you doing…this?'

'Why? Because it's necessary.

'Is it money you're after?' She took a small purse from her coat pocket. 'I don't have much with me, but take it. I've some jewellery, also.' She fumbled at her wrist, the watch her mother bought her all those years ago.

The car started with a low growl, before easing outwards. Sarah watched it disappear into an impenetrable haze of swirling snow, with only headlights holding off the weight of the flakes. In her mind she could still see the taillights of the car, long after it had gone. It made her feel terribly alone.

He reached and touched her shoulder.

Bizarrely, a comforting calmness began spreading throughout her body at his touch. She suddenly felt light. Nothing seemed to matter anymore.

The shot hit her in the head and she flew back with a grunt, her breath swept away in the sharp, unholy wind of winter. Landing on her back, glazed eyes opened to the sky. Blood began spreading out under her, mingling with the pressed snow.

For a few seconds the killer closed his eyes, head bowed, lips moving in silent prayer. Then he gently placed the rejected offering in Sarah's left hand, before leaving the cemetery to the dead.

CHAPTER TWENTY-FOUR

DARK CITY

'A big hard-boiled city with no more personality than a paper cup.'
Raymond Chandler, *The Little Sister*

Karl shook snow from his overcoat and leather gloves while entering the all-night cafe on Great Victoria Street. The exterior of Debbie Does Dinners looked like something from a Charles Dickens' novel, but inside served the best coffee and grub in Belfast.

He removed the overcoat and gloves before parking his bulk at a small table right beside the front window, and waited for service. It wasn't long coming, in the form of a middle-aged waitress, notepad in hand.

'Hello, lover boy. Haven't seen your craggy mug in weeks. Where've you been hiding?'

'Busy as sin, Janice. Any late breakfast?'

'Breakfast? It's eight o'clock at night. Have you been boozing?'

'Nope. Just working my arse off. Now, what can you do me for? I'm starving, babe.'

'That's what you get for tying up with a gorgeous-looking girl, half your age. You missed your once-in-a-lifetime opportunity with me.'

'I know, and I've come to regret every second of it.'

'Liar.' Janice smiled. 'How about an almost Ulster fry?'

'Almost?'

'Sausages, eggs, potato bread, fried tomatoes, and mushrooms. Sorry, but we're all out of bacon and soda bread.'

'Cancel the sausages, and shovel the rest in my gob. Don't forget a big pot of coffee, you lovely thing.'

'No sausages? What's wrong with you?'

'It's a long story, and one that you wouldn't want to hear. Besides, I'm working on a new, slim me.'

'I like you the way you are. Something a woman can grab.'

'You say the loveliest of things, you lovely thing.'

As soon as Janice left, Karl focused his attention on Great Victoria Street Station, directly across from the cafe. The place was screaming with people, despite the last train having pulled out of the station over an hour ago. Tourists were everywhere, mixing with late-night drinkers and Thursday night shoppers. Unfolded maps and brochures of Ireland were being scrutinised by the beleaguered foreign visitors. Tour guides were herding the unfortunates from buses just back from the Giant's Causeway and other and 'must-see' scenic routes of monotonous, winding roads and sectarian towns painted in wonderful colours of the rainbow. Some of the tourists sported loud t-shirts depicting Donald Duck wearing a bulletproof vest, proclaiming: *Please don't shoot. I'm only a tourist visiting Belfast. Quack! Quack!*

Only yesterday, bus crews had admitted to wearing bulletproof vests, after threats from a shady organisation, suspected in some quarters to be disgruntled taxi drivers angry at their meagre income being lessened by the big bus companies.

Who the hell in their right mind would want to tour this bloody place, anyway, and in this god-awful weather – or any other weather, come to think of it? Karl had to smile at his own thoughts. *Speaking of right mind, you've a cheek...*

This afternoon's letter from dead man Phillips had galvanized him, forcing him to comply with the madness in his head and going against the rational thing to do: ditching the plan completely.

Janice returned ten minutes later, thankfully interrupting his conflicting thoughts.

'Enjoy, lover,' said Janice, leaving the bill on the table before departing.

Almost immediately, Karl began cutting into the eggs. The fry was greasy, but not as greasy as some of the customers directing their suspicious stares at him.

Antique Rouge Show, thought Karl, doing his best to ignore the stares.

The cafe was a well-known haunt of hookers and johns, thieves and fences, along with bent cops and double-tongued informants. Karl hated admitting it, but he blended in perfectly with this particular brand of society's purgatorial lepers.

Despite the grease, the fry was delicious, and the coffee excellent. Just as he was about to bite into the potato bread, two off-duty policemen stopped beside his table, one of them belching loudly.

'Nice meal, Billy. Pity about some of the scumbags they let in here, though.'

Billy grinned, but said nothing in reply.

Another time and place, Karl would have made a smart retort.

But now wasn't the smartest of times to be smart. He continued eating, allowing Belcher and Billy to depart verbally unscathed.

Just as he was about to sip on the coffee, out of the corner of his eye he noticed a movement; someone trying to exit the cafe and not wanting to be seen – at least not by him.

'Lipstick…?' said Karl.

Lipstick stopped immediately, like a rabbit in headlights.

'Karl?' Lipstick smiled. It looked forced. 'I…I didn't notice you there.'

Despite the heat from the cafe, Lipstick's skin was brailled with goose bumps.

A burly man accompanying Lipstick looked infuriated at Karl's interception. To Karl, the man appeared to be higher than a lost balloon, bloodshot eyes bulging angrily from their sockets.

Looking directly at Lipstick, Karl patted the seat beside him. 'Join me.'

Lipstick looked nervously at her companion, before replying. 'I'm really in a hurry, Karl, and need to be–'

'You need to be sitting beside me – *now.*'

'Just who the fuck do you think you are!' snarled Mister Burly, stopping beside Karl's table. 'She's going with me, so don't go sticking your nose where it isn't wanted, otherwise I'll bend it out of shape.'

Karl stood, face tight with anger. Quickly pushing away from the table, he eyeballed the man, nose to nose. 'It's not my nose you need to be worrying about, dopey. It's my boot.'

'Huh? What the fuck did you just–?'

Grabbing Mister Burly by the balls, Karl began squeezing. Tightly.

Mister Burly moaned in a bad way. His entire face seemed to have lock-jawed. Tears began forming in his eyes. He looked on the brink of collapsing.

'Can you hear me better, now?' whispered Karl into Mister Burley's left ear.

Mister Burly nodded weakly. 'Please…the pain…'

'Wrong answer.' Karl tightened his grip.

'Arghhhhhhhhhhhhhhhhhhhhhhhh!'

'How's the hearing, now?'

'Okay! Okay!'

'Good. When I release my grip on your tiny balls, you'll do an about-turn, head straight for the door, and no back-lip. Deviate whatsoever from my instructions, and you'll find your coat in the Mater Hospital – along with most of your body. Understand?'

Mister Burly quickly nodded.

'Goodnight, sweetheart,' said Karl, releasing his grip, before unceremoniously shoving his victim towards the door.

The man staggered out like a drunk at a wine convention.

'You,' said Karl, pointing a finger at Lipstick. 'Sit.'

'Where do you learn such frightening stuff?' asked Lipstick, a mixture of awe and terror on her tiny face.

Karl seemed deep in thought, before answering in a soft voice. 'I learned that little trick from a lady I had the privilege to meet, not so long ago. A lovely lady named Sandy.'

Then, just as quickly, the softness was gone, replaced with a forced crustiness. 'Now, what the hell are you up to?'

'It wasn't what it looked like, Karl. Honest,' said Lipstick, sliding in beside Karl.

'I know what it looked like, and it was.' Karl fumbled in his pocket and produced a mobile. Hit a few numbers.

Lipstick looked terrified and very vulnerable. 'You…you're not going to call the judge and have my bail revoked?'

'Worse,' said Karl, before speaking into the phone. 'Naomi? Listen. I've a visitor coming to see you. It's Lipstick. Make sure you have a word with her. I must speak some foreign language because she doesn't seem to understand me.'

Karl clicked off the phone before fishing for some money in his pocket. 'Here. Get a taxi outside, and head straight to my place. I'll be watching from this window.'

Lipstick looked horrified. 'Can't you give me a break?'

'You've had more breaks than a KitKat.'

'I can't face Naomi, Karl. She's going to be so angry with me.'

'You don't need a crystal ball to know that. Now get moving. I'm going to call her in twenty minutes. If you're not there, I *will* make that phone call to the judge.'

'You wouldn't,' said Lipstick, uncertainty on her face.

'Wouldn't I?' said Karl, looking at his wristwatch. 'Now it's nineteen minutes…'

'I'm beginning to dislike you, Karl Kane!' said Lipstick, quickly sliding back out.

'Join the queue. Eighteen and a half minutes…'

He watched her running for the door. A minute later, he stood and put his overcoat back on, before heading for the counter.

'How was it?' asked Janice, taking bill, payment and tip.

'Top notch, as usual, Janice. Goodnight, you sexy thing. Take care,' said Karl, putting on his gloves.

'Goodnight, Karl, and watch yourself out there.'

Great Victoria Street Rail Station was still packed to the gills with tourists and locals when Karl eased through the side entrance adjacent to the Europa Buscentre.

His intuition continued warning him as he walked with a forced casualness towards the rows of nondescript grey lockers down the dimly lit corridor. The ageing lockers resembled a fleet of tombstones.

Nearing the designated locker – number twenty-eight – Karl quickly took in his surroundings: an elderly male cleaner wiping the floor with a mop that had seen better days – a bit like the cleaner. The man seemed to be creating more of a mess than anything else. He glanced at Karl for a second, before continuing his slow pendulum movements with the mop.

Another man was standing a small distance away, scanning a freebie newspaper. He looked like an iffy businessman with a cheap suit and attitude to match.

Undercover cops? Those two have the look and smell, especially that sneaky-looking bastard pretending to read the paper. Karl glanced up the corridor before checking the guy with the paper again. *This could be a classic stitch-up and you're providing them with all the needles and thread they need for your sorry arse, Karl Kane.*

Seconds later, Karl stopped hesitantly at the locker. Bending on one knee, he pretended to tie his shoelace while sneaking a glance under his arm. The iffy businessman was dumping the newspaper in an over-flowing bin. He appeared to be staring straight at Karl's back. The cleaner, meanwhile, had stopped mopping the floor. He was leaning the dirty mop against a door, while wiping his mouth with what looked like a filthy rag. He seemed to be eyeing Karl, too.

Is that a rag, or a walky-talkie in his hand?

To Karl's relief, the cleaner suddenly gathered his tools-in-trade, and began moseying out of sight towards the direction of the main part of the building.

You're becoming bloody paranoid. Strap on your balls and get the job done.

Easing himself up, Karl glanced again at the other man, who was now speaking into a mobile phone.

Shit!

Against his better judgement, Karl's gloved hand quickly removed the key from his pocket, grateful for the corridor's bad lighting. Opening the locker, he peered inside. The oniony stench of sour feet hit him straight up the face. An old battered pair of Nikes and hardened socks the culprits. The contents of an upturned bottle of Brut aftershave had gelled, creating a gooey mess. The scent was weak but tangible, immediately reminding Karl of Edward Phillips in the departed days of his living.

A used disposable razor encrusted with yellowing shaving cream and face stubble accidentally nibbled Karl's gloved hand. He shuddered slightly. Alongside the disposable razor, a family of clipped, dirty fingernails nested inside a used Kleenex tissue.

Disgusting…

Even though he knew it wasn't healthy to think ill of the dead, Karl had to question Phillips' personal hygiene.

A pinup of a beautiful nude woman attached to the inside of the locker door caught Karl's probing eye. The nude had the largest ponderosa of pubic hair he had ever seen. He wasn't a cartographer, but he would have said it resembled Alaska, if questioned on 'Mastermind'.

Just about to take his eyes off the picture, he noticed the dark-brown envelope taped to the hirsute forest. Freeing the envelope immediately, he tore a great hole, giving an unintended Brazilian to the Alaskan countryside.

'Oops…sorry about that, lady…' he whispered.

Hurriedly, Karl slipped the envelope covertly into the inside pocket of his overcoat, feeling like a thief in the night before continuing with the rummaging.

Badly soiled boxer shorts dangled from a hook, alongside a thickly knotted tie.

An omen? Shitty underwear and a hangman's fucking noose…

Beneath copies of thumb-worn *Hustler* and other porn magazines, a large pouch protruded. He eased it out gingerly, as if it were a bomb about to explode in his face. It was made from faux reptile skin. A bulge rested in the middle of the bag, like a crocodile with a tiny animal lodging in its stomach.

What the hell have you got yourself involved in? Just leave the–

Without warning, a hand gripped Karl's shoulder.

Fuck! Karl's heart popped. Back stiffened, ready for combat or arrest. Both, perhaps.

Turning quickly, he saw that it was the dodgy businessman. He was brandishing what looked like a weapon.

'You a smoker, pal?' The man spoke with a Canadian inflection. An unlit, enormous cigar was clamped between two fingers.

'What the hell do you think you're doing, grabbing me?' Karl tried desperately to control the pumping in his heart.

'What…?' The man looked taken aback. His face paled. Lips trembled. 'I…I'm sorry, pal. I didn't mean to startle you. I…I walked out of the hotel without my lighter.'

'Can't you read? Big sign over there stating that this is a designated no-smoking area,' snarled Karl in a voice he hardly recognised. 'Now, piss off back to your hotel before I have the Mounties arrest you, *pal.*'

'Sure…sure thing, pal. I…I don't want any trouble.' The man did a quick about-turn, before walking speedily down the corridor out of sight.

Leaning against the locker, Karl released all the tense air from his lungs, trying to calm the hammering in his heart.

'You're getting too old for this kind of shit. Way too old…'

Back to the task at hand, he quickly removed the pouch before slamming the locker closed.

Moving now with purpose down the corridor, his fingers gripped tightly on the pouch, as if fearful of some purse-snatcher stealing it.

He smiled wryly at that particular thought. *Perhaps that would be the best thing to happen to it, stolen, gone from my life for good?*

The freezing weather outside was becoming suicidal, yet he was sweating bullets as he quickly stepped onto the zebra crossing near the Europa Hotel. To make matters worse, the damn pouch seemed to be breathing in his hand.

As he headed for home, there was little doubt in his mind as to what was in the reptile's stomach, and it sure as hell wasn't antelope meat.

CHAPTER TWENTY-FIVE

OUT OF THE PAST

'They say money don't stink. I sometimes wonder.'
Raymond Chandler, *Farewell My Lovely*

'I didn't hear you coming in last night,' said Naomi, staring at herself in a full-length mirror, adding final touches to her hair.

'I was supposed to meet a new client outside the Europa, but they were a no-show.' Karl was typing out a few lines on his latest unappreciated masterpiece. Unbeknown to Colin the barman, he was quickly becoming the central character.

'That makes me really angry, Karl. They must think you have nothing better to do.'

'Goes with the job, darling.'

'I'm glad to see you writing again, and ignoring those stupid publishers.'

'Publishers? What do they know about publishing!'

The radio began playing Smokey Robinson's *Being With You*.

I don't care what they think about me
I don't care what they say...

'I desired you this morning, when I woke up,' said Naomi, hamming a husky voice while fluttering her eyelashes at the mirror.

'I don't know if that's me or yourself you're talking to, but you were snoring your head off like a lumberjack this morning – at least I *hope* that sound you were making was snoring, and not farting.'

'Karl Kane!' exclaimed Naomi, looking offended. 'You know I'm too much of a lady for that.'

'Makes no difference to me. I had sex with you, anyway, and you didn't even notice a thing. Must be getting smaller as I get older.'

Naomi giggled. 'Are you sure about not wanting to come shopping with me?'

'You know I hate shopping. I'd rather spend the rest of the day chewing on steak knives.' Karl hit a few more keys on the typewriter. 'I see Lipstick has gone. Didn't even hear her sneaking out, this morning.'

'I gave her some money to buy a new pair of jeans,' confessed Naomi. 'The ones she had on were torn and filthy.'

'Very charitable of you. I'd have given her a needle and thread along with some Persil, instead.

'Sure you would,' said Naomi, smiling. 'You're a big softy.'

'Why be half a sucker when you can go the whole way, eh?'

'I have to say that this is a lovely gesture, telling me to buy something nice for myself,' said Naomi. 'Are you feeling okay?'

'Leave the jokes to me.' Karl considered the sentence he had just typed. It didn't seem to be gelling with the previous paragraph. Too much on his mind, no doubt.

'Sure you trust me with *our* new credit card, though? I might get carried away.'

'Just don't rip the arse out of it or melt it, otherwise I might be the one getting carried away – by the men in white coats.'

Karl couldn't figure any way to get Naomi to leave the apartment, other than an enticement. He just hoped it wasn't too expensive an enticement.

Smokey Robinson slowly faded, his lovely smoothing voice replaced by a newsreader's dull and rambling tone.

Police have released the name of the woman murdered in the City Cemetery yesterday afternoon...

'I didn't even hear any news concerning a murder,' said Naomi. 'Just shows how commonplace it's becoming.'

Sarah Cohen appears to have been the victim of a robbery...

'Disgusting,' said Karl, taking his attention away from the typewriter to listen.

The murder was soon replaced with news of job losses, and a forecast of more snow on the way.

'Let's not let that bad old news get us down, Karl. Get ready for some hot action when I get back.' Naomi's voice was full of promise and things to come. 'As a treat, I'm going to buy some very sexy lingerie for you.'

'I stopped wearing sexy lingerie a long time ago. It kept cutting the arse off me.' Karl went back to typing.

Suddenly Naomi pushed his head up away from the typing, kissing him long and hard. The kiss was full of tease. He could taste her mouthwash. Mint. It made him feel dirty, in a clean and sexy way.

'See you soon,' she said, finally breaking the kiss before heading for the door. 'Tiger.'

'That word always brings out the animal in me,' said Karl, screwing his hand into a paw before clawing at the air.

'*Grrrrrrrrrrrrrrrrrr!*'

Naomi laughed. Closed the door.

Karl listened to her footsteps fading and the front door closing before going into the bedroom and removing the pouch from beneath the bed.

'It's now or bloody never,' he mumbled, unzipping the pouch slowly. Easing a reluctant hand inside, he began removing the large item contained within.

The gun was wrapped protectively in polythene. It stared out at him like a mummified foetus. He lifted the weapon gingerly via the corner of the polythene, scrutinising the metal more closely through the clear material.

'A Beretta M9? A beautiful weapon for ugly deeds. As deadly as they come.'

He sat the gun down before tipping the pouch over, emptying out the stomach's remaining contents: one large brown envelope and a half-pack of Polo Mints – Phillips' favourite mint for trying to camouflage the stench of whiskey breath during duty hours.

Karl removed one of the mints from the open stack and began sucking slowly, his tongue negotiating the famous hole. Looked intently at the envelope. Then the wrapped gun. Sucked some more on the mint, before finally lifting the envelope. Tore it open, removing a wad of pages from inside.

'I'm sure this is going to make interesting reading...' Karl sucked harder on the mint.

It made him think of Naomi, the taste of her mouth. Then Edward Phillips' mouth, dead in the grave, worms munching on lips.

He quickly spat the mint out into a tissue, and began reading.

Well, Kane

Still pursuing? I knew if anyone could be counted on to be pig-headed enough, it would be you. If you've come this far, then I guess my worst fears have been realised, and I'm no longer feeling any pain. Apart from this letter, you will also have discovered the double action Beretta M9.

But before I get to that... I suppose you still don't remember too much of that particular day when we bumped into each other and I mentioned the King David Syndrome?

I know you're not a great believer in religion, or the Bible, but, many aeons ago, King David of Israel spotted a beautiful woman named Bathsheba taking a bath. He instantly fell in love with her. However, he had one major problem. Bathsheba was already married, and not just to anyone. Her husband, Uriah, was one of David's most fearsome and loyal soldiers, who just happened to be at the front, fighting against the ferocious Ammonites.

Not one to let a good soldier get in his way, David sent a letter to the commander of his forces, ordering him to send Uriah to the hardest and bloodiest fighting, so that the sword of the Ammonites will assure Uriah's death. And that is exactly what happened.

Karl was quickly tiring of Phillips' arcane gibberish, but curiosity forced him to read on, rather than expecting any real hope of enlightenment from the dead cop's biblical tale.

About fifteen years ago when your brother-in-law was a mere holes-in-the-pants detective, we got a tip-off from a source about a big robbery due to go down on the outskirts of the city.

he source was your great friend, Chris Brown. That's right. Mister Squeals On Wheels himself. Brown got a nice wee pile of blood money for the info.

'Shit...' Despite the revelation, Karl wasn't entirely surprised at the wheelchair-bound informant's name being mentioned. 'You always had to be in the middle of dirty money, Chris. Any wonder you had so many enemies before you were gunned down?'

Assigned to intercept and apprehend the would-be robbers was an 'elite' (I have to laugh at that word, now) team made up of Wilson, Duncan 'Bulldog' McKenzie, Peter Cairns, Harry Cunningham, and my good self.

Karl's stomach did a trap-door movement at the names of Bulldog McKenzie and Cairns glaring at him from the paleness of the page. His mouth became dry.

What I would give to see the expression on your face, Kane, at the mention of Bulldog and Cairns! There has always been speculation that you were somehow involved in their murders, but I disregarded that. You're a lot of things, Kane, but murderer isn't one of them. I doubt that you'd have the balls for that sort of thing. If I had been a gambling man like you, my money would be on Wilson's dirty hands, in all honesty.

'I suppose that's why you'd never have made a good gambler, Phillips, in all honesty.'

*To cut a long story short, two of the robbers were killed (we never took prisoners in those days because the shoot-to-kill policy was well cemented into our brains). Harry Cunningham, a decent sort of bastard, was also killed in what was initially and **officially** termed 'in the crossfire'. Is Harry's name becoming clearer to you, Kane? Surely you remember Harry's dutiful and gorgeous wife, Desiree? Do you think it a simple coincidence that Wilson was the man in charge of the bungled operation? Think again. Think harder.*

'Fuck...'

It was all becoming a bit clearer to Karl, if slightly murkier. Years ago – perhaps ten or eleven – Karl, along with his wife at the time, Lynne, attended the wedding of her brother, Mark Wilson and Desiree Hamilton. The local newspapers had given the wedding ceremony maximum and sympathetic coverage. A fairytale ending for a police widow whose courageous husband had been gunned down mercilessly in the line of duty. Desiree was now finding happiness at last, marrying her knight-in-shining-armour and one of the up-and-coming stars of the police force, Detective Mark Wilson. It brought tears to every eye.

Karl could feel himself tensing as he read on, anticipating more dark discoveries.

Examine the Beretta, Kane. Check the firing pin. See how it's been filed down into a flat surface and made redundant? This was the gun given to Harry on the night of the robbery. Someone didn't want Harry to be able to protect himself. I think you can figure that one out...

Just remember that this is dirty territory, Kane. Speaking the truth about power is a dangerous business. It can get you killed. Keep looking over your shoulder. Sometimes it can tell you what's ahead. But only sometimes...

Edward Phillips

This letter – like the previous – had a signature scrawled over the typed name.

Karl's knees suddenly felt weak. The alcoholic euphoria he had been feeling from last night's indulgence was quickly dissipating. In its place were the beginnings of a dull headache and a sense of emptiness and dread.

He quickly sat down on the bed. Debated what to do next.

Craved desperately for a cig. Scratched his upper arm at the annoying nicotine patch, hating its artificialness and lack of spontaneous kick.

'What now...?'

Reluctantly, he came to the conclusion that the only sensible thing to do was either to put the gun back where he found it, or dump it in the River Lagan – now, not tomorrow, along with the letter. There was still time to shove the dangerous genie back in its bottle before it smashed into smithereens all over him. That was the only rational decision.

Unfortunately for Karl, if rationality ever became a currency, he knew he would be a very poor man indeed.

His mobile phone rang just as he began putting the items away.

'Hello?'

'You bastard! You killed her,' said the angry voice at the other end. 'I'm going to kill you, and that's a promise.'

'Whoa a second, fella. I think you've got the wrong number. You'd be as well to stop–'

'*Murderer.* The others were fools, but you didn't fool me.'

'Look, I don't know who the hell you are, or what the hell you're talking–'

The phone suddenly went silent. For a few seconds, Karl stared at his mobile as if it were a dead thing.

'What the hell was that all about?' Then, just as he asked the question, a thought grew so large in his mind that he could think of nothing else.

Quickly he moved to the TV, turning on 'BBC News 24', before frantically scrolling down the regions finder. Hit the button on local news. The murder in the graveyard was still prominent.

He stood watching a female reporter pointing at the scene, the camera panning the area. The reporter started talking.

Sarah Cohen had more than her share of tragedies in her short life…

While the reporter spoke, a family photo of the murdered woman appeared on the screen. Sarah was smiling, yet the eyes were full of sadness.

The face in the photo kicked Karl in the stomach. It was the face of the woman who had called herself Jemma Doyle.

Her three children were burnt to death in Ballymena…

Karl continued staring at the photo. He couldn't move. Shock rooted him. The voice on his mobile phone. It was slowly coming to him. Even though it had been muffled when he first heard it, there was no mistaking it now. The voice in the abattoir. Knifeman.

PART TWO

KANE'S ABLE

'If only there were evil people somewhere insidiously committing evil deeds, and it were necessary only to separate them from the rest of us and destroy them. But the line dividing good and evil cuts through the heart of every human being.'
Aleksandr Solzhenitsyn, *The Gulag Archipelago*

CHAPTER TWENTY-SIX

THE NIGHT OF THE HUNTER

'People of the same trade seldom meet together, even for merriment and diversion, but the conversation ends in a conspiracy against the public.' Adam Smith, *The Wealth of Nations*

It was almost two in the morning when the small, stout figure of Nelson Roberton crept quietly down the carpeted staircase of his Victorian manor house, trying not to disturb his sleeping wife, Belinda. The house was situated in the affluent Malone Road area of Belfast, and had appeared in the prestigious *Ireland's Homes Interiors & Living* magazine an unprecedented three times in the last five years.

Snow was falling heavily outside as he eased open the door of the spacious drawing room, before padding towards an Edwardian drinks cabinet stationed beside an impressive library of unread books.

Opening the drinks cabinet, Nelson reached for a decanter of his favourite liquor. Poured the Hennessy XO slowly into a Waterford crystal brandy glass, watching the glorious fluid easing upwards enticingly. Seconds later, he sipped it gently. Straight.

No sacrilege. No bastardisation.

'Lovely…'

Walking to an enormous window, he looked out at the winter wonderland scene forming rapidly in the impressive front grounds.

'Not bad for a kid from Newtownards Road.'

It was a rare acknowledgment of his family's lineage that hailed from the rustbelt of the shipyard; a lineage he would much rather forget about.

As a teenager, the hardness of nuts and bolts in the shipyard appealed little to Nelson. He never wanted to be like his father, coming home exhausted each day, skin burnt from careless welders, and covered from head to toe in indelible rust. No. Not for him. Nelson much preferred the soft and pliable materials of drugs and prostitution, becoming master of both before he had killed his first rival at the tender age of seventeen. He didn't just have balls, he had the brains to match – a lethal combination in the cutthroat, bullet-in-the-eye world of Belfast drug-dealing and racketeering. The fact that he was built like a wrestler became an added bonus. But then came the bad days of loyalist hard men with even less principles than Nelson and more reptilian in their ruthlessness. It was time to retire with the significant and ill-gotten fortune he had amassed. Time to come in from the cold of eastside Belfast; time to move south to the healthier and prosperous climate of Malone and the fur-coat-no-knickers-brigade. Time to go legit.

Almost.

He sipped once more on the brandy before resting the glass on an antique night desk. That was when he saw the figure paled on the window's reflection, staring straight at him.

Nelson's shoulders immediately tensed crosshair. The figure was armed, ensconced in one of the chairs, his shadow blanketing much of the far wall.

A sensation like dry ice brushed over Nelson's skin, making him shiver.

'What the fuck are you doing in my house?' Nelson said, stealthily running his hand along the ridge of the night desk.

'Sit your arse down. There's little point in pushing the silent alarm button stationed in the desk. I've already deactivated your entire system.' The intruder's voice was hushed and calm, as if he had no wish to wake the sleeping Belinda. Even the gun in his hand looked relaxed, if deadly.

Nelson's knees now felt like soggy sponges. A rush of dread began sizzling his brain. He sat down slowly at the desk, understanding now that the past always presents itself in the future when least expected in the present. A debt collector from the old days had finally caught up with him. Blood, not money, the balance demanded.

'How...how'd you manage to get in here?'

'A skill learned over the years. Don't blame your bodyguard. He's sleeping soundly in the boot of your Mercedes. Even if there had been two minders, they wouldn't have been able to hinder my presence in your lovely home.'

Nelson was doing his best to think, work out this conundrum of past enemies: Which one would have the balls? *And why was there something strangely familiar about the intruder's voice?*

'Who sent you?' Nelson finally asked.

'Lucky for you, no one sent me, Nigel. If they had, you'd be dead by now.'

'Nigel? Look, you…you've got the wrong man. My name's Nelson. Nelson Roberton. I'm…I'm a well-known business man and–'

'Six years and you've forgotten me, Nigel?' The intruder reached over and turned on a small lamp beside the chair.

In the new light, Nelson stared at the man, the devastating scars mapping the face. He was emaciated, nothing but skin and bones. Yet, despite the thinness, there was a menacing aura about him. Then, like a hammer hitting his chest, Nelson recoiled, as if seeing a ghost.

'Peter…? My god…'

'Yes, I just might end up being your god, saving your worthless neck.'

Nigel stood unsteadily, then walked towards Peter, before wrapping him in a hesitant hug. 'I…I can't believe it, mate. You…you're alive. The…last I heard…you were killed in an explosion in Iraq, a roadside bomb.'

Peter stood, but remained stoic, easing out of Nigel's hold. 'Some people might say death would have been a better outcome.'

'Those fucking Arab bastards,' Nigel said, almost spitting out the words. 'I wanted to kill a few of them, when I heard what they did. I…I'm sorry, mate. Truly I am. I wish I'd known you were still alive. I could've helped you get back on your–'

'Cut the false compassion. It doesn't wear well on you. You never cared about anyone, bar yourself. While I was serving Queen and Country, you were busy serving King Nigel. Besides, I'm not here for pity, I'm here for business.'

'Business? Yes, of course! I can fit you in with – '

'*Unfinished business*, Nigel, not some pathetic handout.'

'Unfinished…?' A frown appeared on Nigel's forehead for a few seconds. 'You mean Ballymena?'

'That's right. Ballymena. Your unmitigated disaster.'

'Don't worry, mate I'm sorting that out. Big time.'

'Yes, you were always good at sorting things out, weren't you? That's why you posted a big-time reward with your name plastered all over it.'

Nigel laughed nervously. 'No one knows that's me. I used my pseudonym, Nelson Roberton.'

'Pseudonym? After Harry's and Billy's hands being found, it took me all of five minutes to figure out it was you who posted the reward money. Despite your rich surroundings, you still have your working-class inferiority complex. You want everyone to know you've made it. Look at me, Ma, top o' the world. And talking of your ma, you really shouldn't have let her know where you live and how well you're doing. Couldn't stop blabbering when I visited her.'

Nigel paled. 'Shit! I…I've told her a hundred fucking times never to open her mouth about me to anyone.'

'Makes you wonder just who else she's been talking to about her son's great achievements.'

'What the hell's that suppose to mean?'

'It means you've left yourself vulnerable to attack. A trail of breadcrumbs to your door. Now that I'm involved, those very same crumbs could eventually lead to me.'

'You know I'd never mention you in anything, don't you?'

Peter looked straight into Nigel's eyes. 'I know you know better than to even contemplate it. For your sake, I hope it stays that way.'

'Look, mate, I had to do something after Harry and Billy disappeared. I even went as far as to contact some of my old mates in the paramilitaries from the old days, and they assured me they know nothing about it. I gave them some money, just to keep their ears to the ground. What? Why're you shaking your head?'

'You told the paramilitaries and you can't figure out what's wrong? They're filled with touts. They'll let their handlers in Special Branch know that you've been sniffing about, asking questions. The cops are under a lot of pressure to get this sorted, so it won't be too long before the Branch come asking you the same questions you were asking your so-called mates.'

'I...I never thought of that,' Nigel said, walking to the table and retrieving the brandy. He sipped, no longer enjoying the taste.

'You can add Blakey to the list of disappeared,' Peter said, quite calmly.

Nigel almost chocked on the liquid. Snot spluttered out his nostrils. He quickly wiped it away with the sleeve of his shirt. 'Disappeared? Fuck the night! You think they've got him?'

'I went looking for him in his old haunts. Nothing. Not a trace. He was last seen about a week ago, then simply vanished. Now, a number of things could have happened. He could have fled the country, once he got wind of what was happening – except he hardly has the resources for an unexpected trip aboard. Unlike you, he was never good with money...' It sounded like an accusation.

'I'd've helped him. All he had to do was – '

'Or, he could be hiding locally, somewhere I don't know about. Or...well, you can fill in the dots.'

Nigel quickly refilled the glass. Downed the contents even quicker. Refilled. His hand was shaking now. Badly. 'What do you suggest, Peter? I'll go along with anything you say.'

'I suggest you stop drinking, for a start, and get your act together. I've sent them a message. Hopefully, they'll listen to it. If not, then let it be on their own heads.'

'What kind of message.'

'I shot Sarah Cohen dead, in the graveyard, last night.'

'Sarah Cohen...' Nigel flinched as if he'd just been slapped. 'That was her? The cops haven't released any names yet. The media said it was a robbery gone sour.'

'I wanted them to think that. Tev Steinway will think differently, though, once he's informed about the origami I left behind.'

'Origami? That weird thing Japs do with little bits of paper?'

Peter nodded. 'I took it up as a diversion from my injuries, while recuperating in hospital. Hopefully, Steinway'll understand I mean business. If not, I intend to finish what we started.'

Nigel looked worried. 'Look, mate...we really have to be careful how we tread. It's not...well, it's not like the good old days, anymore. We can't get away with things the way we did back then. Cops no longer turn blind eyes. The peace process bullshit changed all that.'

A slit of a smile appeared on Peter's face. The scars on his face deepened. 'Nobody can stop me. Don't you understand? I'm on a mission. When that bomb when off, it killed three of my squad, instantly. Good men, every one of them. The rescue team took hours to find us – what was left of us. That was the longest day of my life. The pain was horrendous. My face felt as if acid was being poured over it.'

Nigel cringed. 'Fuck, mate…'

'Had my weapon not been blown to pieces, I would have shot myself.'

'How the hell did you survive that?'

'Christ.'

'Christ indeed, mate.'

'You don't understand. Christ talked to me.'

'Christ…talked…?' Nigel didn't know if he should burst out laughing at Peter's joke. Then he remembered Peter didn't do humour, at least not on purpose. Nigel forced his face to go serious. 'What…what did…Christ say?'

'He said I'd survive this nightmare, just like he did the Cross. Said I still had things to do. Great things. He was right. I did survive, confounding doctors and specialists who gave me days, a few weeks at the most, to live.'

'That's incredible, Peter.' Nigel shook his head in wonder. 'A bit like Saul on the road to Damascus, only in Iraq, instead of Syria, and a brighter light.'

As soon as he said that, Nigel realised he shouldn't have. It didn't come out the way he had meant it, and he quickly went about trying to undo it with the safest, sanest words he could think of. 'What can I do to help you on…this mission?'

'How much money can you get your hands on?'

'How much do you need?'

'Fifty thousand.'

Nigel whistled. 'Fifty big ones? That's not pocket money, mate. I've already put up twenty for the reward money in the newspaper.'

'That reward money will never be collected, so stop worrying.

The money I need will be put to good use.'

'Good use?'

'I know a couple of ex-cops. Tight lipped, and with good contacts in the force. They helped me locate Sarah Cohen. They'll help find the rest, if the price is right. Need to give them something to keep them sweet.'

'Shit, expensive sweets for fifty thousand.' Then seeing Peter's eyes narrowing, he quickly added: 'I've a few thousand scattered here and there. Give me a week and I'll have the rest.'

'I'll come by in two days. Have it then.' Peter walked to the door. 'Oh, by the way, do you know a private investigator by the name of Karl Kane?'

'Karl Kane?' Nigel shrugged his shoulders. 'Name doesn't ring a bell. Why?'

'My contacts tell me he might be working for the Jews.'

'Big deal. Some would-be cop trying to make a name for himself,' said Nigel, smugly. 'Wouldn't worry one guy.'

'Wouldn't worry? My contact told me Mister Kane is not to be – how did he put it? – oh, "not to be fucked with, under any circumstances." Quite a dangerous individual, when needs be, apparently.'

Nigel no longer looked so smug.

'No need to see me out, Nigel. I know my way. Stay safe.'

As soon as he heard the front door closing, Nigel breathed out shakily…

'Useless Arab scum. Why the hell couldn't youse have killed the crazy bastard…'

CHAPTER TWENTY-SEVEN

IN A LONELY PLACE

'The world's an inn, and death the journey's end.'
John Dryden, *Palamon and Arcite*

Beside an enormous yielding tree, Karl watched the solemn procession making its way slowly into the cemetery. Thirty plus mourners followed behind the simple pine coffin containing the remains of Sarah Cohen. In a terrible twist of fate, she was to be buried in the spot where she was murdered, next to the graves of her three children and husband.

A long black stream of screaming crows slid effortlessly across the sky, disrupting an otherwise perfect ceiling of rare icy blue. Their wings could be clearly heard, battering against the sky's tightness.

Karl, dressed appropriately in sombre attire, stood well back from the gathering mourners, both out of respect and not wishing to cause a scene with any family members who believed his involvement may have somehow contributed to Sarah's death. Perhaps they were right. In all honesty, he wasn't one hundred percent certain of anything at the moment.

The only information he could obtain from Hicks, for now, was that a piece of origami, shaped into a black widow spider, was found in Sarah's hand. The police had yet to determine if it was simply found by Sarah at the graveyard, or something more sinister.

A rabbi from the family's synagogue on the Somerton Road began officiating while the coffin was being lowered into the grave's orifice. The rabbi's voice was strong. Karl could hear it clearly, even if he couldn't understand the words at first.

'*Baruch atah Hashem Elokeinu melech haolam, dayan ha'emet,*' recited the rabbi, pausing a few seconds before translating into English. 'Blessed are you, Lord our God, Ruler of the universe, the true Judge…'

A few minutes later, men began shovelling the mounds of freshly dug soil, filling up the grave. Karl recognised Tev Steinway. He seemed inconsolable, weeping while bending into the soil, releasing the dirt from hand, not shovel.

'Mister Kane?' asked a voice, close behind Karl's neck.

Karl turned to see Detective Malcolm Chambers, with a police photographer beside him. The photographer looked sleazy, unshaven, with hangover eyes. Karl remembered him from Ivana's funeral.

'Still taking sneaky pictures, I see,' said Karl, glaring at the photographer.

'What are you doing here?' asked Chambers.

'None of your damn business,' snarled Karl, angry that he hadn't spotted Chambers lurking between the trees. 'Just make sure your friend doesn't take any more mug shots of me. I'm not in the mood for it.'

Chambers nodded to the photographer. The man walked away, but not before smirking at Karl.

'I don't like doing this, taking photos at funerals,' said Chamber. 'But violence was involved. We've no other choice.'

'Really? Then why the hell weren't you and your sidekick at Edward Phillips' funeral, taking photos?'

'I…I was on desk duty, that day, and Richard the photographer was off. But I'm almost certain another police photographer was there. It's procedure at all times.'

'Not that time, it wasn't.' Karl's upper lip curled with distaste. 'You'd think the cops would want to find the murderer of one of their own, wouldn't you? Take plenty of snaps?'

'I think you're mistaken, Mister Kane.' Chambers was starting to look flustered.

'Believe what you want. I'm telling you the photographer wasn't there. Fact.'

'I…I'll check that out when I get back to headquarters. I'm sure there's a simple explanation.'

'Simple Simon seeks simple solutions, sonny.'

'What's that suppose to mean?' Chambers' face knotted.

'Mean? Nothing. Then again it could mean everything.' Karl's eyes knifed into the detective's. 'Time will tell what kind of a cop you *really* are, by the washing you put out on the clothesline.'

Chambers suddenly looked uncomfortable. 'I know what you're hinting at. I've been told you're obsessed with the idea that there's police corruption under every stone.'

'Not every. Most.'

'Well, think of me as you wish, but if it's not in the rulebook, I'll question it.'

'Just make sure the book doesn't rule you.'

'You can't needle me, Mister Kane. I've been told how you

work, deliberately winding people up, just to find their weakness.'

'I just don't like people sneaking up on me,' said Karl, deliberately smoothing his voice to honey rather than vinegar. 'What have you got on Sarah's murder?'

'Sarah? Oh, Mrs Cohen. I'm sorry, but I can't discuss on-going investigations.'

'Can't you stop being "Dixon of Dock Green", just for a bloody second?'

'Dixon of what?' Chambers looked mystified.

'Forget it,' said Karl, suddenly feeling old again in the presence of the young detective. '"Dixon" was a bit before your time.'

'I see.'

'Any suspects?'

'I've already told you, that we–'

'Stick that bullshit right up your arse.' The vinegar was back in Karl's mouth. 'Now, if you've nothing to contribute I'd advise you to stop wasting my time and get over there with your boyfriend and his camera.'

'Why are you always so belligerent with me?'

'Belligerent? And there's me thinking I was being bloody benevolent. Let me tell you something, and I won't even charge you for it. Cops – *good cops* – share information with people they know will one day share information with them. It's called *quid pro quo*.'

'I know what *quid pro quo* is.'

'Well, know this, too. You want to remain a lowly and lonely detective for the rest of your arresting career? Then just keep operating they way you do. You'll get your nice wee pension and fake gold watch. But that'll be the total reward. Now, if you don't mind, I'd much rather you moved on.'

Chambers looked on the verge of saying something before turning and walking a small distance. Then he stopped. Glanced over towards the photographer. Walked slowly back to Karl.

'I'll tell you this much,' said Chambers. 'We're treating it as robbery gone wrong.'

'Or murder gone right.'

'Why do you say murder?'

'You really think this was a random robbery?'

Chambers glanced wearily over at the photographer, before nervously answering through an almost clenched mouth.

'There was an item found, clasped in Mrs Cohen's hand.'

'Item? What kind of item.'

'A delicate piece of origami.'

'Origami?'

'It's a traditional Japanese form of paper folding and—'

'I bloody well *know* what origami is. What about the piece in Sarah's hand?'

Chambers glanced again at the photographer who was now taking photos of some of the mourners making their way back out of the cemetery.

'I really shouldn't be doing this, Mister Kane.'

'That's what the vicar said to the call girl.'

'The item in her hand was shaped like a spider.'

'A spider?'

'A black widow.' From his pocket, Chambers removed a notebook, flipped a few pages before saying, 'It was made from a page in the New Testament, 2 Thessalonians, Chapter 1:8. *In flaming vengeance on them that know not God, and that obey not the gospel of our Lord Jesus Christ.'*

'Sick scumbag,' Karl said, trying to control his anger. 'I wish to hell all these religious nuts would just disappear, leave the rest of us to the daily grind of normal life.'

'Talking of disappearing. Remember you told me about the suspect, Thomas Blake, how he might have been implicated in the torture and murder of Laura Fleming?'

'Yes…'

'It seems he's fled the country. Not a trace of him anywhere. Almost as if he just vanished.'

'Perhaps he was a practising magician, and one of his tricks went wrong.'

'The other suspect, the actor look alike?'

'Lee Marvin.'

'He was taken in for questioning, a few days ago. His name is Stanley Williamson, a career criminal. Claims he never heard of Thomas Blake, and that he never fired a gun in his life.'

'You expected him to tell the truth?'

'In my business, Mister Kane, very few people tell the truth.'

'I see,' said Karl, not liking the tone in Chambers' voice.

'It's good you see, Mister Kane.' Chambers nodded.

Karl wasn't convinced of Chambers' nod. Karl nodded back. Chambers didn't look convinced of Karl's nod, either.

'What happened to Lee bloody Marvin?' asked Karl.

'Williamson was released pending further investigation. We've instructed the local police to keep a close eye on him.'

'Really? And who's going to keep a close eye on the local cops?'

'I'll leave you and your suspicions in peace, Mister Kane.

You know how to contact me, if you think of anything helpful.'
Chambers stared at Karl for a few seconds, before finally walking
away towards the gates of the cemetery.

The brevity of the Jewish rite surprised Karl. He had hoped to
have a word with Tev Steinway, offer his condolences, but now
realised that would be impossible and probably inappropriate.

He turned to leave, but for the second time, was caught off-
guard by someone standing covertly behind him.

The young man was willowy, dark-skinned, and his face had
an angry handsomeness. He was adorned in the clothes of a
mourner. He stared intensely at Karl.

To Karl, there was an eerie familiarity about the young man, a
bizarre feeling of déjà vu. He couldn't quite place what it was, and
it began annoying the hell out of him.

'Yes? Can I help you?' asked Karl, tiring of the staring contest.

The young man continued staring. Then spoke.

'What are you doing here? You're neither friend nor family.'

'This place is open to the public, in case you didn't know,' said
Karl, trying to dampen his annoyance at being interrogated for
the second time this morning.

The young man brought his face to Karl's.

'Scum like you are not wanted here,' he hissed, his mouth
splattering Karl's face with spittle.

Just as he planned to lay hands on the young man, the revelation hit Karl smack in the gut. Those eyes. Those terrible, mur-
derous eyes. He could never – *would never* – forget them, or their
owner. Knifeman.

Putting aside for the moment thoughts of punching the young
man in the face, knowing such action would serve no purpose

other than to cause a scene, Karl immediately became aware of the police photographer, pointing the camera in his direction.

'Smile sadly, arsehole, and then reach and shake my hand,' said Karl, reaching out his hand.

'I'd rather touch a snake's skin, you murdering bastard,' said the young man, the veins in his neck looking ready to explode.

'The cops are taking your photo as we speak. If you really don't want them investigating you and your angry face, then you better do as I say – *now*.'

The young man suddenly looked hesitant, uncertain.

'*Now*, arsehole,' reiterated Karl. 'He's about to take that shot of the both of us.'

The young man reached and unsteadily began shaking Karl's hand.

Karl gripped the hand in a vice-like hold and began tightening. He could see the pain registering in the other's eyes. 'That's right, keep looking sad, and nod, arsehole.'

The young man gritted his teeth, and began nodding.

'Listen to me, you fuck dog. No-one – and I mean *no-one* – puts a knife to my neck and tortures me, then has the balls to phone my home, threatening to kill me. Understand?'

There was no reply.

Karl tightened the squeeze. '*Understand?*'

Pain ballooned in the young man's face. '*Yes…*'

'Good. Now, I'm going to tell you something. I'm only going to say it once, and when I do, you are going to hug me, and then abruptly walk away. Understand?'

No reply.

Karl tightened down on the squeeze. '*Understand?*'

'Arghhhhhhh! Yes!'

'Good. Now pay attention. I didn't murder Sarah, or have anything whatsoever to do with her murder. I *am* going to try and find out who did, and I don't give a flying fuck if you believe that or not. Now hug as if you mean it, and walk away.'

Unenthusiastically, the young man hugged Karl.

'Good,' whispered Karl, into the young man's ear. *'Now fuck off, and don't ever let me see your face again.'*

While watching the young man walking away, Karl's heart began beating like a bodhrán on steroids. No matter how he tried, he simply couldn't erase the sneaking suspicion that he was being watched by Detective Chambers, or that the young detective wasn't nearly as naive as he painted himself to be.

CHAPTER TWENTY-EIGHT

ODD MAN OUT

'We sneered at each other across the desk for a moment.
He sneered better than I did.'
Raymond Chandler, *Farewell My Lovely*

The Europa Hotel was buzzing with madness when Karl entered through the revolving doors leading into the marble and cherry wood lobby. Bombed thirty-three times, the grand hotel had earned the unenviable sobriquet of the most bombed hotel in Europe. Or as Belfastians flippantly referred to it: that blasted hotel.

The last time Karl had been in the hotel was in the mid-nineties, helping Brad Pitt hone his accent for his role in *The Devil's Own*. The elocution lessons – or *'spaking Balfast'* as Brad liked to call them – went well enough, but the promised part for Karl in the film never materialised. Still, he couldn't complain. The pay-off financially had been sound, and seeing his name on the screen credits at the end of the film went a long way to soothing his wounded ego. Naomi, of course, was enthralled by the tale, though he grudgingly had to admit she seemed more interested in Brad Pitt than Karl Kane.

Inside the hotel, Karl quickly took stock. Travel-weary guests were being shuttled to designated rooms by harried staff with sore-face smiles, while a foreign television crew – armed to the teeth with high-tech apparatus – aimed their weapon-like cameras at any moving target. A documentary seemed to be in the making, and everyone was a star, including Karl.

'Are you a visitor?' asked a bearded man, pushing a microphone into Karl's face. The man's accent was German. 'What do you think of Belfast?'

'Not much,' said Karl, forging a polite smile, while expertly sidestepping the man and quickly making his way toward the Grand Ballroom on the first floor.

Everywhere Karl looked, pictures of famous people lined the walls, but none more so than Bill Clinton whose portrait seemed slightly larger that the rest.

Perhaps because Belfast loves nothing better than a rascally rogue or sinner, thought Karl, smiling back at the smiling ex-president. *A sinner caught by the balls – or zipper, to be precise.*

Things didn't look too promising as Karl approached the entrance to the Grand Ballroom. A slew of bear-like bouncers, faces aglow with menace and ball-crunching snarls, were prowling outside. They seemed to be feasting on vibes of danger.

Here goes nothing, thought Karl, taking a deep breath before sauntering confidently forward with a bluff the size of his shoulders.

'Can I help you, sir?' asked one of the bouncers, blocking Karl expertly.

'No, thanks. I know my way in. I've been here–'

'This is a black-tie formal, sir. If you don't mind me saying, you don't look dressed for the occasion.'

'I know. I just got off the plane. They lost my damn suitcase, would you believe?'

The man obviously didn't believe. 'Do you have your invite, sir?'

'Invite? Oh...' Karl's hands went from pocket to pocket. 'Invite...? Oh, now I remember. I left it in my suitcase. Damn!'

'I'm sorry, sir, but I can't allow you in. Ticket invite only.'

'Don't be ridiculous, man. I've been asked to speak at–'

'Karl?' said a voice directly behind him.

Karl turned. A bouncer was grinning. He resembled Steven Seagal, only taller, and no ponytail.

'Pat? What the fuck are you doing here?' said Karl, smiling, putting out his hand. 'Thought you were touring Europe with a group of wrestlers from Russia?'

'Broke three ribs and a toe, practising in the ring.' Pat grinned. 'Ended up back home, wet-nursing this bunch.'

All the bouncers grinned in unison. Creepy. A family of jack-o'-lanterns at Halloween.

'How's things with you, Karl?'

'Fine. Could be better; but then again could be a hell of a lot worse.'

'I heard about Katie, when I was in away in France. Terrible. Thank God that scumbag got what was coming to him, blown to bits.'

'Yes. Didn't he just.' Karl wanted to say that no god played a part in Katie's rescue, and that it was all down to a mere but brave mortal named Brendan Burns. Instead, he stayed focused on getting into the ballroom. 'Look, Pat, I really need to get in there to see Mark Wilson. What's the chances?'

'Yeah, I saw him about an hour ago.' Pat's grin melted like summer ice cream. 'Didn't even acknowledge me. He'll always be a stuck-up wanker.'

'We're in full agreement there, my friend.'

Pat nodded to the bouncers. One of them turned, before opening the doors.

'I owe you, Pat,' said Karl, quickly entering the Grand Ballroom.

Two steps in, Karl swept the entire scene with vigilant eyes. Delegates from all over the globe sat banqueting on top-notch nosh. The difference with these particular delegates was the dress code: all cop uniforms. A criminal's worse nightmare. Chicago, New York, Sydney, London, Paris, et al – as well as the old divide of Belfast and Dublin.

Plenty of wannabe hard men – and maybe even one or two of the genuine article, thought Karl.

Local politicians – never shy about getting their eager snouts in the troughs – were dining joyously on the free nosh. Normally 'sworn enemies' for the benefit of watchful cameras and the mugs who vote them in, they were backslapping each other like long lost cousins. It never failed to baffle Karl how anyone in their right mind didn't manage to see through the farcical charade, each polling day.

'Can I get you a complimentary drink, sir?' asked a smartly-dressed young waiter, interrupting Karl's thoughts.

'Complimentary?' Karl was suspicious of anything free.

The waiter nodded. 'All drinks are free tonight, sir.'

'Tell the tax payers that at the end of the year.'

'Pardon?'

'Hennessy, please. Large. I may as well get something back for my hard-earned taxes going to this bunch.'

Karl waited until the waiter returned less than a minute later. The young man politely refused his offer of a tip.

'We're not permitted to take tips tonight, sir. Thank you, all the same.'

'Why am I not surprised? Not much chance of getting money from cops or politicians, is there?'

'Pardon, sir?'

'If you don't tell, then I won't,' said Karl, winking while slipping the tip into the young man's waistcoat.

Karl allowed the Hennessy to stain his mouth, careful of not going overboard with the free booze. It was imperative he kept his head clear – at least for a wee while. It was then he saw Wilson, standing with a group of four, all brass and sharp uniforms. They were all drinking alcohol, with the exception of Wilson and his white lemonade.

Karl made his way over and stood beside them, listening, smiling and nodding along with each smiling and nodding head. They seemed totally oblivious of Karl's gate-crashing, while continuing their one-upmanship spiel of dangerous criminals being brought to the courts of justice.

A large Chicago cop was telling a story about being cornered by two armed men after a botched hold-up.

'Top of the evening, Mark,' said Karl, smiling, tipping the brandy towards his ex brother-in-law. 'Thanks for the invite.'

Mark Wilson's face went from red to white, and then back to red. His skin tightened. He looked on the verge of saying something, but no words came out. His hand seemed to be coiling on the glass it was holding.

Chicago Cop finished the pie of a tale with a slice of humour. All the company laughed, except for Wilson.

'That's a cracker,' said Karl, pretending to wipe tears from his eyes.

'A cracker?' said Chicago Cop, looking slightly perturbed.

'Oh, I don't mean it like that,' smiled Karl, his words sounding slightly slurred. 'A cracker here means a great joke, not junkie. Sorry for the misunderstanding.'

Chicago Cop frowned, and then grinned. 'You guys over here sure have a way with words.'

'Don't we just?' said Karl.

'Daniel Brühl, captain in the police to the good people of Chicago,' said Chicago Cop, holding out his hand towards Karl.

'Karl Kane,' said Karl, shaking the enormous meaty hand. 'Pain-in-the-arse to the good people of Belfast. Isn't that right, Mark, me bucko?'

Captain Daniel Brühl laughed out loud, as did the other three policemen. Wilson continued glaring.

'If you would excuse us for a few minutes?' said Wilson, finally breaking his silence while reaching for Karl's right arm. 'I need to talk to Mister Kane, privately.'

'How else could one talk to a private investigator, but in private?' Karl's words were becoming more slurred. He staggered slightly, allowing Wilson to guide him from the group towards the emergency doors at the back.

'What the hell are you doing here?' said an agitated Wilson, finally stopping beside the doors.

'Me? I just love a man in uniform. Wanted to see what a policeman's balls looked like.' Karl brought the brandy to his mouth, but not before spilling some of it on Wilson's jacket.

'*You clumsy fool!*' hissed Wilson, taking the glass from Karl, before setting it down on a table. 'You're intoxicated – as usual. Thank your lucky stars I don't have you arrested for being drunk and disorderly.'

Wilson pushed through the exit doors, manhandling Karl down the steps and out into the cold night air of Belfast.

'Look at the state of you,' continued Wilson, outside in the street. 'You should be ashamed of yourself. Except you have no shame, do you? Just pathetic self-pity. Don't let me see your face about here –'

The speed of what happened next caught Wilson totally by surprise. Before Wilson could react, Karl's hands gripped his ex brother-in-law's neck.

'If you struggle, I'll be tempted to squeeze the life out of you, Mister Law and fucking Order. *I'm as sober as you with your lemonade,*' said Karl, through almost clenched teeth.

'I'll have you for this, Kane. See if I don't.' Wilson's face tightened with pain. 'Security cameras are everywhere. You'll be lucky if you only get two years for assaulting a police officer.'

'You should get longer for imitating one.'

'Take your filthy hands off me – now!'

Karl released Wilson, shoving a large envelope into his chest. 'Stop sounding so bloody ungrateful. I've come all this way to give you a little gift.'

Wilson stared at the pale envelope, holding it as if it were diseased skin.

'What little game are you playing now, Kane?'

'Open it and find out, Sherlock.'

Snow began falling heavily, covering Wilson and Karl in its pureness.

Wilson tore open the lip of the envelope, before slowly removing the contents. A single colour photo emerged.

'A blown-up photo of a gun? Am I suppose to be impressed?'

'Not just any old gun. Take a look at it. A good *long* look.'

Wilson looked at the photo for some considerable time, before speaking.

'And? What on earth am I looking for?'

'That's the gun you gave to Harry Cunningham on the night he was murdered. Note the firing pin? See how it's been filed down so that it's unable to strike?'

'Just what the hell are you rambling about? Is there no end to your madness and paranoia?'

'Sometimes people get their ends before their starts.' Karl reached inside his coat and removed another envelope, this time containing a photocopy of Phillips' letter. 'Here. Have a good look at this.'

Wilson seemed reluctant to take anything else from Karl.

'What is it?'

'Read it and find out. It's a letter from a ghost, and I'm not talking about the Ghost of Christmas Past – though I advise reading it after the banquet. It might upset your delicate stomach. We wouldn't want you vomiting over all that brass in there, would we? Bad for that manufactured image of your good self.'

'You've outdone yourself this time, Kane. More ramblings from a fool.'

'Really? I'm starting to have some clarity about things; things that until now I found unclear. When the evidence is eventually looked at, your involvement will become very clear indeed.'

'Your imagination as a failed writer is messing with your head, Kane. Everyone knows you're crazy.'

'Really? Well, just in case *you* get any crazy ideas yourself, I have the real McCoy, tucked away, nice and safe. I'm sure you wouldn't like it to fall into the wrong hands, would you?'

'Threatening me, Kane? Perhaps even thinking of murder?'

'At the moment, the last thing I want to do is kill you, but it's still on my list of things to do before dying,' said Karl, slowly walking away from Wilson. 'Go back in there with your police friends, Mark, have a good time. Perhaps you'll even try and enjoy your sleep… tonight.'

CHAPTER TWENTY-NINE

SHADOW OF A DOUBT

She's not your friend. She's just someone you use to feel better about yourself.'
Ricky Fitts in *American Beauty*

In his office two days later, Karl was reading an inside page of a newspaper, a wry smile on his face, when Naomi entered the room.

'What's so amusing, Karl?'

'Huh? Oh, just reading about three men shot dead in an apparent mob killing in America.'

Naomi shook her head, clearly disgusted. Making fun of the dead always made her uncomfortable. Even after all this time with Karl, she still found his gallows sense of humour grating at times. 'And that's funny?'

'No, of course not,' said Karl, flipping the page to show Naomi. 'But the headline is.'

Belfast-type shooting in Chicago.

'Belfast-type...?' Naomi frowned.

'The irony of it. You'd be too young to remember all the headlines here, when someone was shot dead. It was always "Chicago-type shooting in Belfast". Good to see the Americans getting a well-deserved dig at our sanctimonious editorial writers.'

'Karl, do you think it was bad of me, the way I treated and spoke about Jemma – I mean Sarah?'

'So that's what's been bothering you the last couple of days? Look, Naomi, you've no reason to feel guilty. I can assure you Sarah wasn't offended, and if–'

On cue, Karl's mobile phone began ringing on the table. Scooping the phone up, he checked the number displayed. He didn't recognise it. He didn't like getting phone calls from numbers he didn't recognise. They were either a scam wishing to take his money, or scum wishing to take his life.

He sat the phone back down, and went back to studying the newspaper.

The phone continued ringing. Karl continued reading.

'Aren't you going to answer that, Karl?'

'Let them waste their time. They'll give up before I do.'

The phone stopped ringing.

Karl smiled. 'See, Naomi? Vindicated. Patience is a virtue when you don't–'

It started ringing again.

'Answer or turn it off,' said Naomi. 'If you think I'm going to listen to that all day, you've another think coming.'

Karl picked up the annoying piece of plastic. 'Hello?'

'Karl?' said a female voice at the other end. The voice sounded hesitant.

'Who's speaking, please?'

'Desiree…Desiree Wilson.'

Karl's face tightened into a knot. His heart gave a quick jerk.

Naomi whispered. *'What's wrong? Who is it?'*

Karl shook his head, indicating quietness. 'Hello…Desiree. This is an unexpected call. It's been a long time.'

'Yes…a long time, Karl…'

Karl could hear the hesitancy in her voice. even clearer now.

'What can I do for you, Desiree?'

'I…I'd like to talk with you, if that's possible? I know…I know how busy you must be, but…'

'Not so busy that I can't make time. When would suit?'

There was another lull. Karl imagined her being prompted by someone. Probably Wilson, sitting there beside her.

'As soon as possible,' she finally said.

'How about today? Three in the afternoon, or thereabouts, here at my office?'

'Three, at your office…?' The lull again. 'Yes, that would be great, Karl. Thank you. Thank you so much.'

'See you then, Desiree.' Karl clicked off the phone.

'Desiree?' said Naomi.

'Why do you always make that strange face when it's a woman's name? Had it been a Desmond, you wouldn't have batted an eyelid.'

'Because it's always your female clients that spell trouble for the business. The men always pay upfront, but a sob story from a woman and payment is on the never-never.'

'Ten seconds ago, you were filled with guilt about Sarah Cohen. Didn't take you too long to hit your stride again.'

'Who is this *Desiree*, anyway, and what does she want?' Naomi folded her arms in battle-ready mode.

'I can tell you who she is, but what she wants may be a bit

trickier. A whole lot trickier, in fact…'

▲ ▲ ▲

It was touching three o'clock when Desiree Wilson was guided into Karl's office by Naomi. Over Desiree's shoulders, Karl could see the look on Naomi's face, and it wasn't the one of warm welcome she normally held for most clients. Seconds later, Naomi closed the door behind her, leaving Karl and Desiree alone.

Karl debated on offering Desiree one of those ridiculous womanly air-kisses or a manly handshake. He opted for neither, offering a chair instead.

'It's been a long time, Karl,' said Desiree, sitting down. To Karl, she clearly appeared on edge.

'I think the last time I saw you, Desiree, was at your wedding reception, all those years ago.'

Desiree nodded. 'Hard to believe, isn't it?'

Desiree Cunningham – as she was known back then – was a natural beauty, and always reminded Karl of a young Grace Kelly. She had flowing blonde hair and steel-blue eyes, capturing the attention of any healthy male within a ten-mile radius. Karl always regarded himself as extremely healthy in those days, plus he only lived five miles away.

As she looked nervously at him from across the desk, he had to admit that the years had been kind to Desiree Wilson and that she still had a face to die for. But the million dollar question on Karl's mind was: was it a face to kill for?

'Would you like some coffee, Desiree, or something a wee bit stronger?'

'No…no, thank you. I stopped drinking alcohol a long time ago, when I met…' She didn't finish the sentence.

It was easy for Karl to fill in the blanks.

'This is a nice place you have here, Karl,' small-talked Desiree, glancing about the tiny office.

'Good job I don't have a damn cat. Wouldn't be much room to swing one.'

Desiree's face broke into a tiny grin.

'I know I shouldn't be smiling, but remember the time Lynne threw Agatha at you?'

'Sixteen stitches to my gob makes it hard to forget. I still carry some of the scars.' Karl returned the smile. 'I always hated that cat. It was as creepy as Lynne – and that's saying something. I suppose she told you all about it?'

'No, it was Mark, in fact. Know what she told him?'

'What?'

'Quote: "That bastard Karl Kane said that's the last time I'll ever throw my pussy at him." Mark almost fainted, poor thing.' Desiree laughed out loud. '*Did* you actually say that?'

Karl nodded. 'One of my better quips, I have to admit. It sort of eased the pain on my face, at the time.'

'I know what went on with you and Lynne, Karl, why you broke up, but I'm just glad to see you found someone nice. Naomi's a very pretty girl. Doesn't look anything like Lynne described.'

'I can imagine Lynne's description of Naomi,' said Karl. 'Well, enough about my exciting life. What exactly can I do for you, Desiree?'

'Well…' Desiree seemed to be gathering her thoughts. 'It's about Mark, and you. This…this never-ending conflict.'

'You're going to have to be a bit more specific.'

Suddenly, a little zing of tension entered the room, slipping between them.

'Mark showed me the letter from the detective, the one found dead in the docks.'

'Edward Phillips was his name.'

'Edward Phillips. Yes.'

'And?'

'I know what you're accusing Mark of doing, Karl.' Her face cringed with distaste.

'I didn't accuse Mark of anything – yet.'

'Okay, you *hinted* he had something to do with Harry's death. That's preposterous. You think I wouldn't know if Mark was somehow involved?'

'I don't know the answer to that, Desiree. What I do know from bitter experience is that length of time spent with someone doesn't necessarily make us experts on that person – especially if they have secrets they want hidden.'

'You're talking about Lynne's unfaithfulness, aren't you? You think Mark and I were having an affair, and that somehow led to Harry's death?' Desiree's face stiffened defensively.

'I didn't say that, but if the hat fits…'

'That's not fair, Karl. Just because Lynne was unfaithful, doesn't mean every woman is.'

'I know that, Desiree. It wasn't just the affair Lynne was having, but the fact she was having it with a woman, was the kicker.'

Desiree's face flushed crimson. She looked gobsmacked. Her mouth opened to say words, but none came.

A wry smile appeared on Karl's face. 'I'm sorry if I shocked you.'

'I…I didn't know. Lynne or Mark never said it was a woman…'

'No, not something one shouts from the rooftop in Victoria

Square, is it? But your lovely hubby Mark knew. That's what I mean about secrets, Desiree. They're a bit like matryoshka dolls. There's always *another* one hidden inside. Somewhere. But someone always discovers the secret, sooner or later.'

'The way you said that. You think *I* had something to do with Harry's death?' She looked shocked.

'I never said that, either.'

'By inference, you did.' Desiree's calm voice was slowly gaining a high pitch. 'You think that I could be somehow involved in what happened to Harry? Or that Mark had him killed so that he could marry me? That's sick.'

Desiree stood abruptly, knocking over the chair she had been sitting on. Her face went from red to pale in seconds. 'Mark warned me not to try and convince you. He said you wouldn't listen to reason and that you're very sick and bitter. Want to know something, Karl? He's right. You *are* a very sick individual, but I'm warning you that if you continue to—'

The office door flew open. Naomi stood in the doorway, her face filled with thunder. 'You don't warn anyone under this roof, *Mrs* Wilson. Your time is up. Leave – *now*.'

Desiree stared at Naomi, and then at back to Karl's expressionless face.

'Both of you are well suited,' said Desiree, walking quickly past Naomi and out the front door.

It was ten seconds before Karl spoke. 'What kind of way is that to speak to a potential client? Thought you had changed?'

'She's lucky I only used *words* to chase her out. I was always told to respect my *elders*.'

'Oh, Naomi Kirkpatrick, you little minx!' Karl stood and

walked over to her. 'Put those claws away before you do some damage.'

Naomi smiled. 'I did okay, didn't I?'

'You sure did, kiddo.' He kissed her on the cheek. 'You sure as hell did.'

'What do you think? *Is* she guilty?'

'I don't really know. One thing I do know, though, is that terminology is a great thing for revealing what exactly is inside a person's head.'

'What do you mean?'

'She never once described the killing of Harry as murder. At the very least, she's guilty of diminishing what happened to him. A word misplaced can speak volumes. It can also come back to haunt us.'

Just as he finished the sentence, his phone rang.

'Hello?'

'Mister Kane? This is Detective Chambers.'

'And?'

'I just wanted to call and let you know that Charley Montgomery has been released from custody, unconditionally, and cleared of all involvement in the killing of Kevin Johnson. Johnson's main rival, Frankie Murphy, is to be charged with the killing. One of Murphy's thugs, Paddy O'Neill, who was arrested last week for an unrelated murder, has decided to cut a deal and give evidence against his former boss. According to O'Neill, Murphy got fed up with Johnson infringing on his territory once too often.'

'I'm not going to say I told you so, even if I told you so,' Karl said. 'Paddy O'Neill, eh? Another so-called hard man who can do the crime but not the time. At least poor Charley's out to go back to what he does best: shooting people in the back. Very noisy, but not as interesting as chopping hands off.'

'Well, I just wanted to call and let you know,' Chambers said. 'Good day, Mister Kane.'

'Look, before you go... listen... thanks for informing me on the happenings. You didn;t have to do that. I appreciate it. You... you're not a bad cop, which is a good thing.'

'Coming from you, I think that's what constitutes praise. Thank you, Mister Kane. Have a good day.'

As soon as the call ended, Karl felt the echo of Chambers' smile in his ears.

CHAPTER THIRTY

DEADLY IS THE FEMALE

'Those to whom evil is done
Do evil in return.'
W.H.Auden, *September 1, 1939*

'**K**arl? There's someone here to see you. A woman,' said Naomi, standing at the office door. It was two days after the visit from Desiree Wilson.

'Has she an appointment?' Karl didn't even bother looking up from the newspaper. 'If not, tell her to make one and I'll–'

'*Karl?*' said Naomi, almost in a hush.

Slowly Karl's eyes panned away from the newspaper, and onto Naomi's troubled face.

'What? What's wrong? You look as if you've just seen a ghost."

'Says her name is Judith Levy, and that it's important she sees you.'

'More important than tomorrow's race?'

Naomi didn't answer; simply left the room and a puzzled Karl.

A few seconds later, a woman entered.

'Mister Kane?' she said, holding out her hand. 'My name's

Judith Levy.'

Karl was shocked by what he saw. The woman was almost a duplicate of Sarah Cohen, but with the most startling combination of eyes he had ever seen. One green. One blue. Eyes that the late, unlamented Harold Taylor would have recognised as belonging to a woman called Kerry Morgan.

'I'm sorry…' said Karl. 'I didn't mean to stare. It's just…you remind me of someone.'

A faint smile appeared on Judith's face. 'My sister. Sarah Cohen. You knew her as Jemma Doyle, I believe.'

'Yes, Jemma Doyle…' Karl nodded slowly. 'You were twins?'

'Sarah's…' Judith hesitated. 'Sarah was older than me by a couple of years. People often mistook us for twins.'

'Please, won't you sit down, Judith? Can I get you an early morning cup of something?'

'No thank you,' said Judith, sitting down.

'First, allow me to offer my condolences to you and all your family, Judith. I was saddened to hear the terrible news about Sarah.'

'Sarah had great faith in you, Mister Kane. Said you were a good man and a very trustworthy person.'

'I like the sound of that, but there are plenty of people in Belfast who'd disagree with that statement.'

'My brother, Malachi, would probably be one of those people.'

'Your brother?'

'You met him at the funeral. You shook hands, apparently.'

'Oh, yes. He threatened to kill me – a couple of times,' said Karl, almost blasé.

Judith's face reddened deeply. 'Malachi's always been a hothead. His bark has always been worse than his bite.'

'Thank god he's not a dog.'

'He left for Europe, two days ago. He has no intention of ever coming back.'

'Hopefully, my talk with him had something to do with it. In all honesty, can't say I blame him, under the circumstances.' Karl straightened his large frame in the chair. 'Now, what exactly can I do for you, Judith?'

'I've come here to apologise.'

'Apologise?' A bemused look appeared on Karl's face. 'I don't understand.'

'For what my family did to you…at the abattoir.'

'The abattoir?'

'I can understand you being suspicious, and not wishing to talk about–'

'I'm not suspicious,' said Karl, immediately becoming suspicious.

'I was sitting with Sarah, watching TV, the night your picture was sent to her via Malachi's mobile phone, asking to confirm if the picture was you. Sarah was horrified at what the family had done to you – we both were.'

Something wary kicked Karl in the stomach. 'To be honest with you, Judith, I can't really go into that. It was part of a case I was…investigating. I can't divulge any information, because it comes under client confidentiality. Don't be insulted. If the cops asked, they would get the same reply.'

'Do you know what it's like to kill a person, Mister Kane, or at the very least to be responsible for their death, no matter how evil that person may have been?'

The question almost knocked Karl off his seat.

'That's a strange question to ask someone, Judith.'

'You know of the murder of Sarah's three children, in Bally-mena?'

'Bits and pieces, eventually, but only because it came up when Sarah's death had been reported and the media gave some history into the terrible fire.'

'The children – Benjamin, Nora and Judith – died horribly, despite brave attempts by Sarah and neighbours to rescue them. Sarah was scarred for life, mentally as well as physically. Her husband committed suicide shortly after that, blaming himself for being on a business trip, rather than at home to help…'

Karl could see sadness, an ache that appeared as a dull light in Judith's eyes. It was the same sadness he had witnessed in her sister.

'Why was Sarah's house and family targeted?'

'Simply because she was a Jew. Four men – all part of a neo-Nazi gang – were involved, and eventually rounded up by the police. At the so-called trial, all four were acquitted, even though the dogs in the street knew they had committed the murders.'

'Unfortunately, Judith, that wasn't the first miscarriage of justice.' Karl shook his head with disgust. Thought of his mother's murder and subsequent farce of a trial with its indefensible outcome. 'In all probability, it won't be the last.'

'All that was left from the charred remains was an old wall clock, still working perfectly. My father kept it in the abattoir as a witness on those involved in the murders. He wanted them to hear its accusing *tick tock*…'

Karl scratched at a nicotine patch on his arm, wishing for a cig between his fingers. In his head, he thought he heard the clock ticking.

'My father changed the day the murderers were acquitted, Mister Kane, saying he was no longer willing to be an invisible Jew. When…when we started out, seeking justice for the children, I was all for it – we all were. Little did we know what a disaster it would turn out to be.' Judith looked intently at Karl. 'You're probably sitting there, thinking how disgustingly evil I am?'

'No…not at all…'

'You're an intelligent man, Mister Kane. I don't suppose it took you too long to realise that Thomas Blake wasn't Sarah's uncle.'

'I wouldn't oversell the intelligence product, Judith. Intelligence for me is more of a consequence than an option. What was Blake's role in all this?'

'He struck the first match. Harold Taylor was the lookout. Billy Brown supplied the petrol. Brown was the first to pay for his deeds.'

'Why was Brown's hand dumped at my door?' said Karl, suspecting he already had the answer.

Judith's pale face reddened slightly. 'It wasn't planned that way. Things happened.'

'Like a squad car at the top of the street?'

Judith looked taken aback at Karl's knowledge. 'Yes…'

'Why the hand thing? Why not the entire body?'

'An eye for an eye. *If your right hand cause you to sin, cut it off and throw it away,*' Mister Kane. That's what my father's dictum became.'

'Yes, well, if we applied that to everyone in Belfast, there'd be an awful lot of hands floating on the Lagan.'

'That's the statement our father lived by. It was also a message; a psychological message to the gang members, hoping to flush them out.'

'What was the significance of the number eighty-eight on the hands?'

Judith seemed to hesitate for a few seconds before replying. 'The 8 stands for the eighth letter of the alphabet, *H*. Coupled together, 88 or *HH* stands for *Heil Hitler*.' She said the last two words as if she had just tasted poison.

'Sick bastards.'

'Not sick,' corrected Judith. 'Evil.'

'You said four men were involved in the children's murders. So far you've only mentioned three.'

'Nigel Potts. Unfortunately, we know nothing of his whereabouts. We suspect he was the leader. There was talk of a fifth man, but he was never named.'

'If you've come to ask me to find this Potts, then you've wasted your journey, Judith. Had I known what Sarah was seeking Blake *for*, I would never have searched for him, even though I don't have sleepless night over what happened. He was a scumbag, and got everything that was coming in his direction.'

'No, we don't want you to search for Potts. It's all over. The ghastly vengeance is all over. I came here to apologise, and I've done that. Just like my brother, my husband and I are planning to make a new start elsewhere.' Judith stood to leave.

'And your father? He agrees with your decision?'

'My father? Oh…you mustn't have heard. He's dead. Killed.'

'What…?' The news shocked Karl, but not as much as the

fatigued calmness of Judith's voice. 'When? How?'

'A hit-and-run, as he walked home, almost a week ago. Thankfully, he didn't suffer, dying almost instantly.'

'I'm...I'm sorry to hear that, Judith. I truly am. I can't understand why I didn't hear anything about it in the news.'

'It was reported in the local paper, but the bigger papers didn't bother with it. Why would they? After all, he had become invisible again in their eyes.' Judith put out her hand. 'Goodbye, Mister Kane, and thank you.'

'Can I call you a taxi or anything?' said Karl, shaking the hand.

'No, it's okay. My husband's parked illegally outside your office, watching for the ticket wardens.'

'Goodbye, Judith. Take care of yourself...always.'

He watched her from the office window, approaching a car. A solemn-faced driver got out, opening the door. He kissed her gently on the face, and she smiled that sad smile. The man was tall and muscularly built, dressed fashionably. Seconds later, he closed the car door behind her, but not before looking directly at Karl, nodding an acknowledgement or appreciation.

Karl watched the car disappear down the narrow stretch of Hill Street's cobbled stones, hoping that was the last time he would ever see Starman again.

CHAPTER THIRTY-ONE

HILL STREET BLUES

'I'm going to go home and go to bed where I can't get into trouble.'
Robert Mitchum, *His Kind of Woman*

Karl startled awake in bed, gasping for air. A tightness in his stomach felt as if he'd been performing crunches all night. Another nightmare had mugged him.

The nightmares were becoming more frequent, more intense – more visionary than fantasy. His dead mother covered in blood, banging on the window to be let in from her pursuer and eventual murderer. Standing beside her, Detectives McKenzie and Cairns, both smiling, holding her back. Their gun-blasted faces were barely recognisable in the torrential grey rain, and the empty eye-sockets made the two dead detectives look even more angry and cruel than Karl had remembered.

You want your mother, Kane? Come out and get her, mocked a leering Bulldog, while Cairns pulled at her clothing, stripping her. She was a skeleton. Nothing more.

In the background's foggy madness, he could hear his father screaming to be freed, hoping to help his tortured wife, make it up to her for not being there when she needed him so badly.

Please, his father kept pleading, over and over again. *Please...*

There were other faces, too, appearing intermittently. Sarah Cohen, and Laura Fleming, sad and filled with blood.

He glanced at Naomi. Something about her stillness scared him. He reached and gently touched her, and was instantly relieved when she stirred slightly.

Reaching for a tumbler of water on the table, Karl downed the liquid in one gulp. It tasted nasty and slightly dusty. The small clock on the bedside table told him it was almost two in the morning.

How long had it been since he had had a good night's sleep? He couldn't remember exactly.

'Karl?' said Naomi, voice groggy.

'It's okay, love. Go back to sleep. It's still early.' Easing his tired body out of bed, Karl stood.

'What's wrong?'

'Nothing.' In reality, the nightmare had terrified him. 'Too much booze last night.'

Naomi began yawning.

'You sure that's all?'

'Sure I'm sure. Go back to sleep. I'm going downstairs, look at a file on one of our clients.' He leaned in and kissed her gently on the forehead.

'Make sure you wear something decent, just in case you bump into Lipstick walking about. She's still not sleeping the best at night.'

'She can join the bloody club, then. I'm not sleeping too well at night, either, but you never hear me complain. Anyway, when the hell's she moving out? I can't even walk about in the nude any more, showing off my manly figure.'

'You should have thought of that before bringing her here.'

'I thought that was *your* idea?'

'I love you,' Naomi mumbled. Seconds later, she was asleep.

Downstairs, he turned the office light on and looked at his face via the wall mirror directly above the desk. An earlier blush of freshness stimulated by Hennessy had vanished, leaving him looking haggard and defeated. In the darkness beyond his eyes, bloodshot gelled. The eyes held the dazed look of a man not knowing how he got here.

'Fucking zombie eyes,' he mumbled, turning the light off before easing the window curtain back slightly, peering into the street. Nails of rusted rain were hammering from an iron sky, turning paved snow into filthy tents of slush.

To Karl, the spreading night was cold and dead. The main streetlight had fused so the only light on the narrow cobble lane of Hill Street came from the neon lights of dingy coffee hide-outs and an after-hour club of pathetic old guys, usually wearing youngish clothes, clearly trying to hold onto something long gone.

He caught a glimpse of the tiny item resting on the desktop just as he turned away from the window: a beautifully crafted piece of origami, fashioned into a rattlesnake.

'Please don't make any sudden moves, Karl,' a voice said.

Karl stood perfectly still. In the semi-lit darkness, the claustrophic nature of the tiny office came together in a rush, like two hands cupping around him.

'Turn – *slowly*,' instructed the voice.

Karl turned *very slowly* to see a man, standing near the far corner.

'Over there, away from the window. Take a seat.' The voice was cold, blunt and solid, like the weapon in his hand.

Ominously, Karl could make out a bulbous silencer attached. *Quiet murder. Premeditated.* Almost immediately, his stomach began percolating. The dead brandy came to life, swirling about in his stomach like tossed sea. He wanted to vomit. He sat.

'By now, most people would be asking silly questions, Karl. Not you. I expected that. You've probably so many enemies, this inevitable day is stamped in your consciousness.' The intruder flicked on the office light.

In the glaring exposure, Karl regarded the scarred features of the man. He looked to be suffering from acute rigor mortis. The skin looked powdery, shining pale as eggshell. The protruding lips were fat and obscene, like skinned garden snails. The eyes, though, were fully in command. Piercing blue. Winter cold.

A man who could – at the very least – quite easily strangle another human being with piano wire, thought Karl.

'Sorry to destroy the myth, but I *am* going to ask a silly question.' Karl tried desperately to make his voice sound calm. 'What exactly is it you want, Mister…?'

'Peter will suffice. I'm here to tie up all loose ends.'

'That lovely piece of origami wouldn't be me, by any chance, Peter?' said Karl, 'A rattlesnake? I've been called a lot of things in my life, but have to admit rattlesnake was never mentioned.'

'Take it as a compliment. There is no creature more deadly or masterful than a rattlesnake, once provoked. Your enemies have probably never given you respect, Karl; that's one of the secrets of your longevity.'

'And there's me thinking it was Palmolive soap and daily doses of vitamins.'

Karl could smell the man's aftershave. It reminded him of the eighties.

'I know quite a bit about you, Karl, your personal demons, the senseless murder of your beloved mother. I also know you can be a demon when it suits. A very dangerous demon, indeed, as the two dead detectives would testify, if the dead could talk. You're not the sort of person one would want to have tracking them.'

'I've no intention of tracking you down, if that's why you're here. Honestly.'

'I honestly don't believe you, Karl. I know your nature. We're similar in our single-mindedness. You're like a trusted and relentless bloodhound, working for the Jews. You *would* try and track me down, and possibly succeed. I can't afford that possibility.'

'It was you who murdered Sarah at the graveyard, wasn't it?'

'Yes. A necessity.

'Very brave of you.'

'Your sarcasm is eating away at what little time you have left. I'm giving you time to make peace with your god, Karl. Don't waste it with childish insults.'

'Why are you doing this? Money?' Karl's brain was on fire. If he could only get this madman to come closer, make a desperate grab for him. In his mind's eye, Karl saw the third drawer in his desk, the push-out niche containing his gun.

'It's the closing of the book, Karl. All chapters have been completed – except this one. Now I'm down to the last line.'

'Doesn't a condemned man at least get a last request, Peter?

Peter seemed to think about that. 'I suppose that could be arranged, providing it's sensible. What would you like?'

'One last cigarette? I've a packet in my desk.'

'Okay, but just the one. We don't have much time.'

'Thanks,' said Karl, trying to keep his hand from shaking as it eased opened the third drawer. His fingers touched the gun, and then slowly gripped it. In an instant, Karl had it pointing at Peter's head.

'Very good, Karl.' Peter pretended to applaud. 'Now you know why I made you a rattlesnake.'

'I guess I can be a bit of a snake when I want to. Now, why don't you lower your gun, Peter? Both of us can still come out of this alive. You walk out the door. I forget you even came here.'

'And if I don't? Would you shoot me, Karl?'

'It doesn't have to end this way.'

'Don't you know I'm invincible? God ordained me in this armour. Nothing can stop me.' Peter aimed his gun at Karl's head.

Karl immediately pulled the trigger of his gun, hard. Nothing.

'I found your gun about five minutes after entering your office. I removed these from it before returning it to its hiding place.' Peter put his hand in his pocket and produced a family of bullets. 'Don't you know that a clandestine place is usually the most obvious?'

'Obviously not,' said Karl, gaming a smile, feeling his stomach cave-in. 'I do now, though. Have to remember that, in the future.'

'Future?' Peter's face measured out a grin-like shape – just enough to acknowledge the irony of the word. Walking back to where Karl sat, he again placed the silencer against the side of

Karl's head.

To Karl, it felt like the apex of a drill piece. Tingles of agonising tension quickly began forming on his neck and shoulders, channelling pressure through his clenched jaw. The feel of the gun suddenly began electrifying his brain; neurons and dendrites started going haywire. Panic set in. He became immobile. Skin sparked. Breathing stalled. His entire world became heavy with darkness.

'You won't feel a thing, Karl,' said Peter, squeezing down gently on the trigger.

Kaboom! An explosion, a flash of dull light discharging in front of Karl's eyes. Bizarrely, his eyes seemed to pick up the bullet's flight, its power to make cartilage and muscle detonate into obscene nothingness. Bits of bone, flesh and brain matter sprayed his face and entered his mouth. Everything went into slow-mo retro. He began having an out-of-body experience, freefalling, like Alice in the rabbit hole.

*Dizzy…so fucking dizzy…*Karl's head felt cleaved; nostrils and mouth scorched with cordite. His consciousness felt like a macabre dance, struggling to find a partner to lead him.

Someone was standing a small distance away at the office door. A lone figure, mouth opening and closing, pronouncing stuttering words. It was Lipstick, arms fully outstretched and hands wrapped tightly around the pistol grip of the smoking Smith and Wesson, looking as if she had practised this moment in a mirror many times in her young and dangerous life. Her tiny finger kept pulling on the trigger.

Click! Click! Click! said the empty chambers, each time the firing pin hit home.

DEAD OF WINTER

Then just as suddenly as it had happened, everything went quiet. Seemingly forever. A communication of some sort passed between Karl and Lipstick. Her voice seemed to detach itself from her lips, journeying around the room in a scream; a scream Karl hoped never to hear again for the rest of his life.

CHAPTER THIRTY-TWO

NO COUNTRY FOR OLD MEN

'I don't mind if you don't like my manners. They're pretty bad. I grieve over them during the long winter evenings. But don't waste your time trying to cross-examine me.'
Raymond Chandler, *The Big Sleep*

Detective Harry McCormack stood at the door of Karl's office, munching on a hotdog. Over near the far window, Detective Chambers was scanning the room silently, his eyes moving slowly but intently.

Several feet away from the two detectives, Bartlett's lifeless body lay sprawled on the floor, legs branched awkwardly as if in a skiing accident. Face-up, his arms were spread out evenly, much as those of the crucified Christ. Beneath, blood pooled under his body like Superman's famous cape. Partially crusted, it seemed to be shimmering in the dull, cold morning light.

'Looks like you finally did it, Kane,' said McCormack, gleefully. 'Went and fucked yourself in all the wrong places.'

'This was a clear case of self-defence, McCormack. Even a

thick-necked bastard like you can see that.'

McCormack walked over and stood beside Karl, flipping a page in his notebook before scribbling.

'You claim the deceased was killed about two-thirty, Kane?'

'Roughly about that time.' Karl could now smell the stench of the hotdog on McCormack's breath. It made him think of the abattoir and the sausage machine. He wanted to puke. 'The scumbag came in here all fit for shit, looking to kill someone. That someone being me.'

'It's almost eight in the morning. What took you so long to contact the police?'

'I've already told you. The young girl, Sharon McKeever – Lipstick to her friends – was in hysterics. I called an ambulance. Had her taken immediately to hospital and–'

'Where she's now doped up to the eyeballs, and not a soul's permitted to talk to her on orders of the doctor. Very convenient that this Doctor...' McCormack flipped a page of the notebook, checking names on it. '...Moore is an old drinking buddy of yours.'

'Nothing convenient about it. That's how it happened.'

'Are you claiming McKeever fired the fatal shot?'

'I've her solicitor's contact details, if you want to talk to him. See what he has to say.'

'I can imagine what he has to say.' McCormack's face began reddening slightly. 'Why didn't you contact us as soon as the ambulance left with McKeever, if you'd nothing to hide?'

'By the time my own nerves settled down, a few hours had gone. Calling the Keystone Cops was the last thing on my mind.'

'I bet it was.'

'What the hell's that supposed to mean?'

'You showered. Why?' asked Chambers, speaking for the first time since entering the room.

'Didn't like the taste of someone else's brains in my mouth,' said Karl, craning his neck slightly to stare directly at the young detective. 'I wasn't going to sit in a chair, covered in blood, waiting for your boyfriend to come here and take photos.'

'Want to know how I see it?' said McCormack.

'Not particularly, but I'm sure you're going to tell me, regardless.'

'The pair of you – perhaps even the three of you, if we include your *other* girlfriend pacing about upstairs – concocted this fictional tale of an armed intruder about to kill you.'

'Naomi had nothing to do with this.' Karl tried desperately to calm his anger, knowing McCormack was trying to goad him into saying something wrong. But his brain was overheating, making his thinking cloudy.

'Perhaps you're right,' conceded McCormack. 'Perhaps it was only you and your little girlfriend trying to rip-off a john – possibly one of her long-term *clients*. The unfortunate man probably resisted, so she shot him in the head with an *illegal* firearm. Cold-blooded, Kane. No two ways about it. All of you'll go down for murder, if I have my way.'

'He was ready to blow *my* head off, you fucking moron.'

'Tell that to the judge. Pray he has a good sense of humour.'

'That's the intruder's loaded gun on the ground, in case you haven't noticed it. Even has a silencer attached. Not your everyday kind of killer, wouldn't you say?'

'You probably planted it on the victim,' continued McCormack. 'You seem to be able to conjure up illegal firearms from nowhere.'

'What the hell do you think that is, over on the desk?'

'That?' said McCormack, pointing at the item. 'Enlighten me.'

'You know damn well it's a piece of origami.'

'So?'

'Don't try to be cute, McCormack. You don't have the face. We both know the killer of Sarah Cohen left origami as a calling card. I'm sure when that particular piece over there is dismantled, it'll be made from a page from the Bible, also.'

McCormack's face tightened. 'If what you say is true – and I'm not saying it is – then how do you account for having information not privy to the general public?'

From across the room, Karl could see that Chambers suddenly looked wary, as if Karl had deliberately tried to land him in the shit by divulging the information.

'That's irrelevant, at the moment,' said Karl, regretting now that he had opened his mouth about the origami.

'Perhaps you made all the little paper trophies, Kane. Perhaps you're the one we've been looking for, all this time.'

'You really should stop eating sausages, McCormack. You'd be shocked what goes into them. Destroys brain cells. Come to think of it, they probably won't do you any harm, after all.'

'You fooled Detective Chambers with all that Lee Marvin nonsense, sending him on a wild goose chase, but you sure as hell didn't fool me,' said McCormack, his eyes glaring into Karl's. 'You had something to do with Laura Fleming's death, too, and I intend to prove it, along with a list of other names.'

'I'm saying nothing more, McCormack. Arrest me or send for

the clean up squad to get this scumbag's body out of my office. And I want those uniformed cops removed from my door. Today's my busiest day.'

'I don't think you'll be conducting any more business for quite some time, Kane. Your days of playing Rockford are over.' From his pocket, McCormack produced a pair of handcuffs. 'When I get you in the car, I'm going to delight in interrogating you – the old-fashioned way. See how smart your smart mouth really–'

Suddenly, Chambers pulled on McCormack's arm.

'There'll be *no old-fashioned way*, Detective – not in my presence.'

McCormack shoved Chambers towards the wall, pinning him against it.

'Don't *ever* touch me, posterboy,' hissed McCormack, inches from Chambers' face. 'Otherwise, I'll knock your damn block off its foundations!'

Lightning fast, Chambers administered a double-sided karate chop to McCormack's formidable neck. The bull detective staggered back, holding neck and throat, groaning.

Karl could see the next move coming a mile away. He doubted very much if Chambers could.

McCormack charged at Chambers, like a wounded rhino, head down.

Chambers nimbly sidestepped, permitting the wall to take the impact of McCormack's massive head. McCormack buckled over, and dropped to the ground.

'Don't get up, Detective McCormack. I don't want to take this any further,' said Chambers.

To Karl's amazement, McCormack began easing his body up

from the floor.

'Oh, we're going to take it further, pretty boy. A lot further that you can–'

'Detectives!' shouted a voice from the doorway. 'Just what the *hell* is going on here?'

Both McCormack and Chambers stopped moving. To Karl, they looked to have ceased breathing, stunned into stillness.

The voice from the doorway belonged to the man Karl never imagined ever seeing in his office: Mark Wilson.

Despite the anger in Wilson's voice, Karl had the sneaking suspicion that his ex brother-in-law was elated to be here. He looked as satisfied as God with creation.

'We...we were...' McCormack was struggling for words.

'Detective McCormack slipped on the piece of carpet, sir,' said Chambers, quickly interjecting. 'I was helping him to his feet, when we–'

'*Help* get that body covered, instead,' commanded Wilson. 'Show the dead some respect and dignity.'

'Yes, sir...' mumbled a chastened Chambers.

'I take it Hicks has been informed, Detective McCormack?'

'Yes, sir. He'll be here any minute,' said McCormack, sidestepping Wilson.

Wilson torpedoed his eyes directly at Karl.

Karl had never witnessed so much joy in another person's eyes. Wilson had won the lotto and gone to policeman heaven, all in the same day.

'I want you outside now, Kane.'

'Am I being arrested?'

'Just get the hell outside.'

Another local television crew was just arriving as Karl and Wilson stepped out into the freezing morning, bringing the grand total to four. Five uniformed cops were trying to disperse a small group of onlookers.

'If you want to talk to me, Wilson, I'm not doing it here.'

'Where?'

'This way,' said Karl, walking down Hill Street, towards Long Bridge House at the corner.

Wilson quickly followed.

In the lit-up doorway of Long Bridge House, Wilson addressed Karl.

'This day was always waiting for you, Kane. I saw it a long, long time ago. Everyone did. Everyone except you, of course.'

'Did you drag me out of my office just to give me a lecture?'

'You're like the proverbial dunce in the corner, never learning; never *wanting* to learn. Now a young girl is probably going to be sent to prison, all because of you.'

'It was self defence. She saved my life. Once I give my version to the papers, Lipstick will be hailed as a hero.'

'You sicken me, Kane. You've never given a damn about the people you contaminate with your shenanigans.'

'Is that what's really galling you? Or is it something else? Something more sinister?'

'What's that supposed to mean?'

'He knew an awful lot about me, that Mister Horseman of the fucking Apocalypse. He had to get the information from somewhere – or *someone*.'

Wilson's face tightened. 'You think that someone was *me*?'

'You. One of your men. McCormack, perhaps? Even someone

higher than you. You'd have given anything to be looking at my corpse in there, you sanctimonious bastard.'

'Paranoia's taking over, Kane. It's eating away at you, bit by bit. One day it'll eventually destroy you.'

'Unless you intend to arrest me, I'm going back to my office.' Karl turned to walk away.

'The young woman is to be charged with murder.'

Karl stopped in his tracks. 'You're bluffing.'

'The three pieces of paper in my pocket aren't bluffing. One is a warrant for Miss McKeever to be removed from the hospital and released into police custody within the hour.'

Karl's stomach did a little kick. 'You bastard. She's innocent.'

'Her innocence or *guilt* will be determined by a jury, Kane. Not by you. She'll be in jail on remand for at least two years before the case comes to trial. Two very long years. I'll make sure of that. Know what two years on remand will do to someone in her frail state of mind?'

'You're one sick dog. You can't get me, so you're going to take your anger out on a little girl, barely out of her teens? How fucking depraved is that, you cowardly bastard?'

'Did I hear you say I can't get you? Didn't I tell you? Your licence as a private investigator is to be revoked, forthwith. That's the second piece of paper in my pocket. An illegal firearm was used in your premises. That's a mandatory suspension.'

'You think I'm going to beg you, Wilson? Is that your great dream? Me on my knees, sucking your cock? *Fuck you*. I'll find something else to do.'

'Something else? At your age?' A smirk appeared on Wilson's face. He brought it close to Karl's. 'What? Drugs? Prostitution?'

'Go fuck yourself.' Karl pushed Wilson out of the way.

'Aren't you just a little bit curious as to what the third piece of paper is?'

'Stick it up your arse.' Karl began walking back down the street.

'It's for the arrest of Naomi.'

Karl stopped dead. Wilson's words kicked him right in the balls. He turned. Faced Wilson.

'You wouldn't fucking dare, you bastard.'

'Wouldn't I? We believe she's withholding information vital to our investigation into this killing. At the very least, she'll be charged as an accessory after the facts.'

'You touch her…I'll fucking kill you.'

'The way you killed Bulldog and Cairns?'

'No, the way you killed Phillips.'

Wilson's left cheek did a nervous tweak. 'I didn't kill anyone. That's your paranoia acting up again, Kane. Conspiracies everywhere.'

'Anthony Trollope once said: "I think the greatest rogues are they who talk most of their honesty". He must have had you in mind.'

'I'm tiring of all this.' From his pocket, Wilson produced a phone. 'I hit one button, and Naomi's handcuffed, shamefully brought out in front of the news reporters. Her elderly parents will no doubt see it on tonight's news, down south.'

'No…wait…' Karl balled his hands behind his back; thought about grabbing Wilson by the throat.

'You better cool that hot head of yours, Kane, and listen carefully to what I'm about to say.'

Karl tried desperately to control his heart thumping in his ears.

He had a foul, sinking suspicion of where this was heading.

'Okay, Wilson...I'm listening.'

'I want the weapon Phillips stole. It's police property.'

'Police property?' Karl almost laughed. 'That's a nice way of putting it.'

'You can believe all you want that I somehow set up Harry. I don't really care any longer, but I won't have the good name of the Force dragged through the courts and media.'

'Is that everything?'

'No. Not by a long stretch. I also want all the letters Phillips wrote while depressed and unbalanced, making unsubstantiated and wild allegations about members of the Force,' said Wilson, using the eye contact he had employed in countless successful interrogations. 'I want the *originals*, plus *all* copies made.'

'I see.' Karl glanced up the street, and then back at Wilson. 'And for doing this?'

'The papers in my pocket mysteriously disappear forever. Miss McKeever stays in hospital until she is fit to plead guilty to a non-custodial misdemeanour, you get to keep your licence, but more importantly, Naomi isn't brought into this sorry mess you created.'

'All nice and neat, wrapped up in a bow, eh?' Karl's lip curled with distaste. 'What about your detectives? Aren't they going to be a tiny bit suspicious about your dirty dealings?'

'I'll worry about that.'

'How do I know you'll keep your side of the bargain?'

'You have my word on it.'

'*Your* word?' Karl's face measured out into a small grin. 'Please forgive me for not feeling totally convinced. There's a lot of dead men rotting in lonely graves on someone's *word*. I'd hate to be joining them.'

'Take it or leave it, Kane. I have to trust you, too, and *I'm* not totally convinced of that, either.'

For a few seconds Karl said nothing, weighing up his ex brother-in-law's words.

'Okay, Wilson, it looks like I have no other choice. I accept your deal – reluctantly, it should be added.'

'At long last you're starting to show some common sense,' said Wilson, looking visibly relieved. 'Justice always prevails, provided you trust in it.'

'Justice? A pity you and the other cops didn't put in the same effort to bring the scumbags who murdered the Cohen children in Ballymena to *justice*. Think of the lives that would have been saved.'

'Just make sure the originals, along with the gun, are handed to me by this time tomorrow. Oh, one last thing.' Wilson eased closer to Karl, hard-eyeing him. 'You know of my abhorrence of swearing, of course, but for you I'm going to make an exception. Fuck with me ever again, and it'll be the last time you fuck with anyone. Do I make myself clear?'

'I'm sorry. I wasn't listening. Can you repeat all that?'

'You better have been listening, you fucking snail. I meant every word of it.'

'Using the fuck word really doesn't work for you, Mark, coming over all hard as rusty nails. Someone might just call your bluff.'

'No bluff. One-upmanship, it's called, and I *always* win at one-upmanship, Kane. Never *ever* forget that.' Wilson's face was turning sour. 'At the end of the day, I'll do what's necessary.'

'That sounds like a threat on my life, Mark.'

'Take whatever you want from it. Just have everything in my office by tomorrow morning, nine o'clock sharp. Do *not* be tardy.'

'Don't worry, Mark. You'll get Phillips' posthumous letter, along with the gun he claimed you doctored in Harry's death. Just make sure you keep your side of this dirty blackmailing bargain by not arresting people whom you know to be innocent, just to get at me.'

'*I* decide who's innocent in this town, Kane, not you. Now get the hell out of my sight.'

A small distance away, a female reporter was saying something into a microphone, all the while advancing towards Karl and Wilson.

'Looks like you have company, Mark. Better start swallowing all that bullshit filling your mouth. One thing you should always remember: truth is a bit like shite. Pretty ugly when it starts, but in the end it always comes out.'

Before Wilson could respond, the reporter came rushing up to him.

'Chief Inspector?' said the reporter. 'What can you tell us about this terrible event?'

Wilson's face suddenly became a politician's.

'It's too early to speculate, and I can't comment on an on-going investigation.'

'We have it from a very good source that the man killed was actually the Red Hand serial killer. Can you confirm that for our viewers?'

Wilson bristled. 'That's pure speculation. Unconfirmed rumours like that only help impede any investigations. There never was a Red Hand serial killer. The media should be more…'

Watching Wilson and the reporter walking slowly back down Hill Street towards the rest of the gathering media, Karl probed for the phone in his pocket. No sooner was he about to hit the first number, than a voice called his name.

'Karl!'

'Tom?' Karl quickly clicked off the phone.

Tom Hicks was emerging from a car, hair and clothes dishevelled. 'Are you okay, Karl?' said Hicks, looking pale.

Hicks sounded shattered.

'Fine, Tom. Ever want your sinuses cleared, have someone stick a gun up your snout. Works every time.' Karl tried forcing a smile, but nothing came.

'What about Naomi?'

'Staying tough, as usual.'

'I screwed up, not telling you that Taylor, Brown or Blake had been charged with the murders of the children.'

'That's bollocks. How could you have known? Their records on that particular grisly deed were erased because they were found *not guilty* by a biased jury.'

'I should have dug further. I should have found *something*.'

'Stop crucifying yourself, Tom. There are more than enough bastards carrying hammers and nails in this lousy town to do it for you. Trust me. I learned that a long time ago.'

'Thanks…'

'Don't thank me, but more importantly, don't ever talk like this again. That's an order. You've got nothing to feel guilty about.'

'How about we get together next week, just for a quiet drink? Just the two of us.'

'That sounds like a song.'

'It's been a long time since we've had a drink together.'

'Just the boys night out, sort of thing?' Karl finally managed a genuine smile.

'Yes, something like that.'

'Sounds good to me. I'll give you a call during the week. We'll arrange something. In the meantime, I think you better get down to my office. Wilson and his motley crew are there along with some of the media, fucking everything up.'

'What about you? Not coming?'

'In a few minutes. Just getting my head cleared.'

'Okay. I'll see you back at your place.' Hicks looked uncomfortable again. 'Glad you're okay.'

'I know you are. Go on. Do your job. I'm fine.'

Karl watched Hicks proceed down the street, before hitting the numbers again on his phone. If he could only reach his source, this could turn out to be one of the most important phone calls he would ever make.

CHAPTER THIRTY-THREE

THE STING

'The stupid neither forgive nor forget; the naive forgive and forget; the wise forgive but do not forget.'
Thomas Szasz, *The Second Sin*

Karl and Naomi were relaxing on top of the bed, each reading a Sunday newspaper and sipping coffee. An orgy of tabloids and broadsheets was scattered haphazardly on the bed and floor, swamping the entire area. The radio was playing classic Motown hits from the seventies.

'Coffee, Marvin Gaye and fat newspapers. This is what Sunday morning's made for,' said Karl.

'Thought you said Sunday morning was made for great sex with the woman you love?'

'That, too – if I can squeeze it in.' Karl flipped over a page. 'Every damn article seems to be about Bartlett. After almost a week, you'd think they'd give it a rest.'

The newspapers were still prominently carrying the death of Peter Bartlett, the one-time captain in the Royal Irish Regiment and killer who had narrowly avoided adding Karl to his obituary list.

Naomi looked up from the paper she was reading. 'The *Sunday*

World is saying that Bartlett had been serving in Iraq when a roadside bomb killed three of his comrades and left him with horrendous injuries. Doctors said it was a medical miracle he managed to survive.'

'I don't think the devil would be too happy with the use of the word miracle in association with one of his own, Naomi.'

'It goes on to say "He served with distinction and was awarded the Conspicuous Gallantry Cross for bravery. A terrific and fearless soldier, according to one former captain. But others said there was a dark side to Bartlett, that he was a racist with connections to the British National Front and to paramilitaries in Belfast. It's also claimed that he would routinely physically and verbally abuse prisoners in his custody. Prior to the explosion he was being investigated about the murder of two local Iraqi men whose bullet-riddled bodies were found dumped on the outskirts of Baghdad. Apparently, origami was found in the pockets of the dead men, sculptured from the pages of the Book of Revelation."'

'They claim that certain British Army brass knew of Bartlett's involvement in numerous other killings, not only here and Iraq, but possibly in Afghanistan, and that he was *"a functional subsidiary"* of British Intelligence.'

'A functional subsidiary? What's that suppose to mean?'

'An assassin. Or in layman's terms: we don't mind you doing it, provided you don't do something stupid like getting caught, and spilling the fucking beans. Far better you get shot. Dead men have a hard time moving their tongues.'

'Very cloak and dagger.'

'With the emphasis on dagger. Says here that the good captain was part of a notorious unit known as JFIT – Joint Forward

Intelligence Team –based at the Shaibah Logistics Base, thir-teen miles from Basra, in Iraq. The newspaper claims that all of JFIT members were a mix of military, MI5 and civilian staff and that they took their orders directly from London.'

Naomi turned a page in the paper. 'On my God, Karl…'

'What? What is it now?'

'Your name…it was on a list found in Bartlett's hotel room.'

'What? Let me see that,' said Karl, taking the paper from Naomi.

'What does it say?'

'A load of fabricated crap.'

'Let me read it.' Naomi grabbed the paper back.

Karl sighed. 'Look, it's nothing. I already knew my name was on a list found in Bartlett's room. Chambers called me a couple of days ago to inform me of it.'

'*What*? Why the hell didn't you tell me?'

'To prevent exactly what you're doing right now. Worrying over nothing.'

'I wish you'd stop trying to protect me. I'm a big girl.'

'You can say that again, you big girl you.'

'I'm serious, Karl.'

'Okay. In future, you get all the bad news that I get. No point in just me getting the grey hairs.'

Naomi continued reading. 'The names of the people he murdered all were in red; those he intended to murder were in green…'

'Thankfully, I'm as green as they come, otherwise we wouldn't be having this ridiculous conversation.'

'It says here Tev Steinway's name was in red. Thought you said he was killed by a hit and run?'

'Yes, well, according to Chambers, the cops now believe the and-run driver was Bartlett. Seems the sick bastard was extremely imaginative in his warped way of thinking out new methods of killing people.'

'And to think he was in our home…' Naomi shuddered. 'Gives me the shivers, just thinking of it.'

Karl reached over and kissed her on the cheek. 'It's over – for good. He's dead.'

Before Naomi could respond, the noon news came on the radio.

Police have confirmed that they are re-opening the case of an arson attack in Ballymena, six years ago, when three Jewish children burned to death. There is speculation that Peter Bartlett, the man labelled the Red Hand serial killer, may have been the leader of the gang, but somehow managed to evade police by enlisting for military service in Iraq. The police say they have new and definite leads, and that a businessman is helping with their enquiry…

'A bit bloody late,' said Karl. 'Think of the people who would still be alive if they had convicted the scumbags in the first place.'

'You can't blame the police, Karl; it was the jury.'

'The jury can only play the cards given to them – by the cops.'

Unconfirmed reports say the businessman's name is Nigel Potts, and that he had been living under the alias of Nelson Roberton. Money found at the Europa Hotel has been linked to Potts and Peter Bartlett. Detective Inspector Mark Wilson will be heading the investigation…

'Did you hear that, Karl? Mark Wilson's heading the investigation.'

'Anything for a headline.'

'Aren't you being a wee bit hard on him? At least he's re-opened it, and it was through him all charges against Lipstick were dropped, provided she did rehab.'

'She's never taken drugs in her life. She didn't need to be sent to a bloody rehab.'

'He had to come up with something to appease the media. I for one think it was great of him, sticking his neck out.'

'Yes, he's one hell of a guy.'

'I know you don't see eye-to-eye with him, but don't begrudge him the credit due, Karl. Things could have been a lot worse, had he not used his influence to help us all – you included.'

Karl felt his face redden. He wanted to scream. Instead, he quietly sucked in air for five seconds, before slowly releasing it. Thankfully, his face began cooling down.

'Yes, I suppose you're right, Naomi. I'll have to give him a big hug the next time I see him.'

'Thank God for Lipstick,' said Naomi, touching Karl's hand tenderly. 'I dread to think what would have happened had she not been here. She was so brave. I keep thinking would I have had the strength to pull the trigger?'

'You'd be surprised at what we're *all* capable of, Naomi, when the dice falls.'

Naomi eased from the bed. 'I'm going for a shower. Then I intend to visit Lipstick.'

'Don't let misguided guilt guide you, darling. We've been up every day this week to see her. She'll be well taken care of, once she gets out of there.'

'Are you coming?'

'I'm full of misguided guilt, too. Of course I'm coming. But first, I'm popping downstairs. Want to check something on the computer.'

'Don't be long. I need my back washed.'

'Only if you do my front.'

'Deal.' Naomi giggled. 'Hurry.'

Downstairs, Karl turned on the computer, and waited for it to warm up before inserting a disc. He watched the screen come to life, astounded at the details it was revealing, and then flicked on the volume.

'Beautiful…' he said in amazement, five minutes later, hitting a number on his phone.

'Huh?' A groggy voice answered.

'Richard? Karl. Loved it, pal. It's so perfect, I almost cried.'

'Karl? Oh…good. Glad I was able to help. I was kinda worried when you phoned me that morning. You sounded badly shaken up. Only to be expected, of course, after that weirdo tried to shoot you. Man, what a crazy life you lead. No wonder you don't take drugs. You don't need them, man.'

'I won't forget this, what you did for me.'

'It was nothing. Glad to be of help. Now can I go back to sleep? I don't like Mondays.'

'It's Sunday.'

'Those, too.'

'I'll probably need a couple of copies of this, for posterity.' *And bankability.*

'You can have them by the middle of the week. How's that sound?'

'I owe you – big time. Anything I can do, just name it.'

'Really?' Richard went quiet for a few seconds. 'How about buying me *Detective Comics* number Twenty-Seven?'

'A comic? *A bloody comic?* I'll buy you a hundred of them! What? Why're you laughing?'

'*Detective Comics* number Twenty-Seven is the first appearance of Batman.'

'So?'

'It sells for roughly half a million dollars – if you can find a copy in near mint.'

'Half a bloody million? Shit, I'm in the wrong business.'

'Don't worry about it.' Richard laughed. 'I'll think of something else, down the line. Goodnight.'

'It's bloody–' The phone went dead. '…noon.'

In the silence of the room, Karl re-watched the film playing before his eyes on the computer screen. The darkness of night made clear by modern-day technology, and all in lovely stunning colour.

He studied himself and Wilson standing in the lit-up doorway of Long Bridge House. Admittedly, he looked terribly haggard on the screen, but the fact that Wilson looked even more dreadful helped.

Wilson was talking: *Just make sure the originals, along with the gun, are handed to me by this time tomorrow. Oh, one last thing. You know of my abhorrence of swearing, of course, but for you I'm going to make an exception. Fuck with me ever again and it'll be the last time you fuck with anyone. Do I make myself clear?*

I'm sorry. I wasn't listening. Can you repeat all that?

You better have been listening, you fucking snail. I meant every word of it.

Using the fuck word really doesn't work for you, Mark, coming over all hard as rusty nails. Someone might just call your bluff.

No bluff. One-upmanship, it's called, and I always win at one-upmanship, Kane. Never ever forget that. At the end of the day I'll do what's necessary.

That sounds like a threat on my life, Mark.

Take whatever you want from it. Just have everything in my office by tomorrow morning, nine o'clock sharp. Do not be tardy.

'Karl!' shouted Naomi.

'What?'

'Shower's free. Hurry up!'

'Okay. Coming.'

Karl quickly hit eject, and removed the warm disc. Reaching for a black felt pen, he scribbled on the disc: 'one-upmanship', before slipping the disc inside a protective sleeve.

He smiled, and then made his way back upstairs.

BRANDON